PYRAMIDS
OF
LIFE

PATTERNS OF LIFE
AND DEATH
IN THE ECOSYSTEM

HARVEY CROZE

JOHN READER

FOREWORD BY
RICHARD DAWKINS

HARVEY CROZE is a behaviourist and ecologist with 30 years' experience in African ecosystems. He obtained his D. Phil. at Oxford University under Nobel laureate Professor Niko Tinbergen and worked for the Tanzanian National Parks as an elephant ecologist in the Serengeti in the late 1960s and 70s. He established the Amboseli Elephant Research Project with Cynthia Moss in 1972 and was, more recently, co-ordinator of the ecological programme of the United Nations Environment Programme (UNEP) and FAO Kenya Wildlife Management Project. He has written numerous articles and several books. He was co-author on *The Great Migration* (Harvill Press, 1999) and is currently contributing to a volume compiling the results of 25 years of elephant research in the Amboseli Reserve (Chicago University Press). He is based in Nairobi.

JOHN READER, writer and photographer, moved to Kenya with *Life Magazine* in 1969 and travelled throughout Africa. When the magazine closed, he concentrated on ecology and the problems of conservation, and contributed to international publications such as *National Geographic*, *Stern*, *Paris Match*, the *Observer* and the *Sunday Times*. He holds an honorary research fellowship in the Anthropology Department at University College, London, is a fellow of the Royal Geographical Society and the Royal Anthropological Institute, and has acted as a consultant to the UNEP and the Getty Conservation Institute. His most recent book, *Africa: A Biography of the Continent* was awarded the 1998 Alan Paton Literary Award.

PYRAMIDS OF LIFE

Harvey Croze and John Reader

Foreword by Richard Dawkins

HARVILL PRESS
LONDON

For Cristina, at last
And for Brigitte,

"Pour le meilleur, et pour le pire ... mais jamais pour le déjeuner."
H. Bacon

First published in 1977 in Great Britain by Collins an imprint of Harper Collins Ltd
This revised edition first published in 2000 by The Harvill Press
2 Aztec Row Berners Road London N1 0PW
www.harvill.com

First impression

Text © Harvey Croze, 2000
Photographs © John Reader, 2000

Photograph copyright © P.W. Fera for the images pages 242–3

The authors have asserted their moral rights

A CIP catalogue record for this book is available from the British Library

ISBN 1 86046 613 3

Designed by Rachida Zerroudi

Originated, printed and bound in Italy, by Conti Tipocolor

Contents

FOREWORD

Africa was my personal cradle. But I left when I was seven, too young to appreciate – indeed the fact was not then known – that Africa is also humanity's cradle. The fossils of our species' formative years are all from Africa, and molecular evidence suggests that the ancestors of all today's peoples stayed there until as recently as the last hundred thousand years or so. We have Africa in our blood and Africa has our bones. We are all Africans.

This alone makes the African ecosystem an object of singular fascination. It is the community that shaped us, the commonwealth of animals and plants in which we served our ecological apprenticeship. But even if it were not our home continent Africa would captivate us, as perhaps the last great refugium of Pleistocene ecologies. If you want a late glimpse of the Garden of Eden, forget Tigris and Euphrates and the dawn of agriculture. Go instead to the Serengeti or the Kalahari. Forget the Arcadia of the Greeks and the dreamtime of the outback, they are so recent. Whatever may have come down the mountain at Olympus or Sinai, or even Ayer's Rock, look instead to Kilimanjaro, or down the Rift Valley towards the High Veldt. There is where we were designed to flourish.

The "design" of all living things and their organs is, of course, an illusion; an exceedingly powerful illusion, fabricated by a suitably powerful process, Darwinian natural selection. There is a second illusion of design in nature, less compelling but still appealing, and it is in danger of being mistaken for the first. This is the apparent design of ecosystems. Where bodies have parts that intricately harmonise and regulate to keep them alive, ecosystems have species that appear to do something similar at a higher level. There are the primary producers that convert raw solar energy into a form that others can use. There are the herbivores that consume them to use it, and then make a tithe of it available for carnivores and so on up the food chain – pyramid, rather, for the laws of thermodynamics rule that only a tenth of each level's energy shall make it to the level above. Finally, there are scavengers that recycle the waste products to make them available again, and in the process clean up the world and stop it becoming a tip. Everything fits with everything else like jigsaw pieces meshing in a huge multidimensional puzzle, and we meddle with the parts at the risk of destroying a priceless whole.

The temptation is to think that this second illusion is crafted by the same kind of process as the first: by a version of Darwinian selection, but at a higher level. According to this erroneous view, the ecosystems that survive are the ones whose parts – species – harmonise, just as the organisms that survive in conventional Darwinism are the ones whose parts – organs and cells – work harmoniously for their survival. I believe that this theory is false. Ecosystems, like organisms, do indeed seem harmoniously designed; and the appearance of design is indeed an illusion. But there the resemblance ends. It is a different kind of illusion, brought about by a different process. The best ecologists – including the authors of this book – understand this.

Darwinism enters into the process, but it does not jump levels. Genes still survive, or fail to survive, within the gene pools of species, by virtue of their effects upon the survival and reproduction of the individual organisms that contain them. The illusion of harmony at a higher level is an indirect consequence of differential individual reproduction. Within any one species of animals or plants, the individuals that survive best are the ones that can exploit the other animals and plants, bacteria and fungi, that are already flourishing in the environment. As Adam Smith understood long ago, an illusion of harmony and real efficiency will emerge in an economy dominated by self-interest at a lower level. A well balanced ecosystem is an economy, not an adaptation.

Plants flourish for their own good, not for the good of herbivores. But because plants flourish, a niche for herbivores opens up, and they fill it. Grasses are said to benefit from being grazed. The truth is more interesting. No individual plant benefits from being grazed per se. But a plant that suffers only slightly when it is grazed outcompetes a rival plant that suffers more. So successful grasses have benefited indirectly from the presence of grazers. And of course grazers benefit from the presence of grasses. Grasslands therefore build up as harmonious communities of relatively compatible grasses and grazers. They seem to cooperate. In a sense they do, but it is a modest sense that must be cautiously understood and judiciously understated. The same is true of the other communities expounded in this book.

I have said that the illusion of harmony at the eco-system level is its own kind of illusion, different from, and emphatically not to be confused with, the Darwinian illusion that produces each efficiently working body. But a closer look reveals that there is a similarity after all, one that goes deeper than the – admittedly interesting and more commonly stated – observation that an animal can also be seen as a community of symbiotic bacteria. Mainstream Darwinian selection is the differential survival of genes within gene pools. Genes survive if they build bodies that flourish in their normal environment. But the normal environment of a gene importantly includes the other genes (strictly their consequences) in the gene pool of the species. Natural selection therefore favours those genes that cooperate harmoniously in the joint enterprise of building bodies within the species. I have called the genes "selfish cooperators". There turns out to be, after all, an affinity between the harmony of a body and the harmony of an ecosystem. There is an ecology of genes.

Ecology, for accidental reasons, was largely left out of my biological education, and I learned a great deal from this book that I didn't know before. I read it with the wide eyed, childlike innocence that a first adult visit to Africa always engenders. And what a privilege, on this literary and pictorial journey, to be led by two such guides, accomplished and experienced ecologists, old Africa hands yet still fired up as if seeing the mother continent for the first time. The lyricism and biological insight of Harvey Croze's words is matched by the very same qualities in John Reader's stunning photographs. Both are intellectual hunter-gatherers, to use their own phrase, whose complementary talents harmonise and reinforce each other like the parts of a climax ecosystem.

Pyramids of Life was introduced, in its first edition, by my old maestro – an intellectual hunter-gatherer if ever there was one – the late Niko Tinbergen. It is an honour to follow in his footsteps and recommend, with less expert knowledge, but I think equal enthusiasm, a new edition of this splendid book.

RICHARD DAWKINS

INTRODUCTION

Have you ever seen an ecosystem? In a day's drive from the south to the north of the Serengeti you might see a dozen large mammal species – elephants, lions, wildebeest – two dozen small ones from hyrax to zorillas, a hundred or more species of birds and countless insects and trees. Even from so brief a visit, you will forever retain a sense of having glimpsed the edge of secret lives, episodes within a larger play. If you have time, you may come back, but you never visit the same ecosystem twice.

Consider this a rather special guidebook, one that goes beyond a roster of beasts and places. We aim to help readers understand where they are in an ecosystem, and once there, what is going on. African ecosystems are the focus because they are particularly rich in pattern, structure and process; we could have equally well chosen Nordic peat bogs or Australian scrubland.

Why do we feel so good about seeing a seemingly disorganised sprawl of nature in the raw, the paradoxical co-existence of stillness and motion? In a herd of wildebeest, a landscape or the running of water, there is an insinuation of pattern that we find compelling but cannot easily define. Perhaps, within the apparent complexity of it all, we are also sensing patterns that resonate within us, acts played out by organisms with which we share one Earth and one atmosphere, organisms that are made of the very stuff we are. There is a delightful asymmetry in the natural world, a pervasive patchiness that we are only now just beginning to understand – after more than half a century of research on African plants and animals.

Some might argue that nature is best appreciated unfettered by human explanations, best enjoyed as a relief from the man-made world. We have come too far for that luxury. Let us ask instead with Gregory Bateson, one of biology's greatest lateral thinkers "What pattern connects the crab to the lobster, and the orchid to the primrose and all four of them to me? And me to you?"

Our "ravages" of nature have continued to be well chronicled over the years. Typically the emphasis is on the sensational elements of extinction and destruction. We charge in to tackle the problems of the sick and dying before fully understanding the functional success of the healthy and living. Yet because we know it is foolish to tinker with a complicated and valuable watch without first understanding what makes it tick, we often conclude that it is necessary to learn how the natural world functions in order to keep it – and thereby ourselves – in good working order. But sadly, our ability to conserve the natural world has not proved to correlate with the depth of our knowledge of its functioning.

In the meanwhile, ecosystems continue to tick over in much the same way as they always have. There have of course been changes, in abundance and distribution, concomitant with natural and human-induced changes. Some changes are for the better, many for the worse. One element that has changed our view of nature is the use of stronger social and economic filters. We tend now to ask how the abundance of the natural world might be more equitably distributed to "stakeholders", and how those stakeholders can exhibit better manners to use the harvest in sustainable ways. Best estimates put the total value of the goods and services that ecosystems of the world supply at some $33 trillion, twice the total of the world's gross national products.

Environmental ethics and economics aside, our first response to anything in nature is usually concerned with whether or not it "looks nice"; an emotional response most evident when we first visit tropical environments and confront the bewildering array of remarkable objects and events. We delight

in the beauty of a butterfly, and shudder with revulsion at the ugly vulture. The butterfly is immediately acceptable, whereas the vulture, with its looks and predilection for corpses, is more likely to be dismissed simply on the strength of its appearance.

Such prejudices potentially close our minds to important aspects of life, and the emotional concepts of beauty and ugliness become more of a hindrance than a help to our understanding of the natural world. We must take a broader view. We do not have to be lepidopterists to appreciate the beauty of the butterfly, but surely we will view the vulture in a more sympathetic light when we understand how essential it is to the functioning of the tropical grasslands, and how appropriate its grim appearance is to its own functioning.

Ecology is the science that deals with the match between living organisms and their environment. Ethology is the study of behaviour – what animals do to best match their natural environment. This is far from a simple two-way relationship between beast and background: it is a network rather

than a pipeline and adds to both the beauty and complexity of the thing. Even the boundary between ethologists and ecologists has become blurred with the contemporary designation "behavioural ecologist". Whatever we call them, they are naturalists at heart who share our wonder when viewing the beauties of nature. They are intellectual hunter-gatherers: after making the catch, their curiosity leads them to observe life's patterns more closely, to record and organise what they see.

We cannot all be card-carrying behavioural ecologists, yet our understanding and appreciation of how the natural world works will flourish once we look at its objects and events in their ecological perspective. A major facet of this perspective is governed by what might be called the Rule of Non-Randomness. Nothing is superfluous in the natural world. The living Earth is made up of linked biological systems, not a haphazard collection of objects and events. Patterns, sequences and interactions occur in nature in a manner comparable to the disposal of streets, traffic-flow, shop-distribution and electricity-use

in a large city. Although life is not random, nor is it perfectly orderly. There is both predictability and perversity in the way things happen

When you look at a butterfly in a particular place, or a vulture swooping down on to the carcass of a gazelle, you are not observing an isolated event. You are invariably glimpsing part of a system, part of a biological process that is measurable by the fact, predictable in the general, but not controllable at the instant. Given a little more knowledge, the mere presence of a butterfly could tell you something about the vegetation, the soil and climatic aspects of the system it is in. And the condition of the gazelle carcass, the species of the vultures about and their numbers, could tell you a fair amount about the system's prey and predator populations.

Of course, in a global sense, the Earth itself is one vast biological system. But within it we can define thousands and millions of others, quite distinct, internally consistent entities made up of a finite collection of the fundamental elements of life. One system could be a two-square-metre pond, another a 2,000-square-kilometre stretch of grassland – whatever the size, the principles governing the way it functions remain much the same.

It is often tempting to think of a biological system as a complex machine, built with environmental parts – climate, soils, vegetation and animals. These parts are constantly shifting their relative positions but remain closely connected by common biological laws, by their effects upon one another, and by their inter-dependence. But life is not a machine, for several reasons.

First of all, a living system is

paradoxically both closed and open; its organization is closed – you can draw a line around it and enumerate its components – but its structure is open to other systems or just to the atmosphere. Eugene Odum, ecology teacher to generations, encapsulated life's closed-open nature: "Matter circulates, energy dissipates." The second characteristic of life is irreversibility. Once a life process has happened – a cell split, an egg laid, a behaviour enacted, heat generated – there is no going

back. Unlike machines, life follows the one-way arrow of time.

The third non-mechanical quality of life is that it is self-replicating to the point that most of the energy that living things spend has to do with making more of themselves. No machines yet can make copies of themselves. In this book, we do not intend to go down into the engine room of life, into the cells where they carry out the replication of DNA, the stuff that genes and therefore life's forms are made of. We will live with the quip that the organism is DNA's way of making more DNA and dwell occasionally on the surprising fact that we have not yet understood how the whole organism and its lifestyle is made up of the sum of its parts.

The blueprints for body form, the propensity to behave in such-and-

INTRODUCTION

such a way, indeed the sequence of growth and development itself are copied from one generation to the next through reproduction. But the "message" copied is not a one-to-one set of instructions, like how to assemble a model aeroplane. The quantity of information contained in cat DNA is too small to describe a cat; that in human DNA is not even enough to map our brains. Just how a whole functioning cat or human is built, we don't yet know, any more than how water spirals down a plug hole, even with a pretty good knowledge of fluid dynamics and the properties of bonded hydrogen and oxygen.

We may not know how to do life, yet we have come quite far in describing its three main qualities: pattern, structure and process. Pattern has to do with how life's bits and pieces are arranged, rather like a blueprint or a map. Structure is concerned with the physical parts and their linkages, that is, the organism itself, assembled and ready to go. Process has to do with activity – the enactment, the doing, the unfolding of the play.

In nature there is a myriad of patterns and more structures than we can count. But the number of

processes is relatively small, and repeated over and over again in all biological systems. This fundamental fact has determined the form of our book, which is divided into three

parts: the Grasslands, the Lakes and Rivers, and the Forests of tropical Africa. We have chosen African ecosystems to illustrate the processes, but the same ones are played out all around the world.

Grassland, lakes and rivers, forests – these are general designations of ecosystem types, clearly recognisable patches laid over continental landscapes. They each have their limits of tolerance and some critical defining physical characteristics: the presence and abundance of water is the major one, as are altitude and temperature. These types are not arbitrary descriptive labels, for they have complex internal structures. In many respects they are like big sprawling organisms. They replicate themselves and, if conditions allowed, would overrun each other. They are the highest levels of ecological organisation, and for this reason serve as the major divisions of this book.

Following the general process of nutrient cycling, from the Earth to the vegetation to the animals and back again to the earth, we demonstrate how just a few of the Earth's countless life forms deal with the three life processes common to all: how they find their food; how they avoid becoming some other organism's food; how they perpetuate their species. The habitats to which our protagonists belong range from bare rock to forest; from soda lake to semi desert. The life forms themselves vary from blades of grass, trees and microscopic protozoa to elephants, insects, reptiles and cats of all sizes.

And our purpose? It is to show that even amid such an apparent confusion of place, object and event there is always orderliness; the very diversity itself is determined by biological laws that no organism

can escape. And understanding this, the "fearful symmetry" of the natural world is no longer perplexing and remote. It is beautiful and close.

We start our investigation into the underlying order of the natural world with life's building blocks, the chemical elements of the Earth itself. Every once in a while the Earth reminds us that it is still forming: a village disappears, a new

island pops up. Ol-Doinyo Lengai, the Mountain of God in northern Tanzania, is only a few million years old. It last puffed ash over the Serengeti Plains in 1966 and is still changing shape from year to year. The materials bound in its barren volcanic mass contain mineral resources beneficial to a living system, but that must first be freed from the rock. Sun and rain, heat and cold, organic acids and the roots of pioneer plants very slowly insinuate themselves into the physical and chemical chinks of the parent material, which crumbles, mixes with the organic debris and becomes soil thus joining the roundabout of life.

Consider one atom of one element in the soil, say phosphorus – a particle of one of the usable mineral resources in a living system. If we could tag that particle, we might be able to follow its radio-active trail and trace its movements through the system. We would watch as the atom is absorbed by the root of a plant and incorporated into the plant itself. If the plant was a grass, a wildebeest might eat it. Our atom of phosphorus would then perhaps be used in building wildebeest flesh. The wildebeest might be caught and eaten by an African wild dog, and the same atom of phosphorus that was once part of the soil, would now become part of the dog. The dog would excrete, or die, and the atom would thus be made available to the maintenance of yet another class or organism, the decomposers. These are the animals, from bacteria to vultures who complete the disassembly of organic structure; they bridge the gap between life and death and thus return our atom of phosphorus to the soil. It is then ready to be run through the system once more.

The path the atom has taken is called a food chain. There are complex alternative paths in all biological systems called food webs, inter-connected food chains

by which mineral resources move through a system. A gazelle could have eaten the same grass, and the phosphorus been excreted out the next day. Or it could have passed into a cheetah that caught

the gazelle. Thence to a vulture or to other decomposers and back, inevitably, to the soil.

Having followed the path of our element from the soil through the plant and animal communities back to the soil, we would find ourselves close to where we started – probably no more than a hundred

kilometres – having travelled within an ecosystem, an integrated, self-maintaining biological unit. It is the set of all the places through which a particular atom is likely to pass.

Every ecosystem has its own special characteristics. It has, for example, a geographical location. The boundary of the ecosystem often coincides with a number of physical boundaries, like a Rift Valley wall, or a lake shore, or the interface between two soil types. When it does, we might find vegetation boundaries congruent with the physical ones, such as the line between forest and grassland. As we shall see later, most animals usually stay on one side or the other of ecosystem boundaries. Of course, boundaries need not be barriers: it is possible for animals to move across them. But the network of processes that go on between soil, plants and animals makes it more likely that the atom of phosphorus will stay within one particular ecosystem.

Different ecosystems have different weights – or biomasses – of plants

and animals, usually a function of the climate and the amount of nutrients available from the earth. They have different topographies, soils and plant formations. There must be, of course, some form of energy that moves our atom and all the other materials round an ecosystem. The sun is the only natural source of energy in our solar system; its radiance gives light and warmth. But nobody can eat sunlight. The only way the sun's energy can be trapped is by green plants in the process of photosynthesis, that is to say "making with light". What do plants make? They make a miracle: by linking heaven and earth, they make the first food.

Given the energy of the sun acting on water from the Earth, carbon dioxide from the air, and chlorophyll in the plant cells, green plants produce oxygen and simple sugars – the first table-setting of energy

and materials in the food chain. This is the primary production of a living system, the basic "trophic" or nourishment level. Thereafter, the sun's energy pumps through food chains with water providing not just moisture but electrons for energy transfer. Thus energy travels with the minerals from one trophic level up to the next: from *primary production* to *herbivores*

INTRODUCTION

(eaters of plants), to *carnivores* (eaters of flesh), to *decomposers* (eaters of everything).

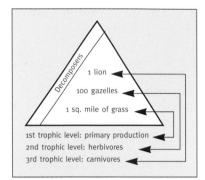

1 lion

100 gazelles

1 sq. mile of grass

Decomposers

1st trophic level: primary production
2nd trophic level: herbivores
3rd trophic level: carnivores

As originally formulated in the mid-nineteenth century, the Second Law of Thermodynamics tells us about the behaviour of energy in a system. Over recent years it has survived scrutiny by quantum physicists and still carries the practical message that if you change the form of energy you lose some of it in the process, as heat. You get hot when you run, because of the heat produced when the chemical energy of your food supply is changed into the kinetic energy of movement. Just growing or replacing worn cells requires energy conversion, so all organisms, even blades of grass, give off heat, the tax of living.

Grass is only concerned with being grass. Much of the energy it absorbs from the sun is dispersed in heat so as to maintain itself. Only part of the sun's energy that became grass remains available to be eaten by, say, a gazelle. Gazelles must maintain themselves too, and in doing so use about a tenth of the energy they derived from the grass. Hence the leopard that eats the gazelle gets in the end only a hundredth of the sun's energy which was originally trapped by the grass. Although studies of a variety of

ecosystems have shown that the trophic level energy transfer varies between 2 and 24 per cent, the average seems to be 10, evidence enough for declaring a general tithe for maintenance.

The Second Law of Thermodynamics thus explains why there could never be more gazelle meat than grass tissue and never more leopards or lions than gazelles: there is not enough energy to maintain them. The mandatory heat loss as each organism in an ecosystem keeps itself going decides the relative amounts of energy, numbers and biomass in the trophic level above. The decomposers, we shall see, are a special class of beasts who eventually feed on all trophic levels. Nevertheless, they too are subject to the law, and must exist at a smaller biomass than their food source.

Thus energy inevitably diminishes as it moves up through the food chains, and a pyramid of life is formed, one that applies to all ecosystems, excepting some marine

systems based on phytoplankton. In this book, we shall use the pyramidal stack of trophic levels to help guide us through our three main African ecosystem types and the basic patterns of their elements and processes.

Primary production is the basic food source in every ecosystem.

Each habitat presents its basic food source in a particular pattern, the form and extent of which is determined by geology and climate (the **controlling factors**), and

modified by fire and by the animals eating it (the **modifying factors**).

When we talk of eating and of the movements of energy and materials from one trophic level to another, we begin to cross the thin line between the sciences of ecology and behaviour. Materials do not move themselves but are moved by animals in their **pursuit of food**. When a lion eats a gazelle, the elements in that gazelle at once change their position in the pyramid of life. Of course, the gazelle will try not to become the lion's food and it is by **avoiding predators** – the obverse of feeding behaviour – that a species attempts to keep its materials in its own trophic level.

Within a trophic level, we observe in **reproduction** the complex rituals and elaborate adaptations of breeding behaviour. These maintain the integrity of a species, and the internal organisation of an animal or plant community. They are part of species' **social organisation,** which quite apart from ensuring breeding success, may also assist in the pursuit of food, or in predator avoidance. We also see animals indulge in "comfort behaviour": scratching, preening, rubbing and rolling all serve to keep plumage or pelage in top condition in order to protect, propel or repel predators and parasites. Such behaviours keep materials moving around within a trophic level, rather than from one to another.

Questions abound: Why is an organism built the way it is? Why does a plant grow in a particular place? Why does an animal behave the way it does? Many answers are not yet known, but we will try to show how a curious naturalist might think about the question and set about finding the answer.

In one sense there are as many answers as there are organisms, answers that have to do with place and time. But these are only part of the basic answer: an organism is the way it is, and does what it does, in order to stay fit and alive long enough to reproduce more of itself. Behavioural ecologists would refer to an animal "maximising its inclusive fitness". Whatever we call the relentless quest for self-replication, it is clearly the most important of life's concepts, one that should be understood at the outset.

We said earlier that animals and plants are not machines: the complex of chemical information encoded in the genes in the heart of every cell cannot be perfectly replicated each time an individual reproduces. For this reason we find variability within species, or even between siblings. Some products of reproduction fare better, others

worse. There is no perfect solution. Every behaviour, every characteristic is a compromise between its costs and its benefits.

The impartial judge in this lottery of breeding and survival is the environment. Those organisms best adapted to life in their surroundings will produce more young, bearing the very characteristics that gave their parents a survival edge. In this way, the environment is said to select the best strategy for survival from the number of alternatives offered each time there is reproduction and a recombination of the genetic

information that defines a species. We have, then, natural selection, the most important concept of life in the natural world.

Yet there may be imperfection in the beauty of natural selection. For over thirty years, biological sciences have continued to wonder why, even as we know more and more about the details of biological structure and functioning, we cannot yet model the whole system. There are still some quite large lingering mysteries, such as the origin of life, of sex and of human consciousness. We are still not certain how a single fertilised cell develops into an elephant or an ecologist. Perhaps we need more data and more computing power to reconstruct the whole with near-perfect understanding

or perhaps we need a new way of looking at the networked structures of the living world.

This book does not pretend to account for the last mysterious leap from component parts to whole systems. Whatever view we take, the only one that can help understanding is a contextual view, structured windows into the teeming and often confusing web of life, as opposed to a list of events or a catalogue of players. After all, experts who think about such things twenty-four hours a day recently admitted that there is as yet no calculus to explain the behaviour of complex adaptive systems, be it weather, stock markets, human consciousness or ecosystems.

This is our taking-off point. We hear some schools of thought questioning whether natural selection can explain everything, and others admitting that they cannot always gather the particulates and thereby account for the whole. It is therefore still meaningful and interesting to use the time-honoured marriage of images and poetry, words and pictures, to do the work for us, to help create a "momentary stay against confusion".

Ecosystem structure determines the page sequence; ecosystem patterns and processes are found throughout

Grasslands

Geology and climate, patches and patterns

Once the world began to cool seriously some four billion years ago, had the first organisms been cognisant, they would have been struck most with the *unevenness* of it all. In fact, through the following aeons, they and their descendants were struck by that very patchiness, like coins of the Earthly realm, into a myriad of patterns and forms along the way. Had the Earth's surface been like a billiard ball, smooth and even all round, it may have been that there would be just one type of inhabitant: bland of feature, self-replicating, self-indulgent and rather boring. Happily, the physical forces that formed the backdrop were brutal and chaotic, and left us with an interesting Earth – indeed, a pretty, smooth, blue-green marble from space. But at the working level, the Earth is a kaleidoscopic jumble of bumps and dips, cracks and ridges, holes and peaks, repeated again and again, from pole to pole, from east to west. A pervasive patchiness reigns.

The patchiness of Earth is not only on the ground, it is also atmospheric (here it is mostly hot and dry, there it is mostly cool and wet) and temporal (now it's cool, tomorrow will be cooler, in six months it will be hotter, in eleven years hotter still, in eleven thousand, cool again). Some of the "time patches" are very predictable, like the alternation between winter and summer as the tilted earth orbits the sun. Others are less easy to pin down, like the massive surge of warm water from the western to the eastern Pacific called "El Niño" that happens more or less every five years and impacts weather patterns in all parts of the globe. It affects more of us than war. The list of

candidate controllers of climate fluctuation appears to include everything Earth and sky are made of: behaviour of polar and oceanic ice sheets, distribution of carbon dioxide in the atmosphere and the oceans, deep ocean water movement, the Earth's magnetic field, volcanic dust in the atmosphere, variations in solar output and the geometry of our orbit around the sun. Even if experts deduce that the last of these seems to explain most of long-term climate variation, there is not much we can do about the way we circle the sun. It is plain to see, however, that if we overlay all those sky and time patches on the physical patches, in some places the living is easy and in others not; some times are good, others bad.

Relatively "young" volcanism and tectonic grindings in the nearby Kenyan Rift Valley have changed major geological stress patterns in the Chyulu Hills no less than five times in the last 1.6 million years. It may seem at first that such variety would engender confusion. In fact, it seems to present opportunities for major evolutionary steps in humans and other species that have had to adapt quickly to drastically altered neighbourhoods. Some scientists hypothesise that evolution moves in jerks: relatively short periods of rapid change interspersed with long periods of little or no change at all, a so-called "punctuated equilibrium". One of the most spectacular of these pulses in our common history was coincident with the huge K/T meteorite that hit the Earth 65 million years ago and probably polished off the dinosaurs through drastic climate change, clearing the way for the rise of mammals. Although others

argue that evolutionary history is marked with periods of "accelerated gradualism" that occur with any opportunity catastrophic or not, there seems to be little doubt that our geological past was turbulent over relatively short periods.

The scale of such patterns is monumental in time and space. The geological backdrop is hewn from huge masses of the Earth's surface, and the Earth's climate mill has been grinding out its cycles and spewing out anomalies for eons. The energy involved in creating a mountain or moving a sea is so monstrous, and plant and animal impact is so puny, that effective human intervention is unthinkable. As we wonder how to deal with a rapidly changing world, it may help to reflect on what we can manage and what we cannot.

Relatively young volcanoes: Kilimanjaro (*opposite*) and Ol-Doinyo Lengai (*above*)

Learning to cope

One of our great contemporary dilemmas is can we sanction a lifestyle demanding raw-material conversion into both creature comforts and necessities, one that then with a kind of "even-handed justice commends the ingredients of our poison'd chalice to our own lips". The noxious effects of environmental pollution are undisputed, but the debate rages on about the price to pay, the costs and benefits of economic growth. The majority of the world's scientists now allow that "the balance of evidence suggests a discernible human influence" on global climate. So the accumulation of so-called greenhouse gas emissions from industry and energy production in the atmosphere will, unless we stop growing in numbers and producing goods and services, make the Earth warmer over the next century. Many of our same activities also increase the amount of tiny particles – soot and the like – suspended in the atmosphere. These block out some sun and make it a bit cooler. When the pluses and minuses are all added up, the somewhat dicey sum indicates we will probably warm up on average by a degree or two over the next fifty years (it has already warmed 0.6 degrees over the past century). The chances of us stopping doing the sorts of warming and cooling things to which we have become accustomed are pretty slim. So we shall have to do what countless organisms have done with many more drastic changes over the millennia – namely, learn to live with them.

But what kinds of things will we all – plants, animals, readers and writers of books – have to put up with? Let us put things in perspective. The Earth's mean temperature (poles and deserts included), has for the past few thousand years always been around 15 degrees C – about the temperature of a cool, spring morning in temperate realms. The worldwide extremes, of course, range from −50 to +50. The last ice age during Pleistocene times saw an overall decrease of five degrees, a chilling thirty-three per cent average temperature drop. In the intervening 1.9 million years, the Earth switched from a glacial to a milder interglacial climate and back again nine times. Core samples taken from the depths of the Greenland ice sheet suggest that in some periods we were subjected to several degree fluctuations in the span of a few short decades. Yet, we made it through, with our fairly recent ancestors becoming very adept at fire-making and processing animals to wear as well as to eat.

In the current changing situation, as in the past, there will be winners and losers. Those plants and animals that can adapt and weather the change, or those able to abandon the inhospitable places and make it to the habitable will be the winners. We are already predicting from satellite data how the patterns of production will change across the face of the globe: patches of dryland will grow in Africa, diminish in Canada. Boreal forest edges may retreat; moist tropical forests may advance. The mean sea level will either creep inland a metre or so, or recede, depending on whether the centres of the polar ice sheets grow faster or slower than the edges melt (the results are not yet in). The only things certain are that there will be change, that it will be difficult to predict the precise outcome and that the outcome will be as patchy as ever. And, as ever, the interesting challenge is in the reality of learning to cope with it and in helping others to do so as well.

The northern glaciers near the Kibo summit (*top*), the peak of Kilimanjaro and the arid Sahelian zone of northern Niger (*above*)

Sum of the parts

The finger-like, branched pattern of interconnected streams we see from the hill slope (*opposite*) is such a common feature of our world that we often no longer see it. Look again. What is there about this fundamental pattern that insinuates itself into virtually every part of the Earth's surface, etches its claw marks on the landscape and invites water to run down hill? Does the water do it to the hillslope or does the hillslope do it to the water? The question may seem rather silly and academic, but it illustrates the notion of connectivity. Things are connected if some pattern or process links them. Once we have recognised such a link between two or more elements of our world – between water and the hillslope, for example – we are a shade closer to understanding them, even though at the moment of recognition we may not know exactly how they work together. To carry on with this example, a perfect knowledge of gravity, the average mass of water falling on the hillside, fluid dynamics and the fine structure of the substrate of this particular hill will not provide a fraction of the insight of the structure of landscapes that the image here does. Moreover, not only can we see that there is a connection between one extreme of the basin and the other through the movement of water, but we are able to conjure up mental images of the trees on one side passing pollen to those on the other via wind or bees. We imagine the patches of vegetation providing nesting sites for birds or cover for stalking predators hoping to establish different kinds of links with their prey. We frame the patches and clumps of trees and all the

potential links they imply within the spatial integrity of their basin, in the clutches of this one watercourse.

In an ecosystem, the lives of plants and animals, their comings and goings, are played out on a stage of drainage basins. Often the whole drama of one or two generations takes place in just one such amphitheatre. The boundaries of the basins are more important and real to the actors than the artificial outlines we impose around our parks, provinces and nation states. We could capture the whole world's landmass by summing up all of its drainage basins.

Setting the stage

Seasonal rainfall distribution has dramatic effects on Africa's grassland vegetation patterns, both in time and space. The difference between the wet and dry seasons has to be seen to be believed: it is often the difference between a lush meadow and a dustbowl. Yet the rainfall in the grasslands is not only low, it is also too unpredictable to produce the kind of steady-state vegetation found in temperate regions. Seventy years in every hundred will receive less than 750 millimetres. And the rain that falls is not evenly distributed for the convenience of plant reproductive cycles. Within the year, most rain crashes down in a couple of months – the wet season; or else in two relatively brief periods – the long (some six weeks), and the short (around two weeks) rains.

Furthermore, it falls too hard and runs off too quickly for the soil, and hence the plants, to absorb it all. The rain that does soak in is just enough to sustain those forms of life adapted to survive through the eight months of the dry season. The effect on vegetation of the rainfall timing and pattern becomes strikingly clear when we consider that the wooded grasslands of Africa receive nearly the same average precipitation as Ireland, the Emerald Isle, where the rainy season is virtually continuous and the evaporation far less.

Again, quite apart from these annual fluctuations, the rain falls irregularly on the larger scale of decades too: for instance, East Africa experienced flood-producing torrents in 1961, and in the following

year the worst drought in decades. A short rain failure produced the region's 1971 to 72 drought; a long rain shortfall caused that of 1984. Just to confuse matters further, the short and long rains occasionally merge making it a wet Christmas, as in 1992 to 93 and 1997 to 98. One begins to wonder what is "normal" rainfall. To survive these moisture extremes, plants have developed and maintain what might be called an ecological agility – an ability to recover remarkably quickly after long periods of drought. They lie dormant for months, seemingly dead; but then, within days of the first rain, they sprout; soon trees are green and flowering, land that seemed certain to become barren desert is transformed into productive pastures for the wilde-

beest and the numerous other herbivores. Even before the rains arrive, some trees begin to flower and certain grasses may start to shift gears in their biochemical machinery, cued by subtle changes in temperature or day-length, or perhaps by the more arcane signals of minute increases in electrical potentials in the air.

Rain would seem to be inanimate. Yet raindrops are born and grow almost like living things, forming themselves in the super-cooled cloud tops ten kilometres above ground around microscopic nuclei. These nuclei have origins on the Earth that may be inorganic, like the sulphur soot from the burning of fossil fuels, or, some believe, organic, such as tiny aerosol particles "excreted" from the leaves of healthy vegetation or stressed marine algae. Each raindrop needs one of these tiny "seeds" around which to coalesce and increase until its mass exceeds that of the nucleus and it falls back to earth, with millions of siblings, as rain. Inanimate it may be, but life-giving it certainly is. Once the Earth has set the stage, the seasonal showers that sweep across the land are the cue for all the acts we observe in the grassland, or indeed anywhere else. The grasslands may come and go, but grass of some sort will always persist, ultimately dependent, like most living things, on water.

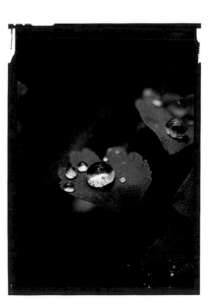

The solar constant

Once rain has fallen, the amount ultimately available to the plants is largely dictated by the inevitable re-appearance of the "glorious lamp of heaven, the sun". Although the sun provides energy for the prolific tropical primary production, it takes its toll by evaporating nearly eighty per cent of the rainfall, as well as sucking moisture from the leaves themselves. If the climate were to become drier, as appears to be happening in some parts of the African continent, the grasslands would tend to become desert. If rainfall were to increase, trees would get enough water to grow in number and literally over-shadow the grasses: woodland or forest would result. But things are not always quite so simple – especially the interaction of water and fire.

Surely as day follows night, it would seem that there could be few things more reliable than the sun. We even refer to the "solar constant", the average density of solar radiation hitting Earth's atmosphere. It is equivalent to the energy of about fourteen hundred-watt light bulbs per square metre up there on the atmosphere's outer edge, more than one hundred kilometres above us. The "constant" only varies by a few tenths of a per cent every three decades. A third of the sun's energy is used up in the atmosphere driving the hydrologic cycle that produces rain and weather. The remainder, after it filters through the atmosphere, hits the Earth as sunlight, on average with the energy of only seven hundred-watt bulbs per square metre. This may not sound like much, but we all know if you leave lights on, it adds up. The sum of energy falling on

Earth over a year is a huge amount of heat. Over four square kilometres on average it is equivalent to the Hiroshima blast; and over the whole world, enough to evaporate the top metre of all the oceans and put tens of thousands of cubic kilometres of water into the atmosphere. The energy trapped in the biosphere works to fuel life on Earth as we know it. This friendly star of ours has been burning hydrogen and helium in its nuclear furnace at more or less the same setting for some 4.5 billion years. It has enough hydrogen in its core to last as long again, so we need not concern ourselves on that score.

What may be of more immediate interest is the behaviour of so-called "sun spots", mysterious magnetic blemishes on the sun's face. These Asia-sized patches wax and wane with a twenty-two-year periodicity, and there are very few things they seem not to coincide with. Statistically agile researchers have found correlations between sun-spot highs or lows with aurora borealis

activity, numbers of births in some European populations, seasonal immunity to infections in dogs (but not people), bamboo flowering in the Chinese Himalayas, annual precipitation and temperature (sometimes), the level of Lake Victoria and the frequency of hip fractures in elderly people in Italy, to name but a few.

Correlation, of course, does not necessarily mean causation. Yet, satellite measurements taken over the past two decades indicate that during sun-spot peaks, the sun actually gets about 0.1 per cent brighter. It is compelling to contemplate that even such small changes in the main source of energy for our weather system, and Earth's food chains, might just tweak atmospheric circulation enough, and in such a manner, to make the African grasslands systematically drier every eleven years.

Grass

Grass is the single most successful visible terrestrial life form, both for its propensity to persist and capacity to increase. Virtually anywhere on Earth, we will not walk far before treading on grass. A relatively large part of the biomass of grassland plant communities goes into the production of offspring – seeds. In the form and structure of a grass plant the emphasis on the seeds is particularly striking – a few thin leaves, one or two stems and a seed head which may weigh as much as the rest of the plant. Clearly these are organisms whose success lies in their ability to flourish when conditions are right. Since the correct conditions may be limited to a few short weeks of rain in the tropical grasslands, the grasses there have evolved to grow and reproduce as quickly as possible. One might call them "increase strategists", particularly the fast-maturing annual grasses that grow, reproduce and die in one short season.

This grassy tenacity may have helped speed along the demise of the dinosaurs. Just before the K/T meteorite, 65 million years ago, grass appeared and started spreading with its characteristic vigour. The new grasses had tiny silica needles in their leaves, which suddenly (in an evolutionary time scale) gave a premium to herbivores with specialised grinding teeth, such as the newly emerging mammals. If the impact of the meteorite had not changed the atmosphere and therefore the climate for dinosaurs, grass might have contributed to their demise in the longer run by providing mammalian competitors with an abundant new food source.

Organisms that produce an abundance of seed are ideal colonisers, especially when the seeds are equipped with devices to enhance dispersal – special hooks to attach to the hair of a passing animal, tasty packaging and an impervious seed coating to attract herbivores on the one hand and survive their digestive juices on the other, feathery appendages to catch and be carried by the wind. If conditions are not favourable for flowering, the plants propagate by vegetative means, literally creeping and rooting over the bare surface.

Many grass species are able to grow where little else can. In volcanic grit that attracts and holds solar radiation because of its blackness, the surface temperature may exceed 43 degrees C. Even when it rains, water is only available to the roots for a very short time because of the porosity of the top layer. Roots of many species have special microscopic hairs that can absorb the minute moisture droplets that condense at night underground. Annual grasses characteristically have deep root systems to divine water down to the parent rock.

Nutrients may be scarce if the soil is in its infancy. Yet pioneer grasses can make do on the very margin of life support. They continue to break down soil particles with their searching roots and add to the organic content of the new soil when they die. They therefore modify their habitat, changing it so that eventually it becomes suitable for successive forms and, at the same time, unsuitable for themselves. But this does not matter; they can move on. The continually changing surface of the

Earth in the form of a lava flow, a hippo wallow or a roadside verge will always provide a home for the plant pioneers.

On more mature soils where the opportunistic lifestyle of the annual grasses is not called for, perennial grasses take over. We call them "equilibrium strategists", for they maintain themselves persistently from season to season, at a high-population density. Their root systems are tenacious near the surface, and capable of storing food for the dry season. They only tolerate a few deep-rooted wild flowers, trees and shrubs; and then only if the local rainfall is sufficient to provide a surplus after the grasses have absorbed all they need at the surface.

Two perennial grasses: the annual or short-lived *Rhynchelytrum repens* (opposite) and *Chloris* (above)

Grasslands

The African grasslands, one of the vegetation patches big enough to be visible from space, support the highest concentrations of large mammals in the world. These habitats are so extensive that if we were to walk from the Sahara to the Cape we would trudge most of the way through various types of grassland. One-sixth of the entire Earth's land surface is tropical grasslands. The rolling savanna dotted with flat-topped acacia trees is part of the picture of Africa everyone knows. To the rangeland ecologist it is known as "wooded grassland". If the tree canopies cover more than about twenty per cent of the ground, the habitat grades into "woodland"; where there are more bushes than trees, it is "bushed grassland"; the nearly treeless areas are simply "grasslands" or "plains". What controls these extremely productive habitats?

Their extent is determined by a blend of altitude (600 to 1,800 metres); undulating topography; an equitable temperature (10 to 27 degrees C) despite intense solar radiation; reasonable if uneven rainfall (500 to 800 millimetres annually) distributed in distinct seasons; and shallow soils, often red on the slopes, black clay in the sumps. Soil differences may be just local changes down a hillside or may be very widespread. For instance, the ashes blasted from Ngorongoro crater when it erupted 5 million years ago fell and covered 20,000 square kilometres to the north and west. The resultant ash-rich alkaline soils inhibit the growth of trees, and the soil boundary therefore marks the edge of the virtually treeless Serengeti Plains.

Beyond the plains where the soil is kinder to their needs, trees and shrubs are able to grow again.

The grasslands, then, are a patchwork mosaic of different forms of vegetation controlled by local differences in topography, soils and rainfall. These inanimate patterns determine the animal patterns we encounter in the grasslands. Thick riverine bush (*opposite top*) shows clearly the drainage patterns of the area because its growth along those particular lines is encouraged by the additional rain water retained in the dips and depressions of the Earth's surface by the fine soils which have been washed down from the higher slopes.

We are drawn like terrestrial mariners to inselbergs or kopjes (*opposite below*), granite islands in the grass sea. They look like intrusions poked through the plain surface, but in fact are the hard bits left after millennia of erosion of the peniplain. Sun, wind and rain then sculpt flakes off the rock surface in a living process of exfoliation. Thus jutting out of the relatively smooth surface of the plains there are steep slopes, cracks and crevices, rock pools and crusts. The combination of surface variety, isolation and a micro-climate that is cooler, wetter and a shade more stable than the surrounding grassland enriches the kopjes of eastern and southern Africa with plant and animal endemic species. Like all islands, they are both refuges and sources.

All of this underlying patchiness of local topography, water availability, soil richness and animal utilisation contributes to what is called "pattern diversity" within the grassland plant communities; that is, dozens of different grass

and herb species living in mixed neighbourhoods. Far from leading to confusion, this very diversity may contribute to a community stability that is better able to withstand extreme perturbations, like fire and drought. United they stand...

Grassland inhabitants: lions (*top*) and the ground hornbill (*above*)

Prolific pastures

The primary production of the grasslands is prolific; during the rains, for example, every square metre of grass can produce almost a kilo of edible material each month – some 1,000 tonnes to the square kilometre. This rapid conversion of materials into an edible, available form creates the opportunity for numerous herbivores to exist, and the very grazing of those animals stimulates the grass sward to produce even more than it would without animal mowing. In terms of kilos of large animal flesh per unit area (called "biomass density"), the Mkomazi Game Reserve in Tanzania and the Queen Elizabeth National Park in Uganda each support something like 200 times as much as the forests we shall look at later. In the Serengeti ecosystem, the live-weight of the twenty-eight species of herbivore, from elephants to dik-diks, is in the region of 250 million kilogrammes – roughly the same as the weight of the inhabitants of Greater London. And that does not include the five species of primates, twenty-six species of carnivore, more than 500 species of birds and the uncounted thousands of invertebrate species which themselves probably weigh as much as all the vertebrates put together. The animal biomass of the wooded grassland is unequalled in any other living system, and there is as yet no evidence that affordable pasture management can surpass what natural communities produce.

For the plants, production and survival are determined both in the dimensions of space and time. Any gardener knows that things grow better on nutrient-rich soils, a quality that makes the Serengeti something of a Garden of Eden. But unlike the predictable squares of a garden allotment, nutrients are not evenly available. Both their amount and accessibility to plants depend first on physical factors,

like local topography and soil texture. Nutrients tend to slip with water through the soil down slopes and accumulate in the bottoms, getting chemically or physically stuck, or not, to sands and clays. And the water necessary to make nutrients available for growth and reproduction tends to be mainly available in the rainy season. Apart from some seed-dispersal tricks, plants are bound to cast their lots in one place. Undaunted by immobility, they nonetheless present herbivores a bewildering variety in a grass sward that looks pretty homogeneous from the middle distance. The wildebeest nosing about in it meets a dozen different grass species, some with more than one variety, with individuals in different stages of growth and flowering, mixed with a number of herbs, all of which may be pristine, recently eaten by someone else, or growing back after a bout of grazing. To bite or not to bite, that becomes the question. And if the wildebeest chooses not to bite, where does it go next?

What plants do in space and time, animals and people do mainly in space. The migratory herds and nomadic pastoral tribes of Africa have evolved an opportunistic way of life; for them, survival lies in continually moving from the dry and withered to the wet and green, trying to extract as much sustenance from as little expenditure of energy as possible. And if geology and topography, rainfall and evaporation are the factors controlling or limiting the form of the vegetation, then it is the moveable animal feasts, combined with fire, that modify it. Such interactions between flora and fauna, between the animate and the inanimate, between fire and water, keep the cycles of the natural world in motion.

A tree for all seasons

The classic acacia is Africa's universal icon. An oak may remind us of England, a redwood of California, a eucalyptus of Australia, and a Protea may bring South Africa to mind. But few images call to mind an entire continent in the way a flat-topped acacia does. Although many species of the genus have the approximate shape, it is only the umbrella acacia, *Acacia tortilis*, that looks perfect against the sunset, perhaps with a pair of giraffes passing in the middle distance. They occur across the continent in the wooded grasslands of the east to the Sudano-sahelian zone of the west. Some imagine "the tree where Man was born" to be a baobab. But we believe the nimble near-humans who left their footprints in the ash mud of Laetoli in Tanzania were more likely to seek shade, perhaps even give birth, under the acacias of the Serengeti and Ngorongoro 3.6 million years ago. A good while later, Moses was commissioned to use the tough, close-grained acacia wood to build a suitable case for his newly acquired, very special Hard Copies. A good choice, compared, say, to the pulpy stuff of the baobab that barely survives a couple of dances as a barkcloth skirt, let alone the millennium guarantee required for the Ark of the Covenant.

The tree is perfectly adapted to a land of heat and sporadic rains, but to appreciate its appropriateness, we need to change the point of view. Underground, we can follow the roots along two strategic lines. One is to send a taproot straight down, twenty metres or more, to reach the moister layers of the drainage basin. The other is to spread to the side, close to the surface, to catch whatever water may soak in from a short shower. From directly underneath we see that the near-perfect circle of the canopy throws a light shadow on the main area of the shallow lateral roots, helping to slow down evaporation from the soil and encourage shade-loving bushes and grasses to help with the task. And from very close to the crown we see that the branchlets are armed with thorns to try to lessen the toll taken by giraffes, and that the tiny bipinnate leaves help, in a way not yet understood, to reduce the tree's infestation by insect pests.

Apart from the Ents of Tolkein's Middle Earth, trees are usually viewed as rather inanimate objects. Yet roots notwithstanding, they do seem to have a form of social intercourse. Some acacias have been observed to provide an "alarm signal" to neighbouring trees. When antelopes browse on their leaves, they emit ethylene into the air and produce leaf tannin in lethal quantities. The ethylene can waft up to fifty metres from the "attacked" individual. The exposed neighbours appear to be effectively warned of the impending danger, for in less than ten minutes they step up their own production of leaf tannin. Presumably after a few minutes of browsing, the herbivore finds his lunch going sour and wanders off to find something better tasting. He may find he has to go farther than the next few trees.

Herbivores are not all bad, and *Acacia tortilis* helps them to eat her seeds by giving them a spiral twist, usually to the left, to make them much easier to pick up with trunk or lip. The old scientific name of the tree – *spirocarpa* – seems more appropriate than the new. The highly nutritious pods are much prized in their season, and the tree is rewarded for its harvest by getting the seeds deposited in a ready compost heap, invariably far away from the shade of the parent.

Thus, despite their defences, the Acacias help nourish the richness of the wooded grasslands. What they give to large browsers is modest compared to their entertainment of thousands of species of arthropod – 1,600 species to the square metre have been counted in Mkomazi trees. One small tree may be home to 70,000 individuals, of which one in five belongs to a species that is new to science.

Fire

In primeval times it was a freak lightning strike or a spark from a volcano that started grass fires. Today it is more likely to be a man with a match, albeit practising what his ancestors have done for the last two million years: setting the heath ablaze either for management or fun. But, whatever the cause, fire has become an integral modifying factor of grassland ecology – over three-quarters of African grasslands go up in smoke every year.

A few tree species have adapted to withstand burning by developing a thick fireproof bark, others "retreat" underground. A stunted but living sixty-centimetre-high acacia in a regularly burned area might have a root stock fifteen centimetres thick – evidence that the part the plant above ground has been burned back regularly for a decade or more. Some grasslands are maintained by fire: others reduced as fire-resistant shrubs creep in. The effects are varied, depending on local conditions.

Although fire may be a quick way to break down materials for re-cycling, it also leads to loss.

In the heat of a dry grass fire, smoke rises thousands of metres. Blown on the wind it spreads a delicate blue haze as far as the eye can see. Grassland ash can drift half-way around the world. It produces spectacular sunsets, but represents the exportation of tons of materials from the grassland ecosystem. The emissions every second from a medium-sized vegetation fire are equivalent to the carbon monoxide and nitrogen oxides produced by several thousand motor vehicles in the same second. A volatile element like nitrogen is lost into the atmosphere in prodigious amounts

and its compounds contribute to the accumulation of greenhouse gases. "Suspended particular matter" – soot basically – ends up reflecting sunlight back into space or as the nuclei of raindrops. Back on Earth, there can be a huge cost to local organisms. For herbivores, the food supply disappears in a flash. In fact so do most of the small mammals and terrestrial insects, if the fire is a late dry-season hot one.

If we put aside preconceptions, born in temperate climes, that lead us to believe all vegetation under-goes successive stages of growth until a climax form is reached, then we are better able to understand the frequently dramatic changes in Africa's wooded grasslands. In many areas trees are dying and woodlands seem to be disappearing. Is this an ecological disaster? Perhaps not, since the wooded grassland is not a climax form, not an end-product in itself, but simply an integral part of a much larger perhaps centuries-long – cycle.

Consider a typical example of a woodland–grassland–woodland cycle. Old trees begin to die, often burned into grotesque sculptures or pushed over by elephants. Their death allows seedlings that would otherwise have died in the shade of the adult canopy to mature. At the same time more robust species of grass can now thrive. But, more grass combined with a "bad" dry season is a fire hazard, and should fire occur, regeneration of the acacia woodland is retarded as the young trees are burnt back. This allows still more grass to flourish which, combined with a series of "good" wet seasons, produces more food for the grazers like wildebeest and gazelles. Increase

a population's food supply and it will, to a point, increase in size. More grazers eat more grass, thus reducing potential fuel for a fire. Young trees begin to grow beyond the fire-critical height of three metres. Grassland begins to revert to woodland. And so on. It may take a hundred years.

Maasai elders in Amboseli recall through oral tradition how the yellow-barked fever trees (*Acacia xanthophloea, previous double page*) all but disappeared a century ago, just as they have been doing over the past two decades.

So, we see that our pyramid of life is a slightly simplistic representation of herbivore-plant interaction, for there are numerous variations on our basic theme of the flow of energy and resources – different habitats composed of different plants, supporting different animals. We need a long-term understanding of the effects of plants and animals upon one another before we can predict the patterns – if indeed we ever can. Nevertheless, the general shape of the pyramid of life stands true in this part of the world where the easiest things to predict are the intensity of the sun and the irregularity of the rains.

Thomson's gazelle, unmoved by a late season grass fire

Animal furniture

Animals, as we shall see, are capable of modifying the vegetation of a habitat. They can also have a considerable impact on its physical structure. Of course, over-use of the vegetation may increase the rate at which rain removes the soil and thus lead to erosion. But in undisturbed animal and plant communities, such serious modification rarely, if ever, occurs.

Mud wallows are an important type of "animal furniture". They are, like our furniture, literally made for comfort and are as inoffensive to the habitat as an easychair is to our living room. The rolling and dusting of a seasonal migration of zebras creates a bared, slightly depressed opening in the grass cover. If the spot happens to be an ancient termite mound, rich in

salts, antelopes paw and eat the "salt-lick" soil to augment the generally sodium-poor vegetation. Elephants pause for a taste of salt or merely to suck up and blow clouds of dust over their backs. The depression deepens; during the next rains, water accumulates. With the onset of the dry season, a muddy patch is left. A family of warthogs may spend the heat of several days

rooting and rolling in the mud. They are displaced by some bull buffaloes who further churn up the mud and carry off more dirt when they leave to feed. The elephants pass by again and this time plaster mud on their backs. The next rains produce a pool that persists even further into the following dry season. After several years of use and modification by a whole string of animals, the result is a mud bath capable of entertaining a dozen hippopotami from a nearby lake.

All these herbivores cool themselves (*overleaf*) and escape from worrisome insects in the mud. They also tend to take the pause in the hot day as a natural time to excrete. Water, mud, and the presence of the dung seem to encourage other animals to excrete, so the wallow eventually becomes a pool of concentrated nutrients. There comes a point, perhaps, when the wallow gets a bit too rich; when it falls out of favour. The animals begin their furniture-building at another spot, and the wallow is left to encroaching plants. Years later, only a patch of particularly lush grass marks the original wallow. Grazers still drop by, but now for another reason.

Animal feeding

From any point of view, the elephant's impact on primary production is as spectacular as its size. In its continuous "predation" on plants, the elephant tears branches from trees, pulls great tufts of grass and roots from the Earth, gouges huge holes in baobabs and pushes over acacia and *Commiphora* trees. Is this destruction? Not really; it is modification, perhaps even enrichment, of the habitat. For a rich habitat is not one which simply makes a pretty picture, but one in which energy is flowing through numerous pathways, and in which materials are changing form continuously.

In the grasslands of Africa, there are no hard and fast rules that dictate that there will be precisely so many trees and so many elephants. If elephants, or voles for that matter, increase their numbers and reduce their own food supply, they obviously become undernourished. Their reproductive rates lessen and a proportion of them invariably die from starvation or disease. As their numbers drop, so does the pressure on the vegetation. Whether or not and how quickly vegetation regenerates, depends on complex intertwining of animal impacts like giraffe browsing and wildebeest grazing, the perennial influence of fire on regeneration (see p. 39), and the vicissitudes of the climate. More patterns on patterns.

Striding through this habitat mosaic, the elephant may cover tens of kilometres a day at a comfortable walk, indulging its catholic tastes on the wide range of food plants that are physically available to it. Such flexibility allows elephants to thrive and leave their mark in nearly every African habitat from semi-arid bushed grassland to mountain forest. They may even stay in one ecosystem for generations and happily weather major changes from woodlands to grasslands and back. The only limiting factor is water, which must be in good supply to support a population whose average member requires seventy litres a day.

Considering that a large elephant can ingest some 600 kilos of green matter a day, stuffing it in for sixteen hours, we may wonder how the habitat can take it. Yet far from being demolition agents, elephants are in fact the greatest natural construction crew in Africa, contributing more to the change and variety in local habitat than any other species. Nowhere, not even in regions of apparent over population where habitat destruction might be expected, has it yet been demonstrated that elephants by themselves degrade habitats to the point of creating deserts. They change them certainly – rather less so than goats, by the way – but they do not destroy them. When they knock down trees in woodland for instance, a greater variety of vegetation frequently results other species of grasses, shrubs, bushes and herbs taking hold. In this way elephants alter patterns and may increase diversity.

Legs and mouths

Materials in an ecosystem may move from the plants to the herbivores, from the herbivores to the carnivores, and thence through the decomposers back to the soil. The gateway from one trophic level to the next is through the mouth. The mouthparts of the harvester ant (*formicidae*, subfamily *Ponerinae*, *right top*) seem a far cry from those of a hippopotamus, yet both animals feed on grass. Like a lawnmower, the hippo trims the grass sward with its wide lips, raking in each bite enough grass seeds to keep one harvester ant busy for most of its life.

The mouths of large herbivore characteristically have lips to gather, incisor teeth to clip, molar teeth to grind. Grazers have wide muzzles to harvest grass. Browsers who feed on leaves of shrubs have delicate mouths to select single leaves. Gnawers have pointed faces and tiny mouths, just large enough to expose the working of the two front teeth. Such morphological (body form) features are invariably accompanied by characteristic behaviours. Hippos bite from the leaf table, gazelles select single leaves, rodents pick seeds apart, harvester ants cart them away.

At the ant's scale, mouthparts seem alien to us, but the mechanical solutions – apart from the piercing and sucking of aphids and weevils – are similar to those of larger animals. Chewers, such as caterpillars and grasshoppers, slice into the leaf cells and extract nourishment from the contents without attempting to digest the celluloid walls. Grasshopper jaws are as well equipped for grinding as buffalo molars; under the microscope, the ridges of their tiny mandibles resemble those of bovine teeth,

despite a thousandfold difference of scale. The mandibles are worked by relatively large muscles that may occupy half the volume of the head: bulbous-pated caterpillars and grasshoppers bear witness to the toughness of their fodder.

A few specialised digestive systems have evolved chemical and mechanical means to unlock the nutritious sugars and proteins in the cellulose armour of plant cells. In the process of rumination, the plant material is chewed and fermented several times in succession. Plant cell walls are further broken down by single-celled micro-organisms that live in ruminant herbivore guts and produce a special enzyme to digest cellulose. The relationship is mutualistic (advantageous to both): the protozoan gets its food delivered, the herbivore gets its digested. Insects, apart from a couple of specialists such as termites (see p. 78), ignore the cellulose as a source of nutrition, and slice or pierce their way through it to tap the vegetable juice within.

There are other necessary adaptations of herbivore body shape and form. The legs of most large herbivores must be long enough to move the animals efficiently over long distances in search of food or for avoiding predators. This means that necks must be long enough to reach the grass made remote by the legs. Once the head is near the plants, the nose, whiskers and lips must be sensitive enough to select the correct parts of the grass by smell or texture. Add these features together and we have the general shape of a typical antelope – a wildebeest or an impala, for

example. Invertebrate legs tend to be jointed and relatively long and, like moonwalker prototypes, can lower or extend several times the body height.

Reaching the richest part of the tree, at the very top, the long tongue of the giraffe slips between the acacia's thorns to pull the foliage into its mouth

Migration

Although plants cannot move, their effective availability changes in time as we have seen. For the herbivore, grass that has withered away might as well have run away. Thus, as the seasons change, herbivores must move on to greener pastures. The movement can be relatively modest, such as that of the resident impalas who cluster along rivers in the dry season and move back up the slopes in the rains a matter of a month or two later. Or, the movement can be a full-scale migration, such as that of the Serengeti's wandering wildebeest (*opposite*) who cover nearly 25,000 square kilometres in their annual 500 kilometre round trip of the Serengeti ecosystem. This moving mass, over 1.3 million strong, is one of the last great animal spectacles on earth.

The question of why they migrate is both simple and complex. The movement itself serves to keep the animals in areas where there is enough grass to eat. During a good rainy season in the Serengeti the daily production amounts to an impressive 300 kilos per hectare, something like a stalk of celery appearing every three paces each day. But beyond protein and bulk for growth and energy, water and probably some essential fatty acids, the migratory herds seek out pasture patches with ingredients that read like the minerals in your daily multivitamin: calcium, copper, nitrogen, magnesium, sodium, phosphorous and zinc – all especially required by pregnant and lactating cows. Once again we see patterns intersecting with patterns: the animals relating to the grass sward, the grasses absorbing from the soil

type, the soil types deriving from the bedrock, the bedrock conforming to topography, all washed the way the water moves.

When drying and grazing reduces the amount and quality of fodder to below acceptable levels, the wildebeest simply move on. Due to a rainfall gradient from the drier southeast to the wetter northwest, the short-grass Serengeti Plains begin to dry up first. So around the end of May, the wildebeest move off to the west and north, through the woodlands, feeding and rutting along the way. The peak of the dry season, July and August, finds them in the still green Kenya Mara. Here they circle around, with the females growing heavy, until November, when the beginning of the short rains greens their path again to the south, where they calve. But what exactly tells the wildebeeste it is time to go, and which way to go?

We hear reports of the wildebeest herds "deliberately" setting off towards distant rainstorms. Do they see the dark clouds and "understand" the implications, or smell the rain and "make the link" between precipitation and production? Perhaps they have such associations built into their genetic information.

Are they able to taste the mineral quality of the grasses in the same way we can tell if a glass of water has come from our favourite spa or the city council? Does going elsewhere satisfy specific mineral "hungers" that need to be sated for successful calf rearing? Then again, herbivores select grass to eat, not so much according to species of grass, but rather according to its tensile

strength. Grass which is easily bitten off is clearly leafier, younger and hence more nourishing. Is the main cue then the physical structure of the grass? Such questions will only be answered with careful observation and experiments both with wild and tame wildebeest.

Distribution, quality and amounts of primary production control the phenomena of the wildebeest migration. But what determines their numbers? The Serengeti population increased steadily after the great rinderpest pandemic at the end of the last century and levelled off in the late 1970s at around 1.3 million. Part of the reason for the growth may be an increase in the amount of open grasslands because of the reduction of woodland by fire and elephants. Or perhaps it was simply a re-growth to pristine levels, in a region largely protected. Scientists following the fate of the Serengeti wildebeest over the past twenty-five years have confirmed that both food availability and predation pressure limit populations: as food becomes scarce, animals take greater risks to get enough. And whilst they are at it, some of them get killed. Causal factors aside, we need to remember that much of this animal wonder takes place outside protected areas. Its future fate thus lies with the levels of development of the neighbouring people and the enlightenment of their governments.

Niches

Different herbivore species, some of which appear quite similar, use particular parts of the same habitat in different ways. They achieve this by adopting what are called ecological niches. A niche may sound familiar, but it is a tricky thing to pin down. It is formally encapsulated in a rather obscure phrase, like "an *n*-dimensional hypervolume". Try to imagine a space that has more than the basic three dimensions of position – length, width and breadth – one that includes also lines of time, climate, light intensity, habitat type, altitude above or below sea level, temperature, food types, and so on. There would be a very large and indeterminate number of dimensions, *n* of them, in fact. If in your imagination you then put marks on the line of each dimension showing what the species needs or simply what it does, you would have a jumble of marks. If you then connect them with your imaginary pencil, you would make a cat's-cradle of lines, a blob in this hyperspace. We cannot actually do all this, of course, but we can imagine that each species' blob would be floating in a different position from all the others. You would have drawn a unique species' niche.

In plainer language, a niche defines everything a particular species does for a living, a concept similar to human vocations. Since the exercise of describing a niche demands such an intimate knowledge of an animal's way of life, it is easiest first to describe *where* it is.

Herbivore food does not run away from the herbivore, but it is effectively available in different measures and qualities in different places. Specialisation on one class of food is, amongst other things, a way of conserving the energy involved in searching – you look in one place, not everywhere. Hence there are some herbivores who are riverine species: waterbuck and reedbuck; those who fill an open grassland niche: gazelle and wildebeest, zebra and ostrich; those who fill a wooded bushland niche: kudu and bushbuck; and those who use the ecotone, the area of intergradation between woodland and grassland: topi and impala.

Throughout the mosaic of grassland habitats, even in those that are wooded or bushed to some extent, you will never find as many browsers as you will grazers. This is because there is simply less browse fodder than grass. The relative abundance or biomass of each species must reflect the abundance of their most necessary resource (or most successful parasitic disease). Agriculturists have for decades called this critical dependency on the least amount of that item amongst those things you need the most Leibig's Law of the Minimum. The limiting factor may be a nutrient like soil nitrogen or a particular species of food plant. If it is not available in what the habitat presents a particular species, then its numbers will surely diminish and other species who are finding what they need will fare better. In the wild the choices are starkly simple: leave, adapt or die.

An important cause of diversity of types and ecological niches is competition for common resources. Back in evolutionary time the species were very similar if not, in many cases, one and the same. When grasses appeared millions of years ago, they spread around the world and provided the fuel for the rise of the ruminants. These "fibrivores" were able to pay the price of the abundance of grass by developing ways to deal with pithy cell walls. Cellulose is the commonest carbohydrate in nature and an excellent source of energy. But it's too tough to handle on its own, and it takes legions of symbiotic bacteria, protozoa and fungi – so-called "gut flora" – living in airless contentment in the fermentation chambers of ruminant guts to break down cellulose. Even with such bounteous fare as grass, niches become "crowded" as the number of organisms using common resources increases. One way to avoid conflict is for one of the contestants to change its tastes. If the divergence increases its chance of survival, it is on its way to becoming a new species, and over the millennia, will slip into another ecological niche. The effect, of course, is to reduce competition between species, to increase the diversity of the animal community and to increase the number of paths energy can take through the ecosystem.

But there is another advantage as well to "being diverse" – namely, to present parasites with a multi-padlocked gate (see p. 110). One species of predator – a hyaena, say – will happily eat any of a dozen odd herbivores, and, as we shall see, there are a few common avoidance strategies that are shared by all herbivores. By the same token, one species of tick carrying a particular blood parasite will latch

The zebra (*opposite top*) fills the open grassland niche and a young impala (*opposite bottom*) uses the ecotone, the area between woodland and grassland

on to whichever of these beasts happens to brush by. If the pest is confronted with a barrage of different immune systems residing in a number of species in the neighbourhood, the chances of that pathogen taking over this patch of the world are considerably reduced (see p. 218). This in turn considerably increases the potential hosts' chances of survival. Thus the niche includes not only where one lives and what one does for a living, but all the tricks of how one lives as well.

The eland is a plains animal, one of the specialists with a rather narrow niche. It feeds predominantly on dicotyledonous plants, on the leaves of small wild flowers that grow amongst the grass. Such plants are very nutritious, so the eland can build a large body. Males can weigh up to a tonne and stand nearly two metres at the shoulder. But its food plants are scattered and relatively scarce. Hence the density of elands must be low and their distribution scattered. The eland is a good example of the ultimate dependency of the upper on the lower trophic level, of the herbivore upon its food supply.

The warthog (*opposite top*) and wildebeest (*right*) whose niche is the open grassland, and the waterbuck (*opposite bottom*), a riverine herbivore

The grazing sequence

Niche separation in space and time can be obvious, as we have seen. It can, as well, be too subtle for the human observer to discern at first glance (which leads us to invent terms like "hyperspace"). Animals may appear to be sharing the same pasture, but every farmer knows that the horses in the field are eating different things from the cows. Amongst African herbivores, resources may be shared in a mutually beneficial way known as a grazing sequence.

Because of its coarse structure, a mature strand of grass is physically unavailable to the little gazelles and even unpalatable to the wildebeest. But the heavy feeders like rhinoceros (*top right*), buffaloes and elephants can tramp into the chest-high grass and efficiently harvest what they need. Once they have trampled and eaten the heavier material and permitted regrowth of finer grass, the wildebeest and zebras (*opposite*) move in. The zebras are also, to some extent, coarse-feeders and do not mind grass with a moderately low leaf-to-stem ratio; they are followed by wildebeest who prefer a bit more leaf and less stem. But both are daunted by the virtually inedible, potentially dangerous strands of tall grass which could conceal predators, so they "let" the larger animals pave the way. In fact, although they are partners in the quadrille, their mutual association is largely driven by having more eyes around at one time to spot predators.

After the zebras and the wildebeest have refined the structure of the pasture even further, and mulched some uneaten material into the soil thereby stimulating the growth of more shoots, the grassland is

"ready" for the herbivores with more delicate mouths and refined tastes, such as the hartebeest and gazelles. During the growing season, the first-wave grazing of wildebeest actually increases the amount of grass left for Thomson's gazelles. These selectively nip off the leafy parts of the grasses or pluck the dicotyledons left by the bigger animals. Egyptian geese (*right*) then graze on the shortest swards, termites clean up the debris, and insectivorous birds take continual advantage of the insects stirred up by the feet of the herbivores. Thus in a grazing sequence, the same hectare of grassland is used sequentially and simultaneously during the growing season by a number of herbivores (and some attendant carnivores). The result is a healthy grass "lawn", often a mosaic of close-cropped patches of favoured species and longer patches of stemmier grasses.

The primary production and plant species diversity under such a regime of use by a mixed herbivore community is actually greater than if the grassland were left untouched.

Use begets growth, as Desmond Vesey-FitzGerald was fond of saying, and secondary productivity maintains a maximum level as long as the dynamics and timing of the succession are not interfered with. If one species stays too long or if fire eliminates the grass, the succession is thrown temporarily out of rhythm. The system is flexible enough to weather such disturbances at their natural, infrequent rate. If drought or human activities, such as burning or the confinement of the grazing herds, disturb the sequence for too long, then the result is over-grazing, weed encroachment, bare ground and erosion. The grassland begins to die.

The evolution of species

Evolution is often thought of as something which happened ages ago, an event which, like the Creation, is now finished. But life forms are constantly, if slowly, changing in response to the demands of an ever-changing environment. Modification of form and behaviour will go on as long as there is life; species will continue to come and go. The contemporary dynamism of evolution is most apparent when we observe species that look almost the same, but which, on closer examination, turn out to be quite different.

From a distance there is not much to distinguish the white and black rhinoceros; or the Maasai and the reticulated giraffe, or the Grevy's and Burchell's zebra. But they are different – the larger white rhino has a distinctive squared-off upper lip (hence its name "white", not a description of its colour but a corruption of the Afrikaans word for wide); the reticulated's pattern is bolder than the Maasai's; and the Grevy's stripes are thinner and the ears larger. But why should they be different at all?

In the first place the similar forms live in different places. For example, the reticulated giraffe is an animal of dry country like northern Kenya and is separated from the nearest Maasai giraffe population by some 200 kilometres. Both must have arisen from a common ancestor. With its Pleistocene populations separated by a geographic barrier, or by a chance one-way migration, each responded in its own way to the new local conditions. All populations of one species separated in space tend to become distinct "ecotypes". different forms of one species. The two giraffes are examples.

Isolation results in changes in behaviour as well as colouration or body form. After thousands of years apart, the Grevy's finds that it has a different social system from the Burchell's zebra: a territorial one designed to conserve a scarce grass supply in arid areas. Their behaviour thus diverged enough to isolate effectively the two incipient species. When such populations happen to come together again after many generations of separation, they tend to remain distinct, as populations of the two zebras do which now overlap in northern Kenya. It is doubtful, however, that they would pass the test of true speciation: if they could

be convinced to overcome their behavioural barrier and mate, they would be quite likely to produce a fertile hybrid. "Good species" would not.

Both giraffes eat acacia leaves and both zebras eat grass, but the two rhino species have gone further in their speciation. The black rhino, as we have seen, is a browser; but the white, as we would guess from its broad lips, and its exceptionally long skull which puts the lips constantly close to the sward, is a grazer. The white rhino lives in predominantly open grasslands, the black in bushier country. The way the mother and young move in relation to each other further reflects their long niche separation. Black rhino babies follow on their mother's heels, letting her plough

a path through the bush. White rhino babies precede their mother through open grass, allowing her to cover their rear whilst sweeping ahead and side to side watching for danger. Body form and lifestyle changes of this magnitude suggest that the two rhinos diverged a very long time ago, and probably have become "good species", although we know of no attempt to cross-breed them.

So speciation is a gradual process of divergence, accelerated in some cases by enforced separation or habitat catastrophes, until not only the form and behaviour differ, but the very structure of the genes has changed too far to allow successful recombination through natural backtracking. The colour differences between the two giraffes

and between the two zebras are probably ones which have come about by pure chance – a judgement admittedly arrived at by examination through human eyes, to which both types of blotches and both stripes are equally effective. We cannot, of course, ask them directly about their ancestries, but there are new techniques – derived from forensic medicine – to deduce family trees from similarities and differences in patterns of the structure of DNA molecules. Not only can genealogies of species be determined, but the degree of relatedness of populations within a species can also be established.

From left to right: the white (top) and black (bottom) rhinoceros, the Maasai an reticulated giraffe, and the Grevy's and Burchell's zebra

Reaching a niche

The giraffe is a product of evolution that has solved its problems through elongation. Scholarly debate rages over whether the extraordinarily long neck evolved primarily to reach up to augment the long front legs in getting food, or to reach down to access water made distant by those very legs. What really matters is that the composite height of the improbable beast lifts it into a highly nutritious and largely unexploited grassland food niche. A food source six-odd metres above the ground is virtually unavailable to most other mammalian herbivores. "Browse lines" on the underside of a woodland canopy, or shrubs shaped like hourglasses, are evidence of the hedge-clipping activities of giraffes, who browse on all the suitable trees in an area, taking just a few small sprigs from the surface of each. Like pruned hedges the trees respond with a thickening of the surface which in turn provides a greater leaf table area for the giraffe.

Giraffes have the same number of neck vertebrae as us – seven – but each is several times longer than it is wide, unlike ours that are wider than they are high. A neck of such unusual length demands that the heart of a giraffe be relatively large – two-and-a-half times larger than its body mass would suggest – in order to pump blood three metres uphill to the brain. When a giraffe drinks or browses from a ground-level shrub, the brain would burst from fluid pressure if it were not for special valves in the neck arteries. In turn, however, maintaining elasticity of these valves and strength of the arterial walls requires a diet rich in just those materials, such as calcium, that are most plentiful in the vegetation at the very tops of trees, and which cannot be reached without a long neck. The long tongue of the giraffe – extendable to nearly half a metre – is just able to slip between the acacia's array of defensive thorns and pull the foliage into the mouth, lengthened and narrowed for the same reason. Its specialised canines are splayed at the ends in two or three lobes to help comb leaves off shoots. Ingested thorns do not much bother the idly munching animal: it engulfs them in a viscous latex-like saliva and compresses them against the horny skin covering its highly grooved palate.

The leverage and muscular masses of the long legs allow the giraffe to lope along at nearly forty kilometres per hour and kick with a force that puts it near the bottom of the list of favourite lion food. The giraffe's visual advantage in spotting danger before more conventionally structured prey animals makes it a valuable and respected member of the herbivore community. When a giraffe stops to gaze, others freeze and listen.

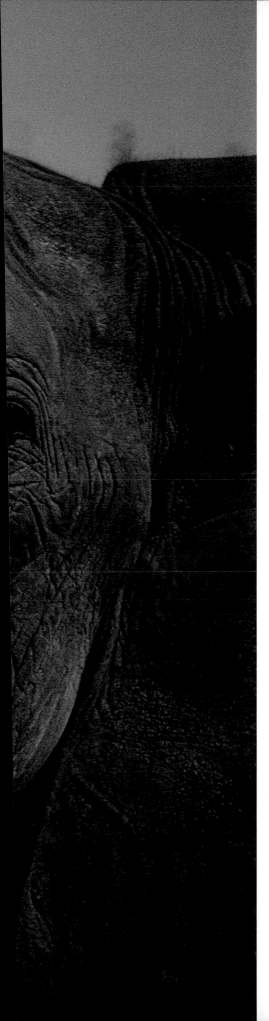

Blood relatives

Blood, as Goethe put it, is a very special juice. It binds us in many ways. We mammals all bleed red if pricked, and our family trees are mapped in the structure of the blood proteins that aid clotting. Analyses indicate common ancestries and paint a peculiar family portrait featuring elephants, sea cows, hyraxes, aardvarks, and elephant shrews (see p. 270). Today, there are few mammal herbivores that could appear less alike than a two-kilo rock hyrax (*right*) and a 2,000-kilo elephant. Yet, not only can biochemists find matching blood proteins, but physiologists point to a number of physical similarities and palaeontologists trace the fossil record back to the antecedents of a 40-million-year-old beast called *Moeritherium*. These animals browsed and grazed their way through Eocene ("dawn of the recent") pastures and gave rise to progeny who solved similar problems in very different ways.

Hyraxes achieve thermoregulation with a behavioural repertoire to augment their curiously inefficient internal thermostat. When the outside temperature drops, they seek the sun or flatten themselves against a warm rock; at night they sleep in cosy piles in rock crevices, insulating one another and decreasing the effective surface area of hyrax exposed to the cool evening air. They have a remarkable interwoven network of veins and arteries in their legs that ensures that the body heat in the outward-bound arterial blood is transferred to the cooler venous blood returning from the feet. Elephants do the same with their ears (see p. 62). Another physiological oddity shared by these two blood

relatives is a special modified gland that secretes a pheromone-laden substance when the animals are excited. The respective glands provide a visual as well as olfactory signal and attract considerable attention amongst conspecifics. There the resemblance stops. The elephant's musth gland is a modified tear duct located between the eye and ear. It streams out in a conspicuous dark patch on the side of the head of, for example, adult cows and young when the group is excited at a reunion or adult bulls when they are in the unique elephant male "season". The hyrax counterpart is an augmented subcutaneous gland in the middle of the back, surrounded by erectile hairs with a conspicuous whitish tinge. It appears active under similar social circumstances.

It would belabour the point to draw any more parallels, such as the high degree of sociability, the homologous foot bones, the fermentative gut, the elongated incisor teeth (tusks in elephants, pseudo-canines in hyraxes) or the internal testes. Their ancient history is common; the animals are unique and both curiously compelling.

Big is beautiful

Paradoxically, the very size of the elephant means it needs less to stay alive than you would expect. The reason has to do with one of the most fundamental design features of living things. Every plant and animal, big and small, has a network of internal tubes that branch down to cell level in order to deliver nutrients and remove waste. Suppose evolution had been bound to a one-to-one scaling rule when building an elephant out of smaller precursors. That mythical elephant would have terminal tubes like garden hoses to feed cells the size of bricks, an impossibility since living cells, like Lego pieces, come pretty well in just one size: very, very small, just enough to package DNA and some accessories. The fact that an elephant's terminal tubes have to be of the same cell-dimensioned size as a mouse's puts a unique constraint on how things grow and metabolise. It is encapsulated in Kleiber's Rule, which states that metabolism relates to body mass not on a one-to-one scale, but to the three-quarters power. Just why it is three-quarters and not some other number is still being debated, but the rule seems to be so universal that even plants obey it. This fundamental economy of scale results in the paradox that a big rotund animal requires less food per kilo of body mass than a smaller animal.

There must be, of course, some compromise between making the most of the energy eaten and dissipating enough to avoid succumbing to heat exhaustion at one extreme, and conserving heat during cool clear tropical nights at the other. The elephant's superlative proportions serve this compromise. Physiologically, elephants avoid overheating by burning relatively little oxygen, by the insulation of the two- to three-centimetre-thick skin on the back, by the great mass of the body that takes a long time to heat up to a critical level and through extensive foldings and bifurcations of the insides – lungs, kidney tubules, blood vessels – to make up in a way for the relative paucity of surface exposed to the outside. Thus the body temperatures of large animals change more slowly when stressed by heat or cold.

Behaviourally, elephants cool themselves by seeking shade at midday, by feeding in swamps with their feet in the water, by plastering themselves with wet mud that lodges in skin folds and evaporates slowly, and by flapping their ears. The elephant's two-square-metre ears are heat-exchange devices. They are almost constantly in motion, and as warm blood from the deep body flows along the veins of the ear, it quickly loses heat through the very thin skin to the moving air outside, and returns to the rest of the body several degrees cooler.

The fact, then, that elephants are thermally efficient animals makes them economical, if sometimes rather messy, feeders. This in turn contributes to their success. And, according to Dr Kleiber, one large two-tonne elephant will actually consume less vegetation per day than the same biomass of smaller species, a large herd of impala, for example, or an entire population of hyraxes.

Reaching for food

Reaching for food is one of the most important things an animal does. Fundamentally this involves a sequence of movements that puts the appropriate part in the right place. This may entail the use of a highly specialised part, like the giraffe's neck, the white rhino's stretched skull or the aardvark's sticky ant-catching tongue.

But reaching may also require a certain type of behaviour on the part of the animal that increases the effectiveness of its existing equipment. The gerenuk (*below right*) goes up on its hind legs to augment its elongated neck, thereby more than doubling its vertical reach and the amount of available forage. The warthog (*below left*) goes down on its "knees" (wrists actually) for grazing to compensate for its short neck. Not only is the particular grazing behaviour inborn, but embryonic structure already demonstrates callosities developing on the carpal joints of the forelegs. Or again, reaching may demand a generalised piece of physical

equipment capable of coping with a variety of special occasions.

The elephant reaches for food with its trunk, which is a remarkable evolutionary fusion of nose and upper lip. It effectively increases an elephant's upward and outward reach, but its main function is to enable the animal to transport food from the ground to its mouth, a distance of over two metres. Although elephants feed primarily on low grass and herbs, any vegetation from ground level to about six metres is fair game for the trunk. It's like having the contents of half a large shipping container within easy reach. Even if the leaves of a tree are beyond that limit, an elephant can simply push the tree over to bring them to a more convenient level.

The hyrax almost matches the elephant's vertical reach by a remarkable agility for one so squat. One of the three East African species, *Heterohyrax Brucei*, is able to climb on to the flimsiest acacia branches and browse there almost as if

grazing. The pads and toes of the feet – similar in internal structure to those of its distant cousin, the elephant – are covered with skin that actually sweats just enough to increase traction and surefootedness.

The elephant's trunk is an amazing tool considering it is basically a nose, but a primate's hand is a thing of wonder. Perfect for omnivores like baboons, chimpanzees (*opposite*) or humans, it is strong enough to kill and tear, dexterous enough to peel and pick. It is used not only to prepare and transport food, but to manipulate, heft, examine, alter and experiment with parts of the environment. Virtually the whole of the rest of the animal kingdom languishes like Gary Larson's cartoon cows listening to the phone ring and lamenting "…here we sit without opposable thumbs". A hand is a perfect appendage for a brain becoming curious enough to be called intelligent, a brain being pushed to new horizons by the hand-brain co-ordination necessary to reach for the sky.

Solitude

It has been said that an individual organism is the gene's way of making more genes. A society is one aspect of this, for the ultimate function of sociability is to increase the chances of survival of the individuals who participate. The possible types of social organisation form a continuous series of co-operating collections of individuals, from the nearly solitary rhinos to the highly gregarious wildebeest. It takes a minimum of two animals to be social, either on a permanent basis like dik-diks or ravens, who pair for life, or temporarily like a male and female rhinoceros who come together only when the female is in oestrous. Either way,

it is a positive attraction of the animals to one another that maintains the social group. A group of vultures on a dead wildebeest is not strictly speaking a social unit, since the "group" is formed by individuals attracted not to each other, but to an external stimulus. Of course, there is nothing to stop them from interacting socially once they sit down to eat.

Social communication is vital in maintaining the integrity of the group. It involves using a set of learned or innately understood signals – visual, auditory, olfactory or tactile. The language is predominantly species-specific, but some messages cut across species

boundaries – a lion understands an elephant's threat, a rhinoceros reacts to an oxpecker's alarm call. Within a species, the messages are unambiguous (to the animals) and hold the group together with such meanings as "I am here, where are you?", "keep back", "come here", "stay still", "follow me"...

The nature of a species' food resource determines, in general, the form of social organisation it has. An abundant food supply means that the animal can afford to be more social and live in groups. But a group would soon deplete a rare and sparsely distributed food supply. Thus, at the least-social end of the social continuum stands the black rhinoceros. It eats herbs and browses on shrubs – food resources that are scarce compared to grass. Its large body size on the one hand means that many rhinoceroses could not get enough to eat in the same small area. On the other hand, its size and unhesitating willingness to use the fused elongated hairs that form its horns, mean that it has an alternative to the safety-in-numbers advantage which social groups enjoy. Its solitude, sadly, was designed to work in other times.

Before the recent international effort to rid the world of rhinos, the population in Ngorongoro crater in Tanzania stood at around fifty individuals. Today it is around thirteen, unlucky enough, particularly as the effective number of breeding animals may be as low as five. This borders on the unviable. All it would take would be a couple of poachers slipping through the conservators' defences, an epidemic or an accidental accumulation of inferior genes to finish them off. Sufficient protection from any of these threats is barely affordable to local authorities, and outsiders are unwilling or unable to help organise or pay for the luxury of rhinos.

Oblivious to its bleak prospects, the bad-tempered recluse lumbers along, socialising only during courtship and mating. The male follows the oestrous female doggedly around his territory, he responding to her scent, she essentially communicating by her actions that he should keep his distance. Bouts of nudging, playfighting, urinating and thrashing the ground with his horn eventually communicate to the female that his temper is suspended and it is safe for her to let him get close enough to mate. Copulation itself is unique in that it can last for half an hour, a herbivore record which may explain some of the pharmaceutical qualities attributed to rhinoceros horn. After mating, she may accompany him for a couple of months, or she may not. Thus ends the rhinoceros social season.

The family

Burchell's zebras have two levels of sociability: we very often see them in large herds, particularly in the wet season, migrating perhaps with the wildebeest on to a locally abundant food source. But if we watch long enough, or especially if a predator threatens, we see the herd fragment into the basic social units, small mobile family groups of up to a dozen, comprising a male, his females and their young.

This response to predators indicates a key function of the family form of social organisation, namely protection of the breeding stock. A male zebra is a formidable fighter who will lead his family in seeing off a hyaena, and has been known to keep lions distracted whilst the family escapes. Such encounters are sometimes fatal for the zebra, but as a result some of his offspring escape and the sacrifice is worthwhile in terms of genetic investment. In the case of the zebra, it is not so much the constraints of the next trophic level down – the food supply – which dictate the form of its social organisation, but rather more the limits imposed by the next higher level, the predators.

The age-old mystery of how the zebra got its stripes may be explained as a by-product of its gregariousness. There are two schools of thought: one involves pressures from without, the other from within. Concerning predator pressures, we are naturally tempted to invoke protective colouration. The mode of deception is not entirely clear. Certainly in dim light, from a distance, the form of the zebra dissolves in a blur where the stripes meet the body contour. Since predators like lions and

hyaenas hunt mainly at night and detect their prey mainly by vision, perhaps the lost contours give a slight advantage to the zebra at a distance in dim light.

Zebras are notoriously restless and never seem to "freeze" in response to the presence of a predator, except to stop and stare for a bit. Perhaps confusion is the objective. A group of running, mingling, head-tossing, boldly striped beasts present a confounding image of a mass of vertical lines to the advancing predator – difficult to get a visual fix on one discrete form for the final leap. In short, zebras in a herd may form their own background against which each individual is camouflaged. The important thing is not that lions should never get zebras at all – they are killed, of course, roughly in proportion to their abundance – but that the lions miss more often than if zebras were all black or all white.

The second school focuses on the glue of group cohesion. Zebras are never alone. They mingle, they jostle, they play. They also mainly

move in follow-the-leader fashion, and so might enjoy something to fix on – like big bold stripes on the leader's rump. They keep close by nibbling and grooming each other, and so might benefit from clear invitations – like stripes – to enhance the invitation: "scratch me just here..." In fact, a neck bent back in a mini-ecstasy of "Ah, yes, just there..." forms folds in the skin that may have provided a visual evolutionary precursor to the crisp pelage patterns of today. Finally, the very flickering of stripes across the retina may trigger a comfortable state of mind. Visual experiments and magic shows have proved that such flickerings can have profound impacts on the brain: vertigo, hypnotic states, fits, harmonised brain waves and tranquility. Zebras are positively attracted to striped panels Who knows? There may be comfort in stripes and an inexorable pull that keeps the group together.

Unfortunately such hypotheses are almost impossible to test, and creative speculation will have to do for now.

The harem

Every adult male impala aspires to hold a territory, to defend his square-kilometre patch of turf from rival males, and to use the attractions of his food resources to lure and keep female herds on his plot.

Impalas are the dominant antelope in most of the less fertile woodlands of eastern and central Africa, and they organise themselves into three social clubs: herds of females and young who move from territory to territory; territorial males either accompanied by one of the mobile harems or temporarily alone; and herds of bachelor males.

The bachelors maintain a strict hierarchy within their herds. Young adults give way to the older animals, and the relative social status of each individual is established by sparring with the others. The system is in a constant state of flux as new animals join the herd, and the dominant adults leave to establish or take over existing territories. Whilst he is an unattached bachelor, the male has little to distract him from keeping in top condition. He may spend eight hours of every twelve just eating and idling. Once he achieves the status of territorial male, however, things get serious. His life expectancy shortens drastically. Life becomes exhausting and risky, as he keeps watch over his females and dashes about conspicuously preoccupied.

The territorial male positions himself as a living territory marker by posturing and vocalising at the boundary. There, he may resort to guile to keep his females clustered in the centre, giving false-alarm snorts at imaginary predators outside his turf. More often he just steers them back bodily as they drift, feeding, towards the edge. Other males are given a whiff of a testosterone-laden secretion from a forehead gland that he rubs on bushes and trees along the boundary. Although he will defend his area against all male intruders, territorial disputes are rarely violent. They more often involve display with the weaker intruder retreating before actual combat ensues. This mechanism ensures that only the strongest males are able to father young. One day, however, sooner rather than later, he will run out of steam, and after a short humiliating bout, will be forcibly retired.

Both the inevitable changing of the guard and the propensity of the females to slip away and wander between territories means that the females are served by a variety of males – thus maintaining a reservoir of genetic variability in the population.

The impalas' speciality amongst the African antelopes is an ability to use a wide range of food plants. This is their particular strategy for dealing with the seasonal changes that dominate the cycle of their year. During the wet season impalas are thinly dispersed throughout all suitable areas, feeding on a generalist's range of green vegetation – grasses, herbs, bushes, trees and fruits. They need shade too, and so avoid treeless country.

As the dry season advances impalas retreat to the woodlands and river valleys where the vegetation is still green, a retreat that is accompanied by a progressive breakdown in the territorial behaviour of the males.

In the wet season the population density of impalas in their habitat is unlikely to be more than twenty to the square kilometre; but the animals will be found in compact groups, the individuals feeding within a few metres of one another. Dry season ranges are much smaller in area, and densities will be as high as one hundred impala per square kilometre. The woodlands are able to support this greater concentration because they provide a diet with a relatively higher protein content. However, since this diet is predominantly browse rather than ground vegetation, individual animals will be more widely dispersed whilst feeding than is the case on the more open wooded grasslands. Thus individuals are most tightly packed in groups when the population is most dispersed (wet season) and most spread out when the population is most concentrated (dry season).

A territory can have a variety of functions, depending on the species. For the impala, there seems to be a premium on keeping the browsing load spread evenly over the habitat. If there were no mechanism to keep hungry female herds scattered, the best areas would be continually over-crowded with impalas and over-eaten. Vegetation needs a chance to recover from concentrated herbivore predation. A territorial male is essentially preserving a part of the population food reserve small enough to defend effectively and large enough to attract and nourish the female herds that wander into his sphere of influence and ensure continuation of his line.

The matriarchy

During the sixty-odd years of an elephant's lifetime, it will wander over a range the size of Lithuania and experience perhaps five major droughts. It has a lot to learn: where there is water; when different food plants come into season; where, in the driest times, some food and water can always be found; and how to avoid its only predator, hunting man. It would be inefficient, dangerous and most likely impossible for a young elephant to learn all the tricks of survival by exploring its habitat alone. Better to draw on the knowledge of older elephants. Better to be taught.

Elephant brains, like primate and cetacean brains are large. We expect no less from animals that are long-lived, extremely social and communicative. Areas of their brains that store and process olfactory and place information – two very important files – take up a relatively large portion. A big brain means an extensive cortex, the outer brain layer where the most reasoning goes on. Recent studies in mammalian brain development suggests that the largest contribution to the cortex comes from the mother's genetic legacy. In humans at least, the cortex is responsible for intellect skills such as language and forward planning. Fathers contribute to the undeniably important, but rather more "primitive" parts of the brain that regulate feeding, fighting and reproduction.

Such fundamental differences in propensities and potentials could help put a premium on matriarchal society. The basic social entity is the family unit led by one mature cow, the matriarch, who is the mother, elder sister or cousin of everyone else in the group. The closest tie a young elephant has is with its mother – she is its earliest teacher. For the first year it will barely stray a trunk's length away. It tastes the food in her mouth and suckles for six years. The secrets of a habitat that must be coped with for sixty seasons cannot be learned in one, or even five. Thus elephants have the longest childhood of any animal, except humans, and stay with the family until puberty, perhaps for fifteen years. Female calves will remain long after and increase the survival rate of the group's calves by helping with the job of mothering.

The low rumbling noise we hear when close to elephants is not, as we might at first surmise, the workings of their huge guts, but rather of their large brains: they are communicating. Elephants have a repertoire of basso profundo utterances, some of which we almost feel rather than hear. Low-frequency sound waves – somewhat lower than the base section of a symphony orchestra – travel well through vegetation and rolling topography. Booming out from the sound box of a three-tonne elephant, they are able to carry information on whereabouts, identity, sexual state, danger over large distances (up to two kilometres has been observed, but as far as ten is possible). And, perhaps in keeping with cortical development, females have a slightly larger vocabulary than males, about five more "words" in the currently-known elephant lexicon of fifty.

Large brains, a complex and loving family life, evidence of altruistic behaviour and sophisticated communications: it is hard to understand how we bring ourselves to kill these "harmless great things". But then, we kill each other often for less.

Herds and troops

The first reactions of a herd of buffaloes or a troop of baboons to an intruder indicate a key function of their social organisation. The adults of the mixed families in these groups look and listen and smell the disturbance. Baboons and vervet monkeys sit up and face the intruder or climb a tree for a better look or to shout a warning (see p. 77). Buffaloes stop grazing and point eyes, ears and noses at the intruder. Some may even advance a few paces with heads raised, giving the impression of myopic curiosity. Young animals move to the rear.

A collection of sense organs detects and examines the discordant stimulus. A consensus of experienced adults appraises the situation and a collective decision is made whether the best strategy is to attack, flee or resume feeding. Subordinate animals may take the cue from the dominant ones, which is not surprising since the animals near the top of the hierarchy are usually the oldest, who have necessarily passed a long series of tests and choices that the environment presents to them. There is early warning, as well as safety in numbers.

Many types of food resources occur in patches so that feeding automatically produces herding in the first instance. Moreover the relative availability of food may be increased if more sense organs are applied to detecting it. A baboon that discovers a bush with ripe fruit will eat the find quickly if there is not much of it. But if the bush is laden, the baboon's actions and excitement will attract its fellows to share the meal. Or the advantage may be a more complex one: the trampling, grazing and excreting of many buffaloes in valley grassland promotes the growth of young, nutritious shoots to the obvious advantage of the whole herd.

Herd movements are similarly co-ordinated by group interaction. Spare the time to watch an undisturbed resting buffalo herd, lying around in the grass, ruminating (*opposite*, with a cattle egret). After a while, one adult will heave itself up and stand, facing in some direction or other. Another stands, then another, until all have risen. Note carefully the direction that the majority are facing. That will be the way the herd will move, almost as though they had taken a vote with their noses.

The mixture of families, the combination of both sexes and all ages, the physical proximity of members, the co-ordinated activities and resource-sharing in herds and troops are rather like aspects of human societies. Even if all the individuals do not know one another, which in fact they probably do, status is instantly recognised by subtle signals, akin to those that humans respond to amongst their own species, but often are not aware of. Body posture, tilt of head, vocalisations, direction of gaze, even body odour are used to signal state of mind, intent or rank in all species. The result is a relatively tranquil order in social groups, which ensures less energy is used in bickering and more in surviving.

One good turn

If we were pressed for one word to sum up – in human terms, of course – the nature of the glue that holds together primate groups, it would be friendship. Literally hundreds of human years of incredibly patient and diligent observations of the behaviour and ecology of chimpanzees and baboons in particular have shown that coalition-building tactics preoccupy these primates almost as much as they do us. When you think about it, having friends in high or even low places, can give you a helping hand and therefore an edge in most daily activities: finding, catching and sharing food; approaching close enough to mate; not getting beaten up by dominant bullies; being warned about approaching danger.

The altruism of relatives is the self-fulfilling prophesy of shared genes and comes more or less automatically. But gaining the confidence of non-relatives requires social skills and negotiation. One of the commonest tricks is grooming, the often ritualised and tactile version of "My, how nice you look today, here, let me flick that speck off your lapel." Eyes directed away from confrontational frontal contact, a neutral gesture, a tentative and helpful touch on shoulder or back, and there you are. As close an encounter as in fighting or mating, but done not in passion but with calculation: you scratch my back and I'll scratch yours, now or later.

Grooming may be so important to social cohesion in baboons that it limits the size of troops. When a troop grows to about two-dozen individuals, that gives on average nearly eight adult females. It becomes difficult in terms of time and motion for them all to maintain their grooming "obligations" amongst the sisterhood, friendships are strained, and groups break apart.

The underground society

Whilst we are watching animals the size of buffaloes, we are usually indifferent to the activities of insects. Yet insects such as locusts that eat live plants, and termites that consume dead ones, probably transport more materials than the spectacular large mammals of Africa. Termites in particular return tonnes of nutrients to the soil by literally carrying dead wood and grass below ground. This would otherwise decay far more slowly in the dry grasslands.

So prevalent are termites that all across Africa they stamp patterns in the soil. Take the Heuweltjies of the Cape Province: circular mounds some thirty metres across and two metres high that occupy up to a quarter of the land surface where they occur. Or the so-called "termite bands", fifty-metre-wide stripes in southern African soils clearly visible from the air or hilltops. Agriculturists are learning to mine the enhanced nutrient qualities of these special patches. They are found in most African grasslands and derive from the erosion of the slopes dotted at regular intervals by termite mounds. The mounds are dumping grounds for earth excavated from the subterranean tunnels as well as cunningly designed flues for venting the heat of termite enterprise. It is a marvel of instinctive behaviour that the mounds are all so similar in appearance, for they are built by millions of workers, none of whom ever see the finished product as we do, let alone the marks they etch across the continent.

Termites are not, as we might think, related to other industrious social insects such as bees, wasps and ants. This misnamed "white ant" is not an ant at all: it belongs in a group of its own, more closely related to cockroaches than to ants. They have no forms that develop from unfertilised eggs, as do worker bees. Instead of starting life as a larva, the young termite hatches directly from the egg into a nymph, a pallid immature copy of the adult.

Some termites are actually able to eat wood with the help of minute single-celled organisms in their stomachs. The so-called "gut flora" produce chemicals that break down the cellulose of plant cells and render it digestible. From the one point of view, these microbial symbionts could be said to run the colonies, since they equal the biomass of the termites whose energy gathers the food for the whole enterprise.

Other termites like *Macrotermes bellicosus* (the "big warlike termite") have no such helpers or masters. Their answer is to become agrarians and cultivate their own food. Underground, in the heart of the lightless chambers, *Macrotermes* shapes the earth into convoluted hanging gardens seeded with the spores of a particular fungus species and fertilised with half-digested regurgitated wood pulp. The little mushroom-like growths that flourish in the dark are the real food of *Macrotermes*.

A termitary operates on a caste system, a strict division of labour amongst builders, soldiers, foragers, cleaners and nurses. There may be several million individuals in one colony, but there is no thought process or reasoning amongst them. Each works or fights instinctively according to the genetic information programmed into it.

The remarkable efficiency and order resulting from this fact has engendered a view of the termite colony as a "superorganism", a kind of "being" in itself, a notion as old as Aristotle (see also p. 255). The superorganism can be thought of as a group of individual organisms whose collective behaviour produces results that resemble the work of a single organism. None of the individuals working on its own could have achieved the same. In the termite colony, the individual termites are analogous to cells and the duties of the castes to physical functions: the foragers are the blood stream carrying nutrients through the organism; the cleaners are its excretory organs; the soldiers, its claws and fangs; the king and queen, its sex organs. The concept of superorganism does help describe a termite colony; but is it metaphor or fact?

Observations of a number of social insect species suggest that when they occur at low densities, they run about and tend to their broods in an apparently chaotic manner. But when their density increases to a certain threshold, they begin to move in a measurable rhythm of rest and work, caring for the young, almost as if from the system itself springs the pattern. This notion is hard to grasp operationally, whereas we can plot relatively easily how natural selection works. What is particularly hard to reconcile is how the work and life of the individual can continue to be sacrificed for the good of the group, unless all individuals are closely related as social insects often are. Still, "why me and not you?" a termite might ask of its fellows, unless all were driven by the inexorable resonation of colonial life.

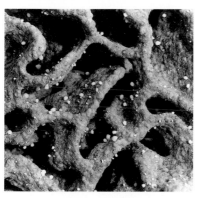

From top to bottom: the winged adult; workers building; the fungus garden on which the termites feed; and the nymphs, immature copies of the adults

The royal family

In the rains when the soil is soft and moist, a caste of male and female termites becomes sexually mature and sprouts wings. One evening, after a heavy shower, workers open tunnels to the surface and the winged emissaries fly up towards the failing light. In the darkness they drop to earth again and having shed their wings perfunctorily, males and females form pairs and scuttle off in tandem to seek a suitable site for the beginnings of a new nest. Only a minute fraction will form successful pairs, and those two creatures are all that is necessary to form a complete new colony. The female even has in her gut a minute piece of fungus to be regurgitated into the seedbeds of their new gardens.

A metre or so below ground, secure within strongly sculptured walls and fiercely protected by thousands of soldiers, lies the queen termite. The very same creature that flew delicately into the evening light has become a grotesque ten-centimetre egg factory capable of the astonishing production of 30,000 eggs a day for twenty years. The king is always beside her to inseminate each crop of eggs, although we do not know if he is the same individual with whom she paired after the nuptial flight. Attendants constantly stroke and cleanse her abdomen. Like a scene from *Alien-3*, her body ripples rhythmically with convulsions of egg-laying, as a continuous stream of workers passes through the cell, bringing food and carrying eggs away to the nursery chambers.

In the nurseries, eggs hatch into nymphs, which, remarkably, are capable of becoming members of any caste. It has been shown experimentally that precisely which caste an individual grows into is somehow determined by the needs of the colony itself. If a colony is in an early stage of construction, most nymphs will become workers; if it has a poor defensive structure,

more will become soldiers. Many simply remain nymphs until the needs of a particular caste become apparent. Apparent? How does an instinctive, genetically programmed, totally "unthinking" colony of insects perceive its needs? What kind of information reverberates through the system to feed back into its behaviour? We do not know for certain, but such questions are pushing evolutionary biologists to look beyond conventional biology, into the realm of complex adaptive systems like economics and metrology. Perhaps the answer is simple, and as with the insider-trading in global financial arenas or teleconnections in the atmosphere, there is a taste of the social state, instigated and integrated, in the case of the termite, through hormonal messages transferred in their shared food – the original word of mouth.

And, what of the untold thousands of termites that flew from the nest only to succumb to the depredations of predators or simply run out of steam and die unmated – are they wasted? The answer must be no. Termites are extremely tasty fare to virtually all predators, including people. On their nuptial flight they are at particular risk as they flutter silhouetted against the evening sky. But there are so many of them! Probably far more than necessary to fill the local predator population who cannot cope with these seasonal excesses, since their numbers are controlled by the average amount of prey available all year round. The enormous sacrifice ensures that some termites survive; and in any event, all the material will be recycled via bird droppings or genet dung and will be used again one day by termites. Thus for the ecosystem, the nuptial flight of the termite begins as a mining operation from below and ends in a rain of nutrients from above.

Prolonged negotiations

Watching the ponderous *pas-de-deux* of necking giraffes, we cannot help but wonder at the extremes animals and plants go to get the job done. What job? Well, simply that of being good enough to leave offspring who are good enough to leave offspring who are good enough... So is that what these two young male giraffes are doing? In a roundabout way, yes. Their ancestors went, step by step, to the trouble of becoming elongated (see p. 58). They paid the price of anatomical modifications to support such extravagance; they took their

chances in attempting to run from danger, like fire engines with the ladders up, through thick bush; and, as we have seen, they burst up into a nutritional salad bar occupied only by insects, tree hyraxes and the odd primate.

Food and safety reasonably well secured, the next item on the list – the main item, actually – is securing a mate. Even though there are many other male giraffes with the same notion, this sparring of young bulls is not primarily to build strength and guile for some future, real fight. Serious fighting amongst giraffes is

almost never seen. As they rub shoulders, entwine their necks and bat each other on the flanks with the sides of their heads and muffled horns, they gain information about each other's size and strength. The necking never escalates; like negotiation, it is a give and take, a peaceful exchange of information to resolve conflict before it starts. The necking may, however, end with the symbolic "winner" play-mounting the other – an overtly enthusiastic burst of fellowship – that underlines the whole business is, after all, really about sex. With the dominance of the usually larger animal ritually negotiated, he has his pick of the local females in oestrus. And they prefer the dominant, larger, stronger, more guileful male, and so combine their genes to produce young who are good enough to leave young who are good enough... And so the dance goes on.

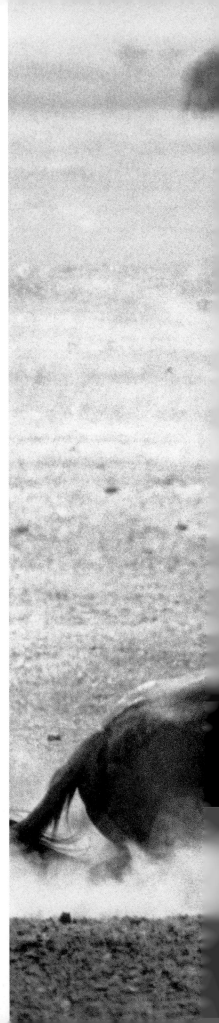

HERBIVORES REPRODUCTION

Male rivalry

Breeding is the class of behaviour concerned with maintaining a species' integrity. No matter how much there is to eat, a great deal of the energy consumed must go into the activities designed to maintain a set of genes that define species, or else the food is wasted. On the other hand, no matter how prolific a species may be, the proliferation will snuff itself out if there is not enough energy to feed it.

A first step in the transmitting of genes is a decision about who will do the transmitting. If all mature animals were to produce young, the population's progeny would contain a considerable portion of substandard material, simply by the laws of chance. A genetic line is constantly at risk: it can lose the struggle against an unfriendly environment at any stage in an animal's lifecycle. Some stages are more vulnerable than others – when new-born, when very old, under conditions of stress in the dry season. The risks can be minimised if the parent's contribution to the next generation is of the highest quality.

Males invest a good deal of effort in competing to decide who will mate. Male ungulates (hooved animals), like Grant's gazelles (*above*) or wildebeest (*opposite*), seem to do little else. They fight to establish a hierarchy and maintain a territory, they fight over females. The decision process ensures that only the strongest, most tenacious, quickest and most cunning will pass on their traits. The screening process of aggressive male contests increases fitness in the population as a whole by letting only the fittest genes through the gauntlet of male rivalry. Of course, a male ungulate

sporting sharp horns, driven by his genetic vigour, fired with an extra seasonal dose of testosterone, is a very dangerous beast. Yet fights are rarely fatal. Clearly, nothing could be more disadvantageous, if practised on a large scale. Thus there have evolved conventions, rituals, almost sporting tests of strength which are just that and not frenzied battles to the death. If contests were fatal, we could imagine a population of wildebeest whose most bloodthirsty males, capable of dispatching lions, would soon dwindle through self-destruction. Just as legs are neither too long nor too short, horns neither too unwieldy nor too small, so most behaviours have a safety valve, a built-in stop that inhibits over-reaction. Gentlemanly behaviour is adaptive; murder is not if it puts your kith and kin at risk.

Common grounds

Imagine all possible ways for an antelope to organise its social life. It could be territorial, with small resident herds living in a traditional home range, with territories containing females and young defended against adjacent males and, if necessary, satelliting bachelor herds. Or it might opt for migratory mode, with large mixed assemblages of animals of all sexes and ages moving steadfastly across the plains, only pausing to rut in small temporary territories when the migration outspans in a particularly good seasonal grazing area. Or, then again, it might evolve to congregate seasonally at longstanding breeding arenas, called "leks".

The topi, or tsessebe in southern African parlance, appears to hedge its reproductive bets and practises all three reproductive strategies at various times and places, depending on the local conditions. In mixed habitat, where there are patches of grass surrounded by less interesting and more dangerous bushlands, topis are traditionally territorial. Where there are nice large floodplains and rolling open grasslands, they will migrate. And somewhere in-between, where they occur at high-population densities and times are good, the topi will gather in at lekking grounds.

"Lek" is an obscure and archaic word that may derive from the old Norse *leika*, the Gothic *laikan*, or the modern Swedish *leka*, all meaning "to play". Indeed there is almost a carefree air on the lekking grounds, where groups of males strut their stuff, displaying and tussling, till the ground is trampled and bare, whilst parcels of females wander about, egging on the males

by their very presence and interest. Having been awake most of the night watching for predators, at first light they start their displaying and dashing about. For the males the object is to be the best and biggest displayer, close to the centre of the arena so the females cannot miss you.

The female mission is to get impregnated by the biggest and the best. Indeed the whole point of the lekking strategy may be to increase the opportunities for female to choose. The female topis may even fight amongst themselves, perhaps captivated by the same male. With such converging agendas it is no wonder the event verges on an orgy. The females often mate with more than one male on the lek grounds. One of our sharp-eyed colleagues pointed out what he called "sperm dumping" (*bottom right*), which, if a common practice, would be a remarkable example of female choice: mate with whomever you please, and then take or leave his genetic offering. Remarkable in animals, that is.

But the lekking strategy of bringing the best to the fore is costly, which is perhaps why it is only engaged in it when there is plenty of grass and lots of topis. Hyaenas in particular have even learned to adjust their hunting timetable in the Mara in Kenya to work over lunch hour in order to take topis that are dozing in the heat on the lekking grounds exhausted after a long morning of carrying on (see p. 131). Even if a few more juveniles and exhausted males do get taken, relatively more females survive, secure at having bagged a good set of genes. Thus topis and other animals that engage in lekking –

the European black grouse being the classic example – illustrate that far from being a rigid, species-specific characteristic, mating behaviour can be altered to suit circumstances. We humans know something of that as well.

Courtship ritual

A male herbivore that has survived till sexual maturity and has established himself with his peers near the top of the hierarchy, has spent most of his adult life keeping his distance from other creatures – fleeing from predators, separating himself from rival males. Females share his aversion to closeness. If he is to fulfil his task in life successfully – to produce children – his whole attitude towards physical contact has to change, particularly with respect to females. Sex hormones – triggered by environmental factors like change in day length, temperature, food availability, or the presence of a mature female – take care of the attitude of the male well enough. But then the problem is to convince the female that this excitable creature confronting her is not dangerous. Not only must she not run away, but she must stay still, and at least for one vital instant be available for the act of mating. Thus we have courtship – an often elaborate combination of attraction, appeasement and reassurance behaviour.

The male Jackson's widowbird is a gallant, if slightly mad suitor. He establishes a territory amongst his fellows in open grassland, and on it performs a circular leaping dance with such vigour that he eventually wears a trampled ring in the grass about the size of a large inner tube. If this bizarre display can attract the attention of humans, it can certainly arouse the interest of females evolved to respond to it. Flocks of females fly over the display grounds as if assessing the performances of the cavorting males, a dozen of whom may be jumping about below. Looked at from a distance, the whole business,

with its concentration of displaying males and appraising females, reminds us of the topi's lekking grounds (see p. 87). When a curious female makes her choice and lands in a ring, a brief bout of hide-and-seek around the central grass tuft follows. The tuft allows her to shield herself from the awful splendour of her suitor; the ring makes the outcome inevitable.

For most of the year there is little to tell between the male and female widowbirds: both are dull brown and mottled: hardly more remarkable than a suburban sparrow. But in the breeding season the male looks like an entirely different creature – rich with shining black plumage, and long, curved tail – resembling his other self as much as a rook does a thrush.

This dimorphism (two forms) and dichromism (two colours) is a tactic that many birds have evolved. It is the ultimate species compromise between advertisement and concealment. The dowdy year-round plumage is good camouflage and, as such, especially important to the female whilst she is carrying eggs. But to ensure she is fertilised in the first place, the male must abandon the security of his camouflage at the start of the breeding season and attract females. There is a risk, of course, that he will attract predators too, so he wears the striking breeding plumage for no longer than necessary. But the risk pays off. An ingenious researcher artificially lengthened the tail feathers of male wydah birds, close relatives of the widowbirds, at the beginning of the breeding season. And sure enough, those males with exaggerated foppish tails ended

up with more new nests in their territories than those with either normal or shortened tails. We hope that in all fairness to the disadvantaged birds, the researcher reversed the favour during the next season.

The Jackson's widowbird (*above*) and the long-tailed widowbird (*Euplectes progne delameri*, *opposite*)

A time to mate

Animals come into season because the season gets into them. Annual changes in things like wetness, dryness, day-length, grass texture and content cause the animals to begin breeding activities. Surprisingly, we do not yet know for certain which of the many possible stimuli actually trigger breeding of the large African mammals – a statement, in fact, which is true for most species. Wildebeest and gazelles court and mate in the dry season. Elephants increase their sexual activity during the rains. Giraffes mate all year round.

Males usually confirm by scent what the hormones of their activated sex glands tell them, or what the females convey to them through their behaviour. The male smells the female's genitals or tastes her urine for a chemical message of readiness. We have whiffs of similar behaviour in our own sexual repertoire wherein certain intimacies are equivalent to burying one's nose in a pheromone bouquet.

Virtually all ungulate males react like the Grant's gazelle (*depicted here*) to the taste and smell of the urine of the ready female with a stretched-neck, head-up, lips-curling posture called "flehmen". We are not sure what the posture means:

it is not likely to be a signal to the female, since she is facing the wrong way and does not even notice. Possibly other males may respond by avoiding the couple, although flehmen will occur with no other males about. It is likely to have a physiological function, namely, to dilate the so-called incisive ducts just behind the nostrils and allow a good spray of urine to waft into the vomeronasal organ, a hyper-sensitive little chamber embedded above the palate. In it, most mammals, especially larger herbivores, conduct an instant chemical analysis on things sniffed.

Although the timing is critical for the actual mating, the act on which humans place such a high premium is a cursory event amongst animals. It is but one of the several steps in the process of gene exchange, and may last only seconds between gazelles and less than a minute between elephants. The only large beast who lingers over the event is the rhino, and the one who most conspicuously loses itself in transports of orgasmic delight is, curiously, the ostrich.

The point of seasonal breeding is usually to deliver young into a world that offers an adequate food supply. Animals of different

gestation periods must clearly start their breeding activities at different times if they are to all take advantage of the same rainy season. The wildebeest has an additional reason. The births of the calves are closely synchronised so that in February, there may be over half-a-million new-born wildebeest on the Serengeti plains. The calves are extremely vulnerable to hyaenas, wild dogs and the cats. But the synchronised calving has the effect of glutting the prey market: the same strategy the termites use on their nuptial flight (see p. 78). The predators spend much of the period lolling around with full stomachs, literally unable to eat more. Consequently, they eat less of the wildebeest calf crop than they would if taking a constant toll the whole year round.

Females choose

Undaunted by their relatively poor performance on the intellectual front, the bulls serve as elephant population pioneers. Compared to the females, they lead an almost solitary life, often on the periphery of the population's range. They thus tend to precede the female herds into new pastures. Again we can see an evolutionary design in this system. On the one hand they are physically more able to explore new regions, since they are larger, stronger, and can go longer without water than younger animals in the family groups. Yet they are more expendable in the short run.

The death of a bull, though individually tragic, is little more than the loss of one elephant out of many. The death of a cow, however, is not only the loss of a teacher or even a group leader, it is also the potential subtraction of ten elephants from the future population, for optimally a cow will produce a calf every four years between her fifteenth and fifty-fifth year.

Young bull calves at puberty begin to stray, primarily because the cows become intolerant, even to the point of tusking them out of the group. This ousting has the function of preventing future interbreeding and also works in favour of the family unit, since there will be one less mouth to feed in the dry season. And it benefits the young bull himself. He may be capable of mating at ten, but he will not become "socially mature" until about thirty, when size, experience and strength allow him to compete for cows in heat. If he stayed with the family group, he would be subjected for almost a decade to the competition of courting bulls, mostly larger than himself. He would continually be giving way to them, and have little opportunity to spar and test his strength with

his contemporaries bull groups.

Bulls do not form permanent groups, but rather loose assemblies of from two to fifty individuals with no long-term social ties. Like all animal herds, they have a primary function of safety in numbers; but beyond this they allow the young animals to meet the other males in a population, and to judge when they are ready for serious contest for the females.

Let us qualify that last notion. The large adult bulls may jostle and sometimes engage in a serious fight over a female in oestrus, but when it comes down to sex,

the females have the final word. The careful, long-term study of the social behaviour of Amboseli elephants in Kenya, for example, has shown that females deliberately go to great lengths to accept or reject males that they deem suitable or not as purveyors of fine genes. They spurn by a toss of the head, by melting into the crowd or simply by running away. If interested, however, they entice by casually brushing past, by coyly hesitating off to one side, or simply by striding up and saying "hello". Sounds too familiar to belabour further.

A trunk laid across the back helps persuade the young female in the above sequence to stand to the bull

A deliquescent nest

The change of seasons, from dry to wet, happens almost overnight. The half a year of rainless weather finishes with a crescendo of atmospheric tension and stifling temperatures. And then it rains, and where there was dust and sand yesterday, today there are pools and rivers. Some of the trees and large mammals have already begun the internal reproductive changes that synchronise their cycles to those of the land and sky. Smaller organisms respond immediately to the rain. Grass begins to grow again that very day, insects hatch, and from out of the parched ground of the bushed grassland in Tsavo National Park, Kenya, creeps, of all things, a frog.

In the semi-arid bushland, it is never certain that water will remain very long, particularly at the beginning of the rains. So the frogs hurry to the edge of a water hole within a few hours of its forming. It is not an event we are likely to see, since the rains usually start at night, probably because it takes a day's heat to build up the clouds to a suitable state of instability. A female frog is joined by one or more of the smaller males, and there begins a frenzied mating scene in which the female produces eggs and a mucus that is worked into a foamy mass by the paddling hindlegs of both animals.

At sunrise we find the frogs sitting atop a soufflé of mucus, eggs and sperm. Even if the water hole dries up before the next shower, the eggs can hatch in the guaranteed moisture of the foam. At the next rainstorm, the deliquescent nest together with the tadpoles is washed away into the pond. By this time, in a normal year, the

rains will have begun in earnest, and the pond should last the few weeks necessary for the tadpoles to grow into adult frogs.

How or where the great grey tree frog (*depicted here*) survives the dry season is not known, for it must aestivate – a hot-weather version of hibernation. It is an amphibian, after all, which must in theory have moist skin to stay alive: much of a frog's breathing is done through the skin. But how does it prevent total evaporation of its body fluids?

Following heavy rain, other dry-country relatives of the foam frog have been observed to rear up on the still-wet earth and literally disappear into it as one watches. They burrow backwards, as far as the earth is wet, which may be a metre down. There they make themselves a mucus-lined chamber, which dries into a seal and protects them during their dry season "sleep".

Amphibians are edge creatures. Halfway between fish and lizards, between water and land, they crawl a thin line between survival or not. It is not surprising then that they are considered to be "indicator species" of environmental degradation. Many of the world's 4,000-odd species of frogs and toads, newts and salamanders are believed to be under threat from local effects of global climate change or pollution. Red flags of systems out of balance spring up when amphibian numbers start dwindling in a formerly teeming wetland or when the local frogs begin to show developmental abnormalities – like extra or missing limbs – as their waters are dosed with chemicals. They may even be victims of "globalisation", through

viruses spread around the world by the ornamental-fish trade or the spores of newly described fungi that float on trade winds. Whether or not we take any notice of what the frogs do is another matter.

Husbandry at the nest

There is nothing very special about an ostrich nest – a perfunctory scrape in the ground, made by a male in his territory – similar to that of most other ground-nesting birds. The all-white eggs may indeed be dangerously conspicuous, but the camouflaged, mottled brown female covers them during the day, the black male at night, and both hundred-kilo animals are formidable in defence. No other bird can claim the distinction of having kicked a lion to death. In any event, most potential predators – lions included – are unable to break an ostrich egg.

The ostrich seems to carry egg production to excess. Nests with over one hundred eggs have been recorded. Since the sitting bird can only cover and hatch about two dozen of these (about the same as a successful goose), we may understandably wonder why so many eggs are necessary. Part of the answer is that ostriches are polygamous: the male invites, courts, mates with and accepts the eggs of more than one female. The females, for their part, lay eggs in more than one nest. There is typically a dominant "major" hen in any one area who also has a "laying territory" that may encompass the territory of more than one male. Added to that are bevies of "minor" hens, who flit about laying eggs wherever they can. As many as eighteen different minor hens have been observed to contribute to one nest. With such a battery of egg producers in the neighbourhood, it is not surprising that nests are large. On top of that, even a two-kilo ostrich egg is relatively inexpensive to produce in terms of energy and materials:

a songbird egg is about one-tenth of the adult weight, an ostrich egg about one-sixtieth. Captive birds can be induced to lay up to ninety eggs at a stretch by continual removal. Such fascinating facts limit us to accounting for the production of a large clutch – the "how" of mechanism rather than the "why" of function.

We might approach the function question by stepping back and looking at the ecology of the bird. Ostriches are selective feeders, who, like elands, rather fussily pluck small, green shoots of wild flowers out of the tangle of a grass sward. A scarce primary resource means, as in the case of rhinos and elands, a low-population density. In addition, a well-defined dominance hierarchy amongst the females results in the same old experienced hen sitting on a particular male's nest every breeding season. Thus, a particular pair would produce offspring sporting recombinations of the same parental genes year after year, if there were not a special mechanism in their breeding strategy that invited other females, as it were, to contribute their genes to the mix. Through the egg lottery at the nest, the offspring of a breeding season have a high individual genetic variability, a healthy thing for any individual in an environment in which climate and primary production can fluctuate as much as they do in the tropical grasslands. Moreover, if one nest is destroyed by, say, a flooding rain, at least some eggs of any one bird will have a chance of surviving if they are laid in several nests. Such considerations go some way to explaining why the males often help

incubate and protect eggs that are not related to them: it is the price you pay to get at least some of your offspring through the lottery.

How do the various players fare in this game? The advantage to the father is that his genes travel forth combined with a wider range of possibilities – like bolstering a hand of cards with more than one suit. The lower-ranking females by laying around get at least some chance of passing on their genes. Like spreading chips across a roulette table, they decrease their risks and increase their chances of a win, albeit with a lower potential payoff.

And the lead hen? There is growing evidence that a major hen recognises her own eggs by pore pattern, size and shape. As she settles down to incubate, she may have under her belly a nest in which only half the eggs are hers. It is not surprising that as she adjusts the eggs, the ones that get left towards the edge of the pile are someone else's. Edges are more vulnerable and charity begins at home.

The economy of numbers

We would expect a herbivorous bird like the ostrich, which hatches fully feathered, mobile, ready-to-feed chicks, to produce a relatively high number of them. Primary production is abundant and immediately available to the hatchlings. The conservative one- or two-chick economy of, say, a bird of prey, who must defend and keep warm the young, as well as travel miles to collect enough food for them, is not a constraint in the ostrich's reproductive strategy.

But whereas ostrich eggs are easy to produce, the chicks are difficult to defend. Their small size makes them fair game to a wide spectrum of predators from eagles to lions. Certainly adult ostriches are effective defenders of their brood, but it is a formidable task to keep a group of twenty-odd chicks together when under attack.

Consequently, ostriches have evolved a unique solution. There is a fairly precise synchrony of hatching within one ostrich population's range, and most chicks follow their parents away from the nest in the same week. Thereafter, when two broods meet in their wanderings, from as far as ten kilometres apart, they join together in a confused shuffle. The dominant pair of adults assert themselves over the other pair with much displaying and end up leading both broods away. This continues until almost all of the broods in the neighbourhood are under the control of one pair of adults. There may be up to 100 chicks in the group: the largest we have heard of was 380-strong.

One can hypothesise a number of advantages, as well as some disadvantages, to such a system. Imagine a predator wandering about looking for something to eat. If there are ten ostrich broods in his range, there are ten possible targets he can encounter. If the broods join into one or two large broods, the effective target area is less and so is the chance of a "hit". On the other hand, a large group is possibly more conspicuous and slightly easier to detect. Then again, if the predator usually gets one chick in an attack, before the adult birds get the rest safely away, then each chick in a large brood has a greater chance of survival than each chick in a small brood. One could go on with such a list of points and counterpoints, but clearly, the advantages must in the long run outweigh the disadvantages.

The lead male who finds himself burdened with all of the chicks, some of them sired by males against whom he has just spent a couple of months defending his territorial boundaries, is not just being a good neighbour. It is difficult to believe he would incubate and defend all of these chicks unless most of them carried some of his genes. As long as individuals continue to wander about, spreading the genetic word, we may one day no longer talk of an ostrich colony or even a population, but of a "metapopulation", spread over thousands of square kilometres.

Symbiosis

We usually think of "co-operation" as being a relationship that involves a more or less conscious sharing of effort to produce a single mutually beneficial effect. Mutualism is a form of "pre-conscious" co-operation in a partnership that benefits two organisms, each in different ways. If the co-operators regularly cohabit, it is called symbiosis, literally "living together". For example, large herbivores like buffalo (*opposite*) and elands (*right top*) frequently share space with oxpeckers, the bird sitting on the buffalo's head – a curious proximity at first glance. But the herbivore provides the bird with a pasture of skin parasites, and the oxpecker offers his perch a danger-detection system perhaps a shade more sensitive than its own. In this case the co-operation is more striking since it occurs between two creatures on different trophic levels.

Plants, of course, do not behave in the usual sense, simply because they cannot actively move in a time scale which we recognise as behaviour. But they do exhibit anti-predator, or rather, anti-herbivore adaptations. The thorns of the African acacia trees and even their chemistry as we have seen (see p. 35), are designed to discourage browsers and therefore decrease the "predation" on vital photosynthetic material. Australian acacias, in contrast, have no thorns, presumably because they evolved in the absence of browsing herbivores. Another example of how comparative observations can give us hunches about function.

The whistling thorn acacia tree (*right*) has bulbous galls at the base of its spines. With a few doors and a little hollowing out,

they provide excellent homes for a small but pugnacious species of ant (*Crematogaster*). The ant gets shelter and a thorn fence, the tree a second line of defence after its armament. Hungry herbivores get bitten as well as pricked if they try to eat *Acacia drepanolobium*. The co-operation has proved so successful to both species that they have virtually evolved together. It is rare to find whistling thorns, even very young plants, without the ants; and the ants never occur without the trees. Ants can, of course, live just about anywhere, but how much more beneficial to have a living home that can evolve structural improvements to accommodate the tenants. The fluting tones produced by the wind blowing across the ants' holes in the galls are delightful to the human listener, but are, of course, incidental to the symbiosis.

Essentially, a symbiotic relationship involves two species doing more or less what they would do in any event, but tolerating the close

presence of one another whilst they do it. It was undoubtedly the benefit, even an originally serendipitous one, which fostered the tolerance. And here toleration, which costs virtually nothing in terms of energy expenditure, increases the chances of survival of both.

First lines of defence

The third major concern of all organisms – after eating and reproducing – is avoiding getting eaten. Of course, both the organism that escapes predation and the one that gets enough to eat have a better chance of breeding successfully. The energy necessary for behaving or for building specialised body parts is most frequently expended in the processes of feeding, anti-predation and reproduction.

The head of a herbivore is a conspicuous indication of its way of life. A main feature is the danger-detection apparatus. The herbivore early-warning system consists of a large nose linked internally to a complex honeycomb of scent-sensitive membrane, capable of detecting molecules in the air and identifying their source with a sensitivity unknown to us. There are the large, well-developed ears, swivelling sound-baffles. And there are the eyes.

Ungulates do not need their eyes to locate food. They can smell it well enough, and to close accurately the gap between food and mouth they are aided by the touch-sensitive whiskers on their lips. But the eyes are essential for detecting danger, and to give the best field of view they are usually located on the side of the head. The dik-dik or the African hare can see what is behind almost as well as what is in front.

After early warning, the next line of defence against predation is simple inaccessibility. Camouflage colouration effectively makes the prey visually inaccessible to the predator. We have already suggested that the zebra's colouration, combined with gregariousness, have the effect of reducing the visual availability of any one zebra in a fleeing group by confusing the predator's target image. "Flash" colouration is another way of confounding the visual predator. Some ground-coloured animals like the bushbuck or the hare have conspicuously white tails that are flashed intermittently at the pursuing cat. The Thomson's gazelle's contrasting side strips may have the same effect in zigzagging flight. This gives the predator momentarily a clear signal on which to fix, but one that vanishes in an instant. In the dark, we are similarly disorientated after a light is flashed in our eyes. The last and perhaps the most obvious form of inaccessibility is simply hiding – going to earth. This strategy works best if the prey is smaller than the predator, who simply does not fit into the suitable retreat. It is not only to get at subterranean food such as roots that voles and mole-rats live in holes smaller than the various species of African cats. Nor is it simply to get out of the cold dry-season night air that hyraxes pile into rock crevices narrower than the average leopard.

Topis (*below*) and impalas (*opposite*) monitoring nearby predators

Slow and steady

There are two paradigms of the Jurassic that persist in African ecosystems: the crocodile (see p. 181) and the tortoise. In fact, the ancestry of the tortoise and its close relatives, the sea turtles and freshwater terrapins, is older even than that of the inhabitants of Jurassic Park, stretching back over 200 million years to the mists of the Permian. It is likely that tortoises looking much like they do today were plodding about under the feet of dinosaurs, munching just about everything encountered from dead meat to living vegetation. Down through the ages it has been buffered from predation by its shell, an ingenious box made from a fusion backbone, ribs and breastbone.

When form follows function without frills, you get some classic designs that persist through changes in fancy and fashion. Incongruously, images of tortoises and Volkswagens spring to mind – low-key time travellers that have surpassed many in the race.

Today's leopard tortoise, one of the dozen African species, is a strict herbivore that stays within a one or two square kilometre home range throughout its several decade life span (in captivity they have reached seventy-five years old). Its laid-back aspect is more than shell deep, since even its muscles are designed to contract at rates fifty to a hundred times slower than those of a mouse or a frog. Conservative, endearing and a little bit boring, its main claim to fame is being a living icon to the I Ching aphorism, "perseverance furthers".

Speed for flight

If the herbivore's eyes, ears and nose do not sense the predator until it is too late to avoid detection, or if the predator sees through the protective colouration, or breaches the retreat, there is only one final recourse – to run. Energy used in flight is costly, but clearly well spent.

The fleeing prey and pursuing predator present what at first glance might be a Darwinist's paradox. It is obviously to the wildebeest's advantage to run a bit faster than the hyaena. Natural selection should favour a faster wildebeest. On the other hand, the hyaena's survival is enhanced if he can run down the wildebeest. So selection should also favour the faster hyaena. We might therefore expect

an evolutionary race in which both prey and predator were producing faster and faster individuals. It has been called the Red Queen effect, since, like Alice's frenetic guide in the looking-glass world, the prey and predator species have to run harder and harder – evolutionarily speaking – just to stay in the same place. By now the contest should have reached a point where the landscape is ablur with supersonic prey and predators hard on their heels, both with reactions and tools honed to impossible levels. This does not happen, in part, because of the essential asymmetry in these evolutionary arms races: as Aesop first observed, the hare runs for his life, the hound only for its dinner. Moreover the superspeed fantasy

ignores the multiplicity of selective pressures which result in any one final form or behaviour. Structural engineering problems such as length of bone and stress in joints; physiological limits set by over-heating and supplying blood to outsized muscle masses; nutritional problems and loss of agility associated with a large body all act as governors on speed. Compromise results, in that today's cheetah and gazelle run as fast as they can in the current set of environmental circumstances. Someone tomorrow will run the hundred-metre dash in less than 9.79 seconds; we will take bets that no-one will ever run it in less than five.

Elands (*above*) and impalas (*opposite*) **in flight**

Weapons to fight

The stag at bay and the wildebeest surrounded by snapping wild dogs are herbivores who have nearly run the gamut of their anti-predator adaptations. When retreat is thwarted, the last-ditch stand is the final recourse to save one's genes and materials for one's own posterity. Poisonous snakes use their venom to threaten or incapacitate their predators as well as their prey. Predators steer clear of the ostrich's vicious middle toe. Herbivore horns have developed, primarily, for the purpose of self-defence so they must occasionally prove effective.

The impressive horns of an oryx (*right*) may be, surprisingly, not only a defence mechanism but also indirectly an adaptation to conserve water. Most herbivores rely on running to escape from predators. Running generates heat that has to be dissipated. This saps precious bodywater reserves through evaporation. Water loss is dangerous for an animal who lives near the climatic boundary of the grasslands, where the credit balance between rainfall and evaporation diminishes almost to zero. To get water where there are no water holes for most of the year, the oryx does much of its feeding at three o'clock in the morning when the withered vegetation has absorbed a little moisture from the cool night air. At the driest ends of the species' range in the Namibian desert, the gemsbok goes for weeks without drinking, conserving water by stopping sweating. A network of interlocking blood vessels – a "rete" – at the base of the brain uses the relatively cool venous blood draining from the nasal sinuses to reduce the temperature of arterial blood from the heart several degrees before it enters the brain. The gemsbok thus avoids thermal shock and brain damage when its body temperature, normally around 39 degrees C, can exceed 45 degrees C in the heat of day – near-fatal for most of us mammals.

Not surprising then that the oryx is not a great runner. In the water and temperature extremes that characterise its habitat, rather than trying to outdistance a lion, it may be cheaper in terms of ultimate survival to take a stand. Such an evolutionary decision requires defensive weapons and a willing-ness to use them. An oryx has both, and is the only herbivore of its size that has been known to wound a lion fatally with its horns.

Although the function of the striking black-and-white facial colouration is not known, one would expect it to be a social signal – to conspecifics and would-be predators alike. The implied message of such a signal is obvious: "a head sporting dangerous weapons is now turned towards you – beware!" Conspecifics avoid useless bloodshed, predators learn to retreat: effects worthy of an unambiguous signal. The skin of the oryx is some six millimetres thick on the neck and shoulders to help reduce accidental damage to itself during head-back displays and to protect it from the thrusts of protagonists during ritualised fights that may get slightly out of hand.

Oryx horns or hyrax incisors would not be of much help without the will to use them. The stress and excitement of the chase increases the supply of adrenaline to the blood that results in untoward muscle performance and aggressive behaviour. The worm literally turns. The Thomson's gazelle faces the jackal; the jackal sees off a hyaena; the plover attacks the jackal; occasional success is clearly better than none.

A Thomson's gazelle holding a Black-backed jackal (*Canis mesomelas, opposite*) and the beisa oryx (*Oryx beisa, above*)

Behavioural flukes

The ecosystem teems with mischief: animals making a living at the expense of others. Of course, good old orthodox herbivory and predation are just that, but they somehow do not carry the moral sting of parasitism, in which the main actor makes use of its host both as food supply and habitat – or at least a staging post for part of its lifecycle. We had best adjust our point of view. Not only are the bitter biological struggles between parasite and host at least as prevalent as the overt eating of plants and animals, they also influence animal movements, social behaviours and even mate selection. Parasites like mosquitoes cause more human misery and death than wars. The lowly parasite may in fact be the prime mover in the ecosystem.

Here's a typical story, an old saw to parasitologists. A nasty miniscule flatworm, a fluke, befuddles its ant host by burrowing into its nervous system and setting off so many short circuits that the usually careful ant throws caution to the winds and perches high on a grass blade, insanely awaiting ingestion by a passing herbivore. The ant sacrificed, the fluke then completes its lifecycle in the herbivore's gut. The ant looses its life, the herbivore is robbed of some nutrition and possibly weakened by the invasion, but the fluke and its offspring get both fed and housed. And this is just one story. Parasite numbers are legion in every animal: nearly every Serengeti lion is feeding half a dozen blood parasites and up to fifteen kinds in its gut, as well as itself.

Whilst the ranks of catalogued parasites is swelling beyond the conventional wisdom list of fleas, flukes, tapeworms and ticks, the breadth of their impact is gradually coming to light: they may be the prime reason for sex. Disease organisms target cells: viruses usurp the host's genetic machinery in the cell to reproduce; certain bacteria and fungi simply eat the cells. These parasites *sine qua non* wreak their destruction by developing protein "keys" that fit into the "locks" of a cell's surface defences. Asexual beasts, many boom or bust invertebrates like aphids, take a chance by handing down just one type of lock from generation to generation: once a parasite comes up with a "key", it will spread like wildfire through a population and all aphids in the neighbourhood will be at risk. Sex serves to shuffle the genetic deck by mixing genetic material from two families and ensures that subsequent generations will have a number of possible "locks" to confound the parasites, and thus reduce considerably the risk from disease.

Being free from internal parasites is important to health, well-being and reproductive success. So much so that the elaborated ritual courtship displays of birds and some mammals may have evolved to carry the explicit message: "not only am I big and strong, but this dance/display/fight certifies that I am quite likely to be clinically free of harmful internal parasites; come fly with me!"

When parasites are not being celebrated for the development of sex, they are being attributed for the development of lack of it and the extreme social sacrifice of colonial insects. The large numbers of sterile workers in ant, bee, wasp and termite colonies may have arisen historically when high-parasite loads decreased female fertility and drove the colonies to put the energy of the evolving sterile working class into foraging and care of the nest and young. If you cannot beat them, outwork them.

Being free from external parasites, like ticks, is also important since such "vectors" are used by the internal variety to breach the skin defence and get inside the host. Even casual observation will tell us that animals spend a considerable amount of time in the "comfort behaviours" of preening and grooming. They do this in part to keep pelage and plumage clean and tidy, but more importantly, to detect and remove skin parasites. Another stategy is to employ – tolerate – a third party to do the job, like the red-billed oxpecker (*opposite*) here on the zebra's back (see p. 101).

The more we look, the more we find out about the evolutionary effort that has been spent in anti-parasite campaigns. Just one recent and rather obscure example: the impala's front teeth are deliberately wobbly: the tips of incisors and canines can bend forward some two millimetres. This is not just an artefact of use or the drying of skulls; it is a deliberate design feature. The tooth sockets are unusually shallow and the teeth are set in a ring of tough fibres with softer tissue below, so they bend out and spring back into place. The impala uses this built-in comb to rake through its hair and winnow out ticks that are both debilitating blood suckers in their own right, and carriers of a host of unpleasant blood parasites. Thus the impala improves both its general health and the range of habitats – ticks or no – that it can exploit.

The design of the hunter

The front-end of a carnivore is as conspicuous to its particular nature as is the front-end of a herbivore. Like a tireless hunter, form follows function and dictates that carnivores be designed to catch food that is usually mobile. Moving food must not only be seen and identified, but its speed and distance judged precisely to ensure an accurate lunge. The complex optical requirements for this job are partially met by eyes that face forward and fix the prey simultaneously. Anyone who has tried to touch the tips of two pencils together with one eye closed appreciates the advantages of binocular vision.

Once reached, the prey must be caught and held. Hence, predators have developed a range of hooks, claws and talons, and the strength to hang on. Once held, the prey must be killed and somehow made manageable for the predator's gullet. Both acts require a diverse array of teeth used for various butchery tasks: holding, killing, slicing, cracking. For killing, the lion or lioness usually clamps the victim's muzzle shut and waits for it to choke on its own blood. The cheetah simply strangles the prey with a prolonged bite at the throat. The serval cat severs the hare's spinal cord. Wild dogs, hyaenas (*bottom right*) and tawny eagles tear the prey to pieces, so that killing and dismembering become part of the the same rather messy process. Knife-edged molars (or beaks) slice up the meat, and in the case of the hyaena, grind up most of the bones too. The smaller the prey, the less reason for the nicety of a clean kill. A praying mantis can easily hold down a struggling fly, or a bird of prey a squealing vole as the meal begins.

Carnivore food is more concentrated than herbivore plant fare. Carnivores consume more protein and energy, and less non-digestible material per time of feeding. Every kilogramme of grass the wildebeest eats contains roughly ten grammes of protein; every kilo of wildebeest flesh the lion ingests is nearly pure protein. One consequence of this is that herbivores spend most of their time feeding, whereas carnivores eat in spaced bouts and then loll about, sustained in the intervals by their high-quality diet. A wildebeest may spend eighteen hours a day feeding; a lion spends the same amount of time sleeping.

Near the top of the terrestrial food chain our attention is drawn inevitably to the large cats of Africa – beautiful and terrifying, perfectly evolved hunting and killing machines. But, sharing the pinnacle of the pyramid of numbers are nearly thirty species of mammalian predators, from lions and serval cats down to mongooses and shrews. There are many predator species quite simply because there are many herbivore species to serve as prey. There are large predators because there are large herbivores. Wildebeest, zebras, buffaloes, hartebeest and gazelles provide the opportunity for lion, leopards and cheetahs to exist.

The nature of an animal's food supply dictates its whole lifestyle, limits its absolute abundance and may regulate its numbers over time. We have already seen that because of the constraints of the Second Law of Thermodynamics the weight of carnivores in a stable terrestrial ecosystem will invariably be less than the weight of herbivores. Even

within these absolute limits, when the herbivores grow scarce, either by dying or wandering away, the carnivores must necessarily starve. Although occasionally carnivores do keep a herbivore population in check, the more general case is that of the herbivore controlling the carnivore's numbers. A curious turnabout – the fate of the fearsome cat decreed by the population dynamics of the timorous gazelle.

But there is another twist to the tale. Cats such as the serval (*above top*) hunt often at night. Good night vision depends on rhodopsin, a chemical made with vitamin A. Cats find the usual sources of vitamin A, namely plants rich in beta-carotene, not particularly to their liking. Instead they "borrow" the necessary chemicals from the flesh of their herbivore prey, who thereby unwittingly provide the necessary ingredients for their own demise.

The solitary hunter

The cheetah walks like an indolent queen, but when it runs, its loose-jointed gait makes sense. Its very lankiness, the peculiar flexion of spine and shoulders, provides the mechanical basis to bestow the distinction of fastest land animal. Cheetahs are designed to run. In hunting they supplement a cat-like stalk to within twenty metres of the prey with a spectacular chase to the finish. The head is small, seemingly out of proportion with the rest of the body, particularly the powerful legs. The claws never retract, like running spikes always on and ready. Such physiological specialities result in the speed and agility necessary to catch Thomson's gazelles, one of the easiest of the herbivores for the weak-jawed cheetah to kill.

The specialisation of speed severely limits the cheetah's range and confines it to open plains or sparsely wooded grasslands where there is a little cover for an initial stalk and enough room to run down small antelopes in short sprints. Even though the heart beats slower than that of most animals of comparable size, and the lungs, heart and adrenals are disproportionately large, the sort of physiological effort that the cheetah puts into the chase would probably kill it if sustained for much longer than a minute. When the prey is knocked down and strangled after a hard chase, the exhausted cat may spend fifteen minutes regaining its breath. The effort is worthwhile. The prey of cheetahs is usually in prime condition, with fully rich marrow fat: no weeding of the weak and sickly for these regal beasts.

They are solitary, or else found in small groups of two or three, perhaps a mother teaching her grown offspring how to hunt. The technique of tagging a zigzagging gazelle at full tilt has to be observed carefully and practised for months until mastered. It is probably the nature of the cheetah's hunting technique combined with competition from fiercer beasts – including cub-killing lions – that limits its numbers, even in a land abounding in gazelles and wildebeest fawns.

The cheetah is normally diurnal, partly because it is simply not possible to run at speed in the dark, but more importantly to avoid both competition and deadly encounters with large nocturnal predators. In the Serengeti, predation by lions and hyaenas seems to be the most serious type of cheetah mortality. The cheetah's spotted camouflaged coat probably serves to conceal the cat from larger predators as much as from its prey. In other areas, the pressure of over-enthusiastic tourists has driven local families of cheetahs to hunt uncharacteristically over the lunch hour when the tourists are feeding or at night when they are asleep.

Pressures on cheetahs and their habitats is leading not only to a decrease in their numbers, but also to a concomitant impoverishment of their very fibre. We find more and more scattered and reduced populations with about as much genetic variability and stamina as a strain of laboratory mice. It is not clear what will eventually finish them off. Experts are debating the relative importance of competition, habitat loss or merely succumbing to a flu epidemic.

Competition between species

It is not unusual to see zebra and wildebeest grazing together, interspersed with Thomson's or Grant's gazelle, not far from a herd of impala or even Maasai cattle. But we rarely see the "big cats" together; the tension at the top of the pyramid is much too great for interspecific sociability.

In the main, the carnivores avoid competition by following different lifestyles – by being large or small, nocturnal or diurnal, solitary or social. But since several predators are dependent upon prey species common to all, clashes of interest are inevitable.

To us, antelopes and gazelles may seem infinitely abundant in the African grassland ecosystems, but for the large carnivore there are only as many as it can catch. Thus, in effect, prey animals are rarely over-plentiful and frequently very scarce, especially when migratory herds move away from a territorial carnivore's range. Furthermore, any herbivore is a chore to catch. It is not surprising then, that even the most "noble" of predators will steal a meal if it has the chance.

The perfunctory displacement (*illustrated here*) of a pair of young cheetahs from their wildebeest kill by a maned lion is a rare event to witness, but probably happens frequently. Cheetah meals are hasty affairs. Other large predators invariably eat the soft belly of their prey first and then consume the

rest at leisure. The cheetah, however, begins with the protein-rich muscles of the hindlegs, as if expecting to be interrupted at any moment, as indeed these two were within five minutes of making their kill. There was no argument, much less open conflict; the cheetahs abandoned their meal whilst the lion was bearing down on them, still over a hundred metres away. The carcass was almost intact, lacking only the two to three kilos of rump steak the cheetahs had managed to wolf down.

Competition within species

The lion is almost an ecological luxury, and, judging from its arrogance and indolence, we might think it knows this but does not particularly care. The size of this 200-kilo cat means that it may select its prey items from the larger species of herbivore such as buffaloes and giraffes, or even, perhaps on a moonless night, have the good fortune to separate an elephant calf from its family and dispatch it in the confusion. The lion's size also means that it can steal food from the other predators with virtually no resistance. In the Ngorongoro crater, Tanzania, some fifty per cent of its meals are poached from hyaenas.

Four out of five lions in the Serengeti live in territorial prides. The prides typically comprise two to nine adult females plus their dependent cubs as well a "coalition" of up to a half a dozen adult males. Although some one-third of the females migrate away from their parent pride, it is still the females that maintain territorial vigilance. They hearken to the roaring of intruders and must reckon the numbers heard, for they only initiate an aggressive foray if the odds are in their favour. The territories may need to encompass more than 200 square kilometres in order to contain enough meat to support a score or so of lions. But even so, lions are only sociable because they have to be. A tight-knit pride is more successful in competing with neighbouring prides for local food resources. This sociability in turn helps fine-tune their most successful hunting technique, the stalk-and-ambush in which two or more animals co-operate.

But once the prey is dead the co-operative spirit evaporates. The strongest of the pride eats first, and if the prey is a small Thomson's

gazelle, there will be nothing left for the others. If prey is scarce then the cubs will die and the young adults will probably leave the pride to seek their fortune elsewhere.

As the largest and the most powerful of the flesh-eaters, lions have few natural enemies (except people, see p. 127). One reason that adult lions are not covered in spots is that they have no-one to fear and hide from. Although leopards occasionally snatch cubs, there is greater risk from within. Male lions, if they get the chance, will murder any cubs that are not theirs – a startling and brutal display of weeding out the genes of others.

There is an enormous potential for increase amongst lions. Females are in season every few weeks throughout the year, and produce up to six cubs in each litter. But lion populations never get out of hand, simply because they are so strictly controlled by the numbers of available herbivores. In turn, lions have little effect on the size of the herbivore populations, except in very local situations where the number of herbivores has been critically lowered by some other factor, such as drought or competition. The top of the food chain is a lonely but usually comfortable niche. The large herbivore diet means the lion lives from one filling, high-protein, fat-rich meal to the next. Often several days are spent over a large carcass, eating and keeping others away. One lioness in Tsavo National Park, Kenya, showed remarkable persistence over a dead young elephant. She spent nearly a week lying down repeatedly licking the same spot on the elephant's hide until her cat-tongue finally rasped a biteable hole in the centimetre-thick skin.

A hierarchy of strength

At a kill, the cat that was greeting and rubbing heads with her pride a short while before becomes an intolerant individual. Chewing is continually interrupted with low growls and bared-teeth snarls, ears flattened in rage and even skirmishes over a choice piece. The more numerous females usually do most of the killing. Males will kill, too, if necessary, for example, in the Kruger National Park where ungulates are evenly distributed. If they are sub-adult, non-territorial or nomadic males, like those likely to be found following the Serengeti wildebeest migration, the larger males find it easier to muscle in and steal the food caught by the females.

There is more tension when there are more mouths to feed. A good breeding season has its pastoral moments of gambolling cubs. But they are just waiting for the next meal to be brought down or brought in. The cubs, being the lowest in the hierarchy, are lucky if they get anything. In the Serengeti each year three out of four cubs may die during the dry season, because all of the migratory herbivores have moved 200 kilometres north into territories held by other lion prides, defended by males who will fight trespassers to the death.

The spectacular fights between two males rearing and rampant illustrates one likely function of the manes – namely, to protect the head and neck from blows with paws the size of soup plates with claws like boat hooks. And, female choice appears to put a premium on darker manes. Ingenious, if a bit bizarre, experiments with life-sized model lions in the Serengeti showed that ladies prefer them dark and handsome.

We are fascinated by these cats because of the functional splendour of their size and strength. We also fear them. One of the most terrifying experiences imaginable is to meet one face-to-face on foot in the African bush – man, the paragon of animals, instantly reverts two million years to a defenceless prey. But we can, perhaps, salve our wounded pride with the thought that in the great mill of the grassland ecosystem, the lion accounts for only a minute fraction of the turnover of materials.

Winners and losers

There is between the so-called "top carnivores" and us an ancient animosity as well as an age-old respect. A group of San hunter-gatherers in the Kalahari (see p. 142) echo that past and today share their foraging range with a pride of lions, respecting each other, generally avoiding each other, occasionally purloining each other's kills. We have been killing each other for millennia, sometimes seeking out the encounters for food or ritual, more often avoiding contact or killing in self-defence. There must have been a time when our brain in its remarkable evolution gave us the edge in the prey-predator race and we started to outwit and outflank the other members of the "carnivore guild" with which we shared the grasslands.

The rules of engagement are somewhat different when the people involved are formidable warriors. Watching two young male lions feeding on a young elephant they had managed to kill (or steal), we were puzzled when they both suddenly ducked their heads and appeared to hide behind the carcass. Beyond them, now visible in the middle distance was the reason: two young Maasai men were striding purposefully along with their unmistakable chin-forward, long-sprung gait, spears glinting on their shoulders.

The Maasai are nomadic pastoralists who have found it a better bet to make their living by having herds than by hunting, particularly if there is enough land and rain to provide fodder for a species mix of cattle, sheep and goats (pastoralists in drier regions like the Rendille herd goats and camels). Not only are these herbivore derivatives more tractable than their wild cousins, but they produce milk. Using milk rather than the dead animal is akin to living off interest without eating into capital. Moreover, at low densities, the domestic stock and wildlife are able to cohabit quite comfortably in an ecosystem. Far from competition, there is even an implied mutualism at work. In earlier, less crowded and commercial times, the Maasai tolerated the wildlife's offtake of grass as insurance against the inevitable years of extreme drought when they would have to resort to wildlife flesh to survive. The wildlife for their part enjoyed protection from a tacit vigilante ranger force: poachers crossed Maasailand with extreme caution.

When their capital wealth is threatened, Maasai take great exception. In the story shown here, two male lions had been satelliting a Maasai *ngang* for several weeks, striking through the thorn fence at night and carrying off sheep and goats, or the odd cow, if lucky. One was a sick and decrepit beast who obviously found domestic stock easier fare for his poor condition; the other, a fat ecosystem freeloader. Whether this ignoble pair worked in concert is not known, but they certainly met their ends together. The Maasai became fed up with the raiding and lay in wait for several nights until the pair struck. With their long-bladed spears and the fires of indignation and ancient rituals burning in them, the warriors set upon the lions and with much shouting and leaping about quickly dispatched them. The postmortem confirmed evidence of calfskin in the belly of the fat one. With respect to human-lion encounters, over the millennia the score must be about even.

There is a kind of bitter irony to the fact that these old foes both seem to be losers in recent skirmishes during the perennial battle against parasites. Periodic outbreaks of canine distemper virus (CDV) have for uncounted millennia laid low jackals, foxes and wild dogs, whilst the neighbourhood enjoyed complete immunity. But in early 1994, CDV suddenly jumped the so-called species barrier and fatally infected large numbers of Serengeti lions. There is no better-observed wild population of lions in the world, and it is quite certain this nasty viral trick was indeed a recent, abrupt and unprecedented event. Well, not unprecedented for viruses, of course. We humans are succumbing in droves to immune deficiency viruses (HIV) that several decades ago made a similar sudden leap between chimpanzees and us. There is a bitter irony indeed in the fact that the scourge is self-inflicted: after all, we built the bridge for the virus by opting to kill and eat our nearest animal relatives. We wonder how many other grim tricks viruses have up their virtual sleeves, and who will laugh last: chimps continue to enjoy immunity to HIV...

Hunting man

In the age-old encounter between people and animals, the odds have come to be stacked in our favour. Traditional encounters are relatively infrequent, often pastoral, as we have seen. Non-commercial hunts for bits of "bushmeat" protein supplement, meagre as they usually are, do not much impact on the wildlife populations. Even modern man's persistence in demonstrating his domination for the sheer splendid sport of it has a trivial biological impact.

The more systematic modern approaches do make their mark. Wildlife-based tourism has grown to be a mainstay of foreign-exchange generation in many African countries. A policy of discipline is necessary to avoid the wildlife being hounded to the edges of their ecosystem and beyond their tolerances for survival; but in general, thoughtful tourists generate more revenue and jobs than they do harm. Game ranching for speciality meat markets is locally lucrative but usually needs supplementing with other activities, such as traditional stock-raising. It is also sensitive to quirks of rainfall and animal reproduction. Attempts at systematic culling and canning of the large migratory herds have invariably ended in a burlesque of mismanagement and misjudged markets.

What a tangled web we weave. One sector of human society, comprising members from all around the world, imputes special ritual, pharmaceutical or decorative uses to various parts of wild prey like heads, horns, skin and teeth. Another sector then initiates command and control policies that cut off supplies and thereby create incentives for poaching and black markets. If

there is a demand, economists suggest we should find a way to husband rationally the supply. No-one in their right mind would wander through the bush hunting for the eggs of gallinaceous birds or shooting them on the wing for the market. Instead we farm chickens. The conservation fraternity has not yet been able to swallow the notion of rhino or tiger farms, even though ostrich ranches start to break the ice. The fact is hunting takes a lot of effort. And what little food it yields is usually riddled with parasites, needs long slow cooking and, being low in cholesterol, simply doesn't taste very nice.

The elephant question is a different issue. Ivory is a hard, if cumbersome, currency and a potentially diminishing resource. People, of course, must come first in the quest for *Lebensraum* in Africa. But whether we like it or not, there is a qualitative difference between sweeping a large-brained, highly social beast like the elephant from our development path and, say, eradicating insect pests. There is enormous controversy over what portion of the observed decrease in elephant poaching can be attributed to the 1989 international ban on trading in ivory. We do not propose to enter this crucial debate here, but would simply observe that if a population of, say, 5,000 elephants suffers a reasonable five per cent per annum natural mortality, the country hosting those elephants accumulates some ten tonnes of ivory every year. Much of it is found: some turned over to the authorities, the rest enters illegal trade routes. The dilemma is how to put that rather

valuable and growing stockpile to some good use, other than a rather depressing photo opportunity. It is hard to decide if the much-touted ivory burnings demonstrate steadfast conservation in action or the absurd outcome of human greed. We wonder if there are not lessons to be learned from the way in which the cartel of diamond-producing countries has solved its peculiar problems of value – and wealth.

The co-operative clan

It was a blow to conventional wisdom when we came to learn the secrets of the spotted hyaena's lifestyle. Prior to research done in northern Tanzania and in the Kenya Mara, the only picture we had of the hyaena was that of a skulking, scavenging coward. This was a natural but erroneous conclusion drawn by hunters and tourists who are mainly diurnal – especially between breakfast and lunch – and who are usually looking for more spectacular game. Dedicated researchers, however, are willing to sit through the night till dawn or sweat out the midday sun if necessary to see what happens in the few hours when hyaenas are not lying around.

A main revelation of hyaena research is that, far from being an outsized decomposer, the hyaena is a highly efficient social hunter that sweeps through the ecosystem in family groups called "clans". The daytime observation of a crowd of hyaenas waiting for a lion to finish its meal may well lead to a false conclusion. In fact, it is the final tableau in the common story of a clan's night-time labours having been usurped by the King of Beasts.

If it can the hyaena will eat just about anything – it is almost a carnivore version of a goat. Even aircraft tyres have been sampled. But clearly freshly killed meat is preferred, if available. The massive jaws and musculature can crunch up and eat an entire wildebeest, leaving only the horns. The digestive system processes nearly all forms of protein so that the droppings are white, nearly pure calcium mixed with a bit of hair. The hair, incidentally, makes it possible to identify the kinds of prey eaten.

Spotted hyaenas partition out the hunting grounds amongst the clans and are as fiercely territorial as Highlanders about their property rights. If one clan chases a wildebeest into the neighbouring clan's territory, the hunt is likely to change into a border skirmish between the two groups whilst the prey escapes.

The function of their territoriality is to guard a food supply; the function of their sociability is to catch it. A solitary hyaena is no match for a stallion zebra protecting his family or a healthy, alert adult topi. So when faced with tightly

social prey and a coherent group defence, hyaenas always hunt in concert and almost always succeed. Migratory wildebeest, on the other hand, are easier to single out, and hyaenas more often tackle them on their own.

The lekking grounds of the topi (see p. 87) set the stage for the rather dissonant and disturbing – to human sensibilities – interaction between the social systems of herbivores and carnivores. Adult topis, dozing in the midday sun after a hard morning's lekking, are an abundant and relatively easy target in the Maasai Mara. Under these circumstances a group of hunting hyaenas would be more likely to alert the soporific herbivores. Thus lone clan members ply back and forth across the grounds until chance presents a sleeping, young or already wounded target. Once a strike is made, other hyaenas home quickly in on the struggle. Although the clan can hunt together with beautiful timing and co-operation, at the kill it is every beast for itself. The prey is literally torn to pieces, and after the initial scrum to get the soft parts, we see hyaenas scattering in all directions, one with a hindleg, another dragging off entrails, a third with the head. Less than seven minutes after the kill, all there is left of the topi is a pile of its stomach contents where it died.

The beauty of the hyaena system is its flexibility: they work in concert or alone, depending on how the prey present themselves. Hyaenas have even evolved a system of "commuting" between the den area and seasonal abundances of herbivores up to sixty kilometres away. Denning females from Serengeti clans have been observed to make fifty-odd three-day return trips, covering over 3,000 kilometres a year. One way or the other, hyaenas rarely starve (more succumb to snaring or poisoning than to lack of food). If the herds of large herbivores have moved away from the clan area, each hyaena can make a living as a predatory commuter, or indeed, if pressed, even as a mere scavenger.

Above: hyaenas seek out and find unwary topi

Sibling rivalry

The hyaena is a curious beast of ambiguous ancestry, coming somewhere between the mongooses and the cats. Since the time of Aristotle, it has been considered to be a hermaphrodite. This legend comes from the anatomical oddity of the female's private parts. She sports an outsized clitoris as large as the male's penis, and even has a convincing if empty scrotum. These sham male parts possibly serve some function in the mutual genital-sniffing greeting ceremony, but what exactly the function is remains known so far only to the hyaenas. Another piece of hyaena trivia: the physiology of their placenta is very close to that of humans. As well as their genital ostentation, the females are pugnacious, physically larger than the males and even dominant in social encounters. Hyaena clans have even been known to alter their sex ratio within one season by suddenly producing more females than males in order, it seems, to populate a newly abandoned neighbouring territory.

Hyaenas start expressing their competitive spirit rather drastically on the very day of birth. In the centre of the clan territory there is usually a den dug in the ground where the animals lie up during most of the day, where the young are born and where they shelter whilst the adults hunt. They invariably come into the world as twins, but only one cub eventually joins the clan. In the darkness of the infant den, one sibling attacks and torments and eventually kills the other, either outright or by helping it to starve in a grisly game of "siblicide". No other mammal young have been observed to do this, only the chicks of some large predatory birds like eagles and herons. In the birds, the reason seems to be limited food supply. But the case of the hyaenas is not so clear.

Since siblicide occurs more often when female twins are involved, it seems that there is some link to female dominance: the cubs of dominant females usually inherit their mother's rank in the clan. Add to that aspiration an unusually high dose of testosterone that the young are exposed to in the womb, and scene is set for a turbulent childhood. Although this may explain *how* the dead cub being carried here met its end, it does not tell us *why*. Researchers continue trying to unravel this grim mystery, through a combination of studies in the wild and observation of captive animals.

The co-operative imperative

Unlike the hit-or-miss and frequently unsuccessful tactics of lions and hyaenas, wild dogs work as a well-organised team and rarely fail. They are coursers who run tirelessly and effortlessly behind a herd of antelopes until fatigue begins to show on the weaker prey individuals. The dogs then confuse, distract and harass their target, cut it off from the security of the herd and run it down in a series of flanking movements that enables fresh dogs from the rear to take over the chase to keep up the pressure. The prey gets no respite and is soon exhausted. Thus we see a large wildebeest calf held at bay by two small wild dogs; the rest of the pack will soon join them. It would be impossible for a lone jackal to kill an animal larger than itself. But a pack of co-operating wild dogs, each not much larger than a jackal, can bring down and kill even an adult wildebeest with remarkable dispatch (*depicted here*). Each dog in co-operative mode needs to hunt around three to four hours a day to get enough to eat, expending up to ninety per cent more energy than a human office worker does during an eight-hour day.

By co-operating like this, wild dogs can kill anything from a hare to a zebra, and hence the absolute amount of food available to their populations is greatly increased. This is the essence of their social hunting and it is crucial to the wild dogs' survival. There is a tempting parallel here with the demands that the slight, fangless and clawless early hominids must have faced – the co-operative imperative.

The larger, stronger hyaena can strike out on its own occasionally and make a living as a solitary roughneck scavenger. But the frailer wild dog is bound to its comrades, for without them he will starve or be killed. The patchy dispersal pattern of wild dogs in South Africa's Kruger National Park has been likened to that of impala – their main prey in that region. But curiously, where impala are common in Kruger, the dogs are generally scarce. The reason is lions, the main predator on wild-dog pups in the Kruger. Lions are not particularly fond of impala, but do like the other herbivores in the neighbourhood, such as buffaloes. So, far from competing for the same food, the dogs are actively avoiding lions and have to nip gingerly into impala (and lion) country when they want a meal. Instant recognition of who is who, and what one's status is, may be augmented by the wild dogs' striking patchwork markings: indeed, their scientific name, *Lycaon pictus*, means "painted wolf". Each animal has a different mottled livery, and if research workers can learn to tell individuals apart, certainly so can the dogs themselves. Of course, smell and attitude must be the key social signals at close range, but at middle distances, for example, during the heat of a chase, perhaps there is a premium on knowing instantly and precisely who is flanking whom.

The chances for field studies to help us understand more about wild dogs are fast dwindling. It is estimated that there may be as few as 3,000 left throughout their range. This is partly as a result of them being shot as vermin by farmers and even by colonial park wardens; and, more importantly, of recent infestations of canine distemper transmitted from the domestic dogs belonging to the growing human populations around protected areas. There is a bitter irony that one splendid co-operator is causing the demise of another.

A hierarchy of respect

A wild-dog kill is not pleasant to watch. The prey is often partly eaten before it is dead; the wildebeest bellows and struggles to escape even as its entrails are pulled out and hunks of meat are torn from its rump. Within fifteen minutes, nine dogs were once observed to devour most of a 200-kilo carcass; an hour later all that remained were a few bones, an uneaten forelimb and a pile of half-digested grass from the dead animal's rumen.

Such a death may disturb human sensibilities, but that is irrelevant. A wild-dog kill is remarkable, not for its inhuman bloodiness, but for the almost polite mutual respect we see amongst the dogs, and their deference to one another. There is no frenzy, no snapping, squabbling or fighting. The dogs eat in their hierarchical order; each calmly waits its turn, presumably in the knowledge that if there is not enough to go round this time, then the pack will kill again and again if necessary, until each has had its fill.

Every hyaena and lion is essentially out for itself, but the African wild dog is a truly social beast. Their packs range in size from just a few to twenty animals, but around a dozen seems to be optimum: enough hands to help in the hunt, and not too many mouths to feed. At any size, the packs are fiercely social melanges of relatives and recruits. The high proportion of related animals encourages the kind of "helper" system seen in many bird species. Non-breeding yearlings help feed their young siblings or their nieces and nephews and thereby contribute to the survival of the new pups who are carrying

some of their own genes. Constant togetherness means continual interactions: touching, sniffing, talking. In contrast to their decorum at a kill, when wild dogs come back together, even after short absences, they demonstrate what appears to be joyful reassurance of their mutual devotion. The leaping about, whining and tail-wagging, sniffing and nuzzling will ring a bell with the owners of some breeds of domestic dogs.

Certainly a rigid dominance hierarchy helps keep the peace and probably increases the efficiency of group hunting. But orderliness has a price. As in other highly social species like mongooses and humans, the dominant members of the pack are often victims of their own social success. The alpha animals, both males and females, show measurable signs of stress. In the case of the wild

dogs, blood corticosteroids have been measured to be fifty per cent higher in dominant males and twice as high in dominant females, compared with their lowly but relatively relaxed underlings. Tough job, maintaining law and order, but someone's got to do it.

The nimble opportunists

Given the relative paucity of protein available to carnivores, compared for example with the sheer weight of grass on which grazing herbivores live, it is not surprising that some of the most successful carnivores are the opportunists. Animals like jackals, crows, mongooses and some vultures and bustards take protein wherever they can get it. They will kill or scavenge. Their choice of food items includes most animals smaller than themselves, or larger animals if dead. They even eat some vegetable matter.

The opportunists literally live by their wits with no special adaptations except perhaps a relatively small size and what we would call intelligence. They cannot afford to maintain too large a body since the source of the next meal is never certain. They occur in large groups or singly, depending on the abundance of food in the area. Their apparent intelligence is born of the need to be exploratory and inquisitive, poking into every niche they can, ready to make use of what they find. The flexibility and ability to adapt to new situations is witnessed by the fact that both jackals and crows can make a living in an environment radically changed by humans – even to within the boundaries of our cities.

There are three species of jackal: the golden, the side-striped and the black-backed. They occur often in the same places, eat more or less the same sorts of foods, and grow up in the same kinds of small family groups. There are very slight dietary differences; for example, the black-backed is thought to be a shade more carnivorous than the others. But the fact that the relative late-comer to East Africa – the golden –

has settled into a diet somewhere between the other two, makes them virtually indistinguishable, in terms of their "niche space".

Here a black-backed jackal demonstrates its hunting side. After touring the perimeter of a herd of Thomson's gazelle, it suddenly cut off one that seemed to us identical to the rest. But when it turned to defend itself, it revealed that it had been previously wounded on its flank. Whether the jackal had spotted the wound itself, or some subtle weakening in the gazelle's demeanour is difficult to say. But clearly it had picked a soft spot in the herd, which it then proceeded to worry to death.

Co-existence of a number of closely related species – like the African cats – is relatively common, as long as they divide up the job of surviving by having different food requirements, different body sizes, different ways of socialising. The jackals pose a bit of a problem to the evolutionary biologist: how can three such beasts of similar habits and requirements co-exist? One would expect them either to diverge further or to become one species. There seem to be two explanations. First, food is usually a limiting resource in competition, but may not be so for jackals. The abundance and unusual diversity of potential jackal prey may take the edge off the razor of competition. If their food were in shorter supply, the three species might not be able to co-exist for long. Furthermore, significant size divergence, a common mechanism for avoiding competition, may not be an option for jackals, given physiological constraints and the bitsy, if abundant, nature of their

food itself. One researcher put it nicely: "success of the golden jackal as an insinuator into East Africa suggests that the carnivore guild might not be saturated." The same might be said of the "omnivore guild": did this help set the stage for the emergence and flourishing of people?

The omnivorous opportunist

From the heights of our mental evolution we sometimes forget that we are animals too: primates, with distant cousins amongst the lemurs and monkeys, and much closer relations among chimpanzees with whom we share a common lineage no further back than one-thousandth of the earth's lifespan.

Even though we consider ourselves to be the paragon of animals, we are governed by natural laws, just as much as every other living organism. We and all our works are no less part of the Earth's finite collection of materials than a termite and its mound.

Whilst giraffes evolved long necks, lions sharpened their claws and gazelles learned to sprint, we developed the brain, initially perhaps to monitor and control the growing demands of efficient eye–hand co-ordination. Our brain is a remarkable tool for living, but makes us unique only in so far as we can imagine the future as well as consider the present and remember the past. Not that the other "unique primates" like chimpanzees cannot make some of those temporal cause–effect links, but we seem to be able to grasp a host of connections all at one go. We are able to analyse cause and predict effect within a constellation of contexts, and the obvious success of our species depends largely on this ability. At this stage we are unlikely to evolve other physical adaptations to aid our survival. The cognitive brain is all we have.

Rightly or wrongly, writers and readers of books regard themselves as the most highly evolved of the species, and surrounded by the trappings of their lifestyles, some individuals may regard the biological

fundamentals of life as remote if not unimportant. But, of course, every single piece of all the artefacts of civilisation is nothing more than a part of the Earth. Destroy civilisation and we would be left with only the Earth and our brain. Could we survive?

Were such a cataclysmic change of lifestyle to happen suddenly it would probably destroy most of *Homo sapiens*, but there would still be some individuals left to perpetuate the species: foremost amongst them would be the few remaining tribes of hunter-gatherers. The Kalahari San Bushmen, for example, are able to survive on what the Earth supplies in a basic form. If freed from the strictures of civilisation, these people could leave the desperate retreats to which they have been driven, and roam the continents as once they used to.

They live by the bow and arrow, the spear and the snare; they eat plants, insects, rodents, reptiles and birds. Survival depends upon total co-operation amongst band members. The social customs they have evolved obviate the ownership of property, and complicated allocation procedures ensure that everyone gets a share of a kill or foraging expedition. For instance, the old man who made the arrow is entitled to a part of the antelope it killed, and the woman who supplied the bag gets a proportion of the berries it brings back, no matter who filled it.

Each band has mutually recognised rights over areas of land, though intermarriage brings with it shared rights. This is particularly important at the height of the dry season when food is very scarce, and the

water available is in moisture-bearing roots that must be dug from underground with sticks and the brain's ally, the hand.

The Bushmen are an integral part of the ecosystem in which they live: they bring nothing to the desert and they take nothing from it. But, whilst they do have some minor physical adaptations peculiar to themselves, they live by the basic tool of the species: the brain tells how to kill the antelope and the brain suggests where to grub for the succulent roots. From our self-styled "civilised" viewpoint, the Bushman's lot appears a hard one in which there is not much choice, only necessity. Yet, as we dash about from nine to five, hunter-gatherers need put in only two to three days a week in order to maintain a surprisingly high plane of nutrition, if times are good. This leaves them an enviously long weekend for cultural pursuits like music, socialising and telling stories. There are days when we might be tempted to trade our cellular phones for that.

A young San child (*above*) eating the bone marrow from an antelope's foreleg

CARNIVORES PURSUIT OF FOOD

Seizing an opportunity

Sources of nourishment are found everywhere in varying degrees of availability. The front-end of most animals is usually designed to deal with particular kinds of food, and feeding in most animals involves the appropriate use of particular tools. Body form and behaviour are always functionally and operationally inseparable: the owl's eye and night hunting; the heron's bill and fish-stabbing; the hyaena's jaw muscles and bone-crushing; the lion's claws and prey-grabbing; the eagle's beak and flesh-tearing – the part and the use evolved together. The propensity to use the right part of the body in the correct way is innate, inborn, but early attempts by young animals are clumsy. Efficient use must be perfected through learning, in play and pratice, and from the rewards and punishments meted out by the environment which result in learning.

Ostrich eggs are attractive sources of nourishment, but relatively rare, so the jackal and the tawny eagle have not evolved the wherewithal, nor have they learned to open them. But the Egyptian vulture has: it throws stones at the eggs.

So intimate are body and behaviour that we are not surprised when a tse-tse fly plunges its proboscis into us, or when an eagle tears off pieces of prey. But when an animal uses a part of the inanimate environment to exploit a food source – like the Egyptian vulture (*opposite*) deliberately picking up and throwing a stone at an ostrich egg – we are amazed. There is no reason to explain "tool-using" by invoking a superior intelligence, any more than such an intelligence is necessary to explain the wood-

pecker's use of its bill to hammer holes in trees. Stones are ubiquitous parts of the environment, even more so than birds' beaks. The components of the stone-throwing movements – picking up something in the beak, lifting the head up and bringing it forcefully down, as in an attack or a strong peck – are not unusual. Given the "tools" in number, the movements already evolved, and a reward equivalent to two dozen hens' eggs, the stone-throwing trick is not so surprising.

We do not see more tool-using because most species have developed built-in equipment to exploit their most frequent food sources. The Egyptian vulture probably has not evolved a large ostrich-egg-cracking bill, swung by enormous neck muscles, because ostrich eggs are not available all year round: foods that put a premium on a slender bill are. On the other hand, when ostrich eggs are in season, the amount of protein they provide makes it worthwhile for at least one member of the community to do something about them.

Dependence on death

At the very top and along the edges of the pyramid of life perch the vultures. We might think of them as predators who happen to prey on animals that are already dead. Indeed, the wooded grasslands provide a large quantity of vulture "prey". Eventually all species fall into this food class. A live Thomson's gazelle and a live zebra present a predator with very different prey-catching problems. But once two such animals die, they become effectively one "prey species" for vultures.

Although all animals eventually die, carcasses tend to be much more scattered in time and space than herds of live animals. Thus, for a group of vultures around a carcass, the essential resource at that particular time and place is limited. As one would expect, this situation produces competition, which in turn provides a selection pressure for the birds to find different ways of attacking the resource: the result is that there are six different species of vulture – the large lappet-faced and white-headed; the medium-sized white-backed and Ruppell's griffon; and the small hooded and Egyptian.

At first sight, vultures on a carcass appear to be involved in a fierce free-for-all struggle for food; but there is much more order than might be supposed. Fights are predominantly between members of the same species. Different species arrive on the kill at different times in a fairly consistent order. They utilise different parts of the carcass and are specially equipped to deal with those parts. The shape of their bills and the parts they have to deal with has caused them to be classed as rippers, gulpers or

scrappers. They have differences in carcass-spotting abilities, feeding behaviour, nesting habits and levels of aggression. Thus, even though they might bicker over space at a kill, each species occupies a distinct niche which allows them to co-exist.

The classical image of the vulture skulking on a dead branch and casting a baleful eye over the ecosystem is apt enough – they are continually watching and waiting for someone to die. They range over thousands of square kilometres. Meals, as we have said, are relatively scarce, so the searching vulture conserves fuel by soaring. It can travel many kilometres without a wing stroke, by cannily choosing a route through thermal up-draughts and air rising on the windward side of hillslopes. So efficient is this low-budget travelling that they can afford to maintain the large, strong bodies necessary for competition at a carcass. And so efficient is their searching, that if you lie down to have a nap in the grass, you may be shortly awakened by a vulture landing next to you.

Endpiece

No matter how spectacular the herbivore, how ferocious the carnivore, all eventually yield their corporeal material to the decomposers.

Any relationship between a vulture and a dung beetle may seem decidedly tenuous, but they both – along with a variety of species of flies, crickets, moths and bacteria – help in the disassembly of organic matter and so speed up the return to the soil of essential chemical elements.

To serve this end and, of course to maintain themselves, most of the decomposers can fly. It is a matter of minutes before the first decomposer finds a fresh carcass or dung pile. The vultures will be there before rigor mortis sets in, the flies within seconds of the animal excreting. Even many bacteria are airborne. They all work with incredible speed. In the wet season, when dung beetles are most numerous, a pile of elephant dung, all ten kilos of it, is worked into balls and rolled away, almost before it cools. The beetle (*Coprinae, above*) deposits eggs in the ball, which it then buries a metre underground. Thus manure is injected directly into the earth. When the eggs hatch, the developing larvae feed on the dung, taking the process of decomposition a stage further.

Lakes and Rivers

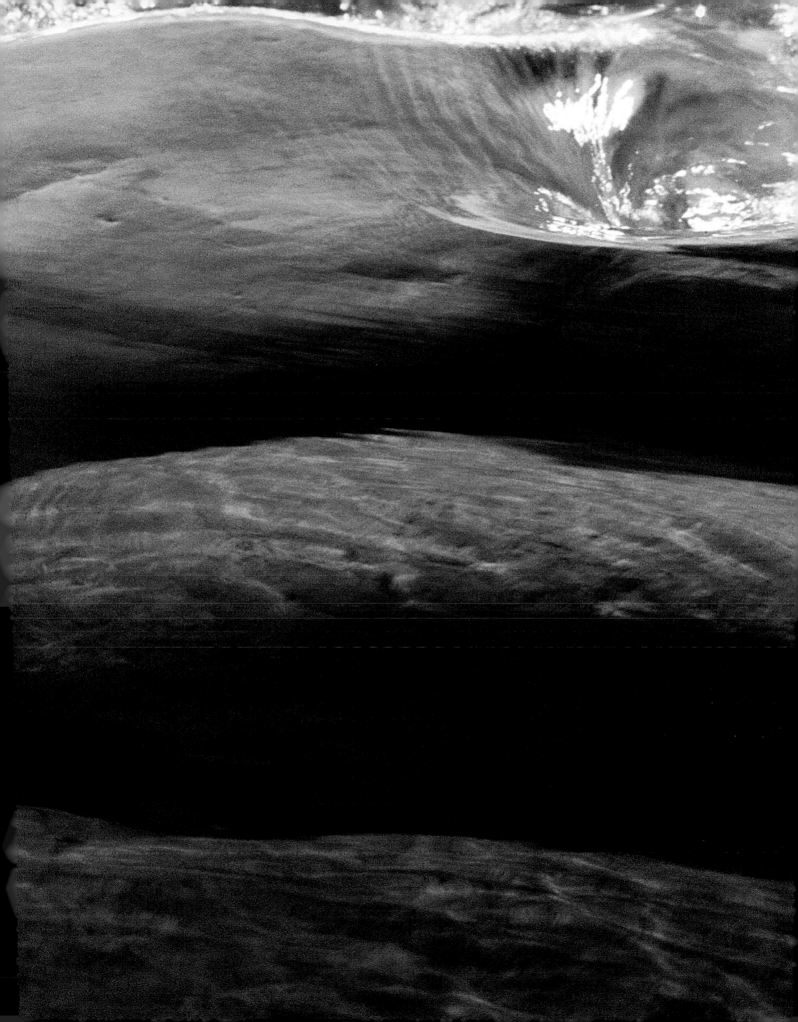

The movement of water

The force that moves water from high places to low places is one of the most pervasive in the solar system, let alone on Earth. The inexorable pull of gravity shapes our very structure and form: it determines how we grow and our absolute dimensions. It waters us along the way, albeit with differing rhythms. Water may fall gently or in torrents, move steadfastly down streams in a high-rainfall river basin, or erratically in drier climes. The comforting predictability of the perennial or the seasonal is rudely punctuated when, for example, natural dams are breached and large amounts of water suddenly and perversely leap free, as in the so-called GLOFs – Glacial Lake Outburst Floods. These scour out whole valleys, sweep people, plants and animals from their paths, and settle down as lakes or mud patches somewhere below.

All life processes are reducible to chemistry and physics. The boundary between chemical and physical effects blur both at the atomic level and on mountain slopes where lake and river water composition is concocted. Water that rushes down mountain streams or thunders over cataracts like Kabalega Falls in Uganda (*opposite*) churns and froths and takes oxygen directly from the air. Still-lake water, in contrast, receives its oxygen from the quieter biochemical process of plant transpiration. Both processes may be a matter of life or death for aquatic animals.

The water's gain is inevitably the soil's loss. Soil degradation – also a conspiracy between chemistry and physics – involves leaching of essential elements from the soil matrix, or just washing it bodily away, "redistributing" it downslope. Erosion occurs everywhere to a greater or lesser degree, and even on a non-abused, well-covered hillside some soil gets transported into the drainage lines. Most soil is lost by the energy of raindrops that knock particles free and then combine in an overland flow to sweep them along in so-called sheet erosion. Excess water trickles down the slope, joins with other rivulets, and gathering power, gouges into soft low-lying places and cuts into the stream-bed sides. This gully erosion looks dramatic, but releases far less soil than its pervasive overland counterpart. On the flat or in the cracks, water moves soil. It also chips out and rolls stones along tumbling off their sharp edges and making of them round pebbles. Streams run into rivers, rivers to the sea, or into swamps (such as the Okavango delta, *right top*), or into lakes.

There is always some movement of this sort going on in the mountain rivers that swell during the floods that follow heavy rain. In fact, very few East African rivers are perennial, like the Nile, the Tana in Kenya or the Great Ruaha in Tanzania that flow all year round. Most are seasonal, running briefly during the rains and dry the rest of the year. The Kerio in northern Kenya is an extremely erratic river that only enjoys enough rain actually to flow into Lake Turkana once every few years. Most of the time it is a "sand river", used as a track. Water is present in plenty, though, well below the dry bed, and it takes the ingenuity of people or elephants to dig wells to get at it.

Where the rivers run into lakes the soil and debris they carry is

deposited on the bottom. As the velocity of the water diminishes, first the heavier stones and gravels are deposited, and then the smaller particles of soil. Finally, the fine silts fall slowly to the bottom, or may even remain in a colloidal suspension, giving a particular colour to the lake. Lake Baringo in Kenya is tinted red from soil washed down last rainy season. Lake Michaelson (*above*) is still green from the fine silt particles carried down by the glaciers of Mount Kenya years ago.

The accumulation of water

Twenty million years ago in Africa the Earth gave a lurch, volcanoes erupted, lava flowed and two of the dozen or so great plates that make up the surface began to drift apart. The result was the Great Rift Valley, 5,000 kilometres long from the Dead Sea to the Zambesi Valley in Mozambique and eighty kilometres wide just west of Nairobi. The faults and terraces of the rift are still as clear as when they were formed. In the bottom of the several arms of this valley lie the most important East African lakes, the surfaces of which still occasionally ripple from volcanic tremors.

Mountains determine the ecological character of lakes and rivers. The water that falls or condenses on them is pure, distilled from seas and lakes. The greater part of it, moving down a well-covered slope, actually flows below the ground until it reaches the junction of two slopes, where it surfaces as a spring – the beginning of a river. Whilst percolating through the soil and over rocks, the water dissolves chemicals and takes on board the flavour of the mountain itself.

Water which flows from heaved-up granitic rocks like the Ruwenzori in Uganda, the Usambaras in Tanzania or the Matthews Range in Kenya, for example, tends to be acidic. Moreover, the granite and sandstone particles filter the water to a state of crystal clearness, almost too pure for the tastes of life.

On the other hand, many of East Africa's mountains are not-so-ancient volcanic ranges, composed of alkaline lavas. Consequently, the water which runs from them carries the basic salts of the rocks into the lakes where they accumulate and concentrate: many of the Rift Valley

lakes are closed basins with no outlets, like Lake Magadi (*opposite*) and Lake Turkana (*above*). Bodies of water, particularly in dry areas, are inevitably strong attractions to the eye and the body. As we scan the horizon for water, let us keep in mind that there is more water in the ground than in all the world's lakes and rivers combined.

The transition from the land to the water is as abrupt as the edge of a lake. Living in water poses problems unknown to organisms on land. For example, getting oxygen, orientating in three dimensions without a horizon and, feeding on primary production that floats unattached all require special adaptations. We say this, of course, from our terrestrial perspective. Evolution of the animal panoply worked the other way round, from the water to the land, and most of the life we encounter in the grasslands or the forests is supported by special adaptations to escape the medium in which life began. Despite the obvious difference between aquatic and terrestrial ecosystems, we shall see that the same basic ecological rules apply to the entire spectrum of life in the water, which ranges from microscopic plants to herbivorous hippopotami and carnivorous crocodiles.

Flood and drought

The processes of solution, erosion and deposition are continuous and slow, except in cases of land degradation. They vary in effect from year to year and from age to age. On the other hand, the rainy season can start overnight, sweeping silt from parched and eroded land, and dumping it into swollen rivers. Water rushes into the lakes, washes away bird nests, initiating the fish migration and spawning, and, whether from above or below, making drastic changes in the lakeshore habitat.

Lake Nakuru rose dramatically following the 1961 floods, and has dried out completely four times since 1951, and very nearly again in the early 1990s. From their girth we estimate that stumps of yellow-barked "fever" acacias were mature trees sixty to seventy years old when the rising lake waters drowned them. Such trees cannot tolerate highly alkaline groundwater, it follows that the lake's water table must have been considerably lower than it is now for the entire half-century the trees were growing. Further testimony to the lake's inconstancy.

Ironically, the trees died not so much from an excess of water as from a shortage of it. This is because in the process of osmosis water travels across organic membranes (such as the cell walls of root hairs) towards the side of highest salt concentration, often in a vain attempt to equalise the concentrations on either side. Thus the trees actually lost more water to the alkaline salt solution of the lake than they could extract from it.

Clearly, such fluctuations are related to climatic trends, but hardly in a simple way. Lake Naivasha seemed to gain a couple of metres in depth during the exceptional rains of 1997/98, whereas Nakuru remained at a living-memory low. Some fear that Lake Nakuru may be disappearing down a subterranean plug hole and thereby keeping nearby Lake Elmenteita topped up. The investigator who discovered that the level of Lake Victoria changes in an eleven-year cycle directly parallel to sun-spot activity would have to admit that the effect is probably one of sun spots on regional atmosphere circulation that in turn alters rainfall in the lake's huge catchment (see p. 25). And, stepping back to a global scale, some climate modellers foresee a causal chain in which increased carbon dioxide in the atmosphere will "fertilise" green

plants and increase their photo-synthetic efficiency. More efficient plants transpire less water into the air and leave more in the soil to run into rivers and fill up lakes. Are we moving to a greener, wetter world?

Through the much longer timespan of thousands and millions of years, life in the lakes has changed profoundly, though gradually. Lake Naivasha, for instance, was once joined through rivers and swamps to another large lake at Olorgesaile in the Kenyan Rift. Around these waters our earliest ancestors lived. That lake is now gone, and, though it may seem difficult to believe when you see its deep clear waters, Lake Naivasha will eventually disappear too, filled with silts, rocks and soils of the higher ground and of the mountains.

So the character of a particular African lake may be quite different from its nearest lake neighbour, depending on the character of the surrounding land. The perversity of rainfall in semi-arid regions also means that a particular lake ecosystem may not be stable for very long. In ten or twenty years the lakes we observe today could be quite different, in size, in numbers and types of species they support – some may even be gone completely.

Nevertheless, despite the ebbing and flowing of African water bodies, the rules governing the workings of their ecosystems are the same as those that pertain to the grasslands and the forests. To show them at work in the water we will look at the eastern African Rift Valley lake ecosystems.

**Lake Nakuru in 1976 (*opposite and above*)
and in 1998 (*above top*)**

A special solution

Several of the Rift Valley lakes are called by the Maasai "magadi", which simply means soda. In these closed lake basins, dissolved materials, mainly sodium carbonates and bicarbonates build up in concentration and produce a fertile, if alkaline, environment. When the lake level falls (because of a prolonged rainless period or simply from evaporation by the sun that volatilises thousands of litres a day) large deposits of salt crystals precipitate on the shore in patchwork sheets of white, brown and red. The crystalline patterns of the precipitated salts are as striking from the air (*below*) as they are under the microscope (*opposite*). In solution they create an unusual chemical environment – one which could kill a thirsty wildebeest but which supports a remarkable profusion of life. The alkaline lakes are extremely rich in primary production, as we shall see, but they provide a physiological environment so alien to most life forms that only a few have evolved to cope. Leave your hand in Lake Magadi for an hour and, apart from getting soda burns, you will lose water through the skin in a vain osmotic attempt to dilute the lake to a reasonable ionic concentration. The twelve centimetre cichlid fish, *Tilapia grahami*, does not shrivel up and die in Magadi because it can tolerate chemical concentrations within its body almost equal to those of the water. It survives in a hostile environment by becoming part of it. It can also tolerate water temperatures up to 41 degrees C, such as occur in the vicinity of the hot volcanic springs that bubble out of the Rift Valley floor and feed Lake Magadi.

Once an organism has adapted to the extremes of an alkaline lake it is likely to do extremely well. It was estimated, for instance, that in its heyday the tilapia population of Lake Nakuru weighed 800 tonnes, very roughly the same as a population of 800 elephants, adults and young taken together. The fish consumed about sixty tonnes of algae a day from their forty-odd square kilometre aquatic pasture. If suitably packaged, this weight of greenstuff could only feed a population of some 450 elephants (and they would have to cover far more than twenty-five square kilometres of wooded grassland to get as much). This illustrates the potential richness of a tropical lake and its concentration of nutrients compared with other systems, and suggests that, if you happen to have such a lake nearby, it's a better bet to farm fish than elephants.

"Slime city"

You slip on a rock crossing a stream and curse the wetness or whatever it was that made you fall. Look again. Your feet are wet anyway; go back to the rock and touch it. Slimy. Scrape off five to ten micrometres with your fingernail. Algae? No, more likely you have just been repulsed by one of the most ancient, prevalent, yet overlooked, communities on earth. On just about every hard surface where there is water and the right temperature and chemistry – rocks in streams and lakes, teeth, guts, above ground and below – there is "biofilm".

Biofilm is the generic name for a community of sheltered and relatively affluent bacteria resting in a happy state. We are more familiar with the free-swimming planktonic state of bacteria – the ones that infect us or feed on our offal. In fact, these represent the relatively brief interlude between the good times – biofilm – and the hard times, typically when temperature or moisture are unfavourable, or hosts are scarce or dead. At this extreme, the bacteria pack up their DNA, switch off their genes, encase themselves in waterproof ultra-micro cysts and wait, as it were, for the good times to roll around again.

Like communities of larger organisms, biofilms often contain many species of bacteria. It is becoming evident that the vast majority of the Earth's bacteria live at some stage in biofilm communities. Some do vital jobs, like working in sewage treatment plants to remove contaminants from water, or in cows' forestomachs to digest grass. Others wreak havoc, for example, by compounding disease

development or secreting acids that corrode the metal of oilrig struts. Even your dentist wages a perennial war on the biofilm called plaque.

Far from being hodge-podge bacterial soups, biofilms appear to have organisation that has inspired researchers to use urban metaphors to describe them: infrastructure, transportation, towers, water supply, neighbours, predatory muggings and twinkling lights (under sophisticated microscopy lighting). They also provide a substrate for invertebrates to latch on to for feeding or launching – like a miniature re-run of *Godzilla*. The more we look, the more life seems to be a reworking of familiar scripts.

Opposite: inhabited rock surfaces covered in biofilm?

The microscopic algae

Alga is the most important primary production of the lake ecosystem. Ubiquitous and successful, the numerous species of single-celled organisms should not be thought of simply as some form of "dissolved grass". Many exist as discrete cells; all have some sort of food chemistry catalyst, usually a form of chlorophyll; some clump together in colonies which have the form of proper plants; others are simple consumers in the sense that they gobble up large inorganic molecules. They reproduce sexually or asexually; they have minute internal organs – organelles – which carry out such functions as excretion and digestion; some can see light, and most can move through their watery medium. They are animate plants, or proto-animals, depending on how you look at them. They are now classified as cyanobacteria. They echo life's first forms on earth.

The water of Lake Nakuru is thick, slimy and green. Your hand is invisible fifteen centimetres below the surface, obscured by the mass of algae suspended in the water. Ninety-five per cent of the cells are in chains belonging to the blue-green algae, *Spirulina* (magnified 10,000 times *opposite*), and are so small that thousands of them laid end to end would be about as long as their proper scientific name: "*Oscillatoria*

 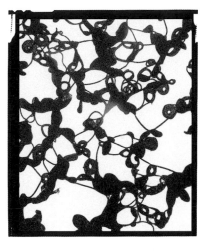

(Spirulina, Arthrospira) platensis var. minor Rich." The whole lake is a veritable soup of nourishing vegetation, an expanse of extremely productive pasture. In an algal "bloom", the weight of *Spirulina* in the forty-square-kilometre lake may be of the order of 200,000 tonnes over a few weeks. That is equivalent to the productivity of over 200 square kilometres of good grassland. Small wonder *Spirulina* is one of the candidates currently being studied as a source of nourishment for space farers.

The algae occur in such enormous quantities because of the combination of strong sunlight, high temperature and high carbonate and phosphate concentration in the shallow soda lakes. *Spirulina*

is a green plant, and needs sunlight. But so opaque are the waters of Nakuru, that only the top ten inches receive enough light for photosynthesis. Yet the lake is virtually filled with living algae. The reason for this is that every day the shallow waters of Nakuru are thoroughly stirred by wind and wave action, which allows all of the *Spirulina* access to some light.

Enriching the water

The hippopotamus is an invader of the water ecosystem. But since it derives no nourishment from the aquatic food chains, and simply uses the water as a daytime refuge from the sun and from predators of its young, it is a benign guest. In fact, its presence is decidedly beneficial. After a day of bobbing about in the water, idling and socialising, at dusk the hippos leave the lakes and rivers and wander along well-defined avenues up to ten kilometres inland to graze. The materials they ingest are imported into the lakes when the beasts lumber back in the morning, have a drink and excrete.

The business of hippo excretion is one of the favourite anal jokes of the African bush. As they defecate, their stubby tails seem to spin like the proverbial fan, spreading dung in all directions. Conventional wisdom has this preposterous display as being one of territorial marking, if the excretor is a male, or displaying oestral state, if she is female. We prefer the Bushman's explanation, namely that the hippo is demonstrating to God that it continues to meet the main condition of having been allocated such a nice life: eating only vegetation and not God's (and the Bushman's) fish. It seems, however, that the hippo belies its strict herbivory; it has frequently been seen sampling bits of found flesh.

The real reason for the dung-spraying may be considerably less romantic, if that's the correct term.

South African researchers have discovered a leech that is decidedly hippocentric. It is a reddish-brown, perfectly camouflaged from oxpeckers against hippo skin. It is a strong swimmer, and even if given a choice of prey to latch on to, prefers hippo blood. Unlike most leeches that move along with a characteristic looping step with a rear sucker following the front, *Placobdelloides jaegerskioeldi* wriggles about on the hippo rather like an earthworm. This leaves it flatter and less at risk of being washed off. It also provides it with the means of getting at its favourite venue for hermaphrodite sex – namely, the dark and cosy confines of the hippo's rectum. Which brings us to the end of this short tale:

it could be that the vigorous gyrations are an attempt to expel or repel amorous leeches.

This diversion prompts a small observation about parasites. Leeches, it has been observed, are like aquatic versions of mosquitoes and vampire bats in the air or ticks on the ground. The interesting thing is that in evolutionary space, the congruence of opportunities – a nice food like blood, mobility of the feeders – produced a scenario, a script, if you will, that could be enacted by different players in different media.

An adult hippopotamus may weigh two tonnes and therefore consumes a prodigious amount of grass around the lake periphery. Its contribution of materials to lake ecosystems may in some cases provide the nutritional basis for an aquatic pyramid of life. Without the hippos, the aquatic nutrient pool would be solely dependent upon the painfully slow process of the weathering of the surrounding rocks.

It is unlikely that the materials the hippo imports to the lake will subsequently move back across the shoreline during their progress through the food chain. The chance is greater that they will travel from trophic level to trophic level within the lake. Perhaps in the long run the hippos' rent is offset by those birds who feed from the lake but then fly off to excrete or die elsewhere.

The point is the materials move round within the lake at a higher rate than they move in and out. This defines the ecosystem. Similarly, the odd wildebeest may wander out of Ngorongoro crater and get eaten by a Serengeti lion, but most see out their lives in the crater. Or, a forest-dwelling bull elephant may come down from Kilimanjaro and succumb in the swamps of the Amboseli Basin. However, this sort of event is relatively infrequent compared to birth, feeding and death within the entity of the ecosystem. The hippopotamus, like us, is one of the few mammals that makes a habit of regularly transgressing ecosystems' boundaries.

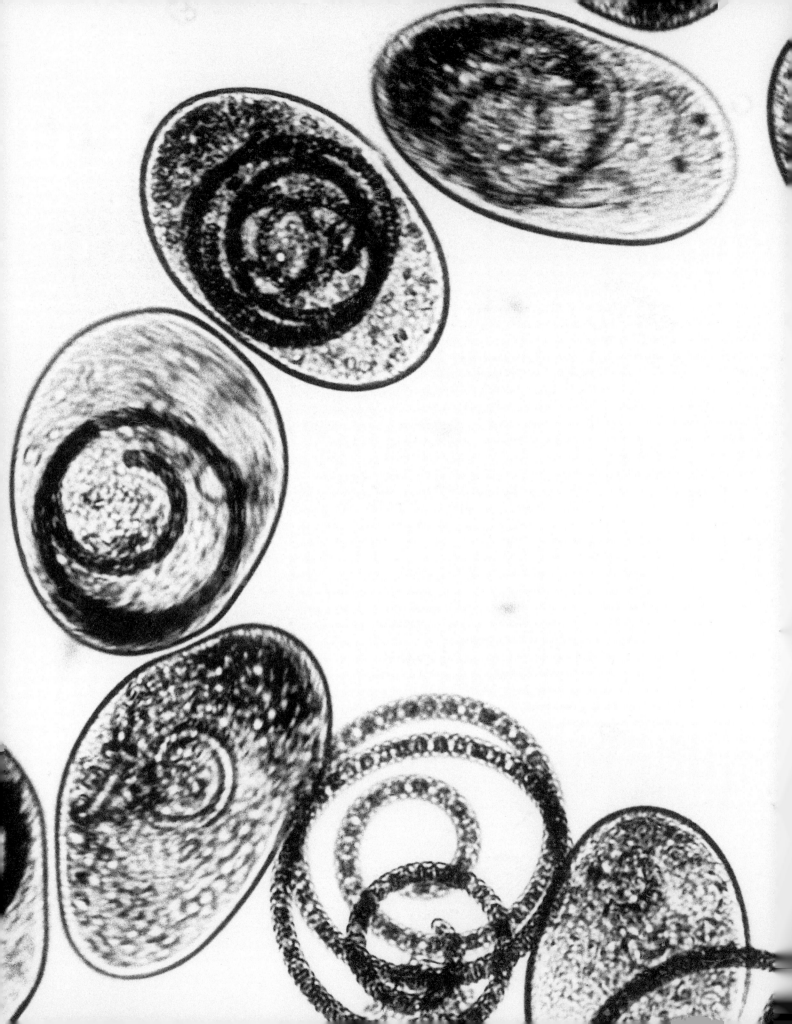

The micro-grazers

A microscopic flora encourages a tiny fauna. Under a microscope in a drop of lake water we observe minute protozoans, single-celled herbivores filled with recently ingested *Spirulina* coils (*left*). They are much like the algae they eat except, lacking chlorophyll, they cannot produce their own food. The protozoan herbivores absorb the tiny plants through their cell walls. The algae are broken down into their chemical parts that nourish the protozoa. Waste products from this process accumulate in a bubble that eventually pops through the cell wall back into the lake – micro-droppings in the lake ecosystem.

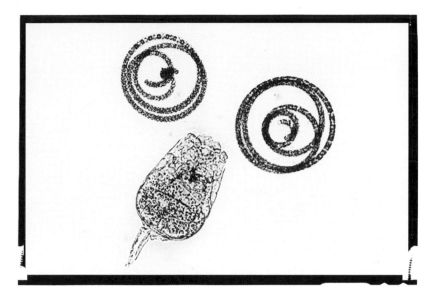

Rotifers are not much bigger, but are slightly more sophisticated than the protozoa. They are curious beasts, rather like primitive mechanical worms with the distinction of being the only member of the animal kingdom to have wheels. At their front-ends, there are circles of constantly moving hairs mounted on rotating axles complete with bearings. These two little sweepers spin eddies of water into the mouth cavity. Particles of food, occasionally bits of *Spirulina*, will also be swept in.

Rotifers make more rotifers by parthenogenesis – that is, without recourse to sex. In fact, males are completely absent in some species, such as the *bdelloid* rotifers (*above*) that appear to have been chaste for the last forty million years. It does not seem to be such a bad strategy since through the ages they have diversified into more than 360 species, none with any close sexual relatives. In one Western Uganda Crater lake, Lake Nyahirya, twenty-four species have been described.

Rotifers are amongst those plants and animals called "cryptobionts": they can lose up to ninety-nine per cent of their body water in drought conditions. They seem to shrivel to lifeless motes, only to "resurrect" when you add water. Against such eventualities rotifers produce a type of egg that stays attached to the adult without hatching. These eggs have a thick, tough cell wall (the typical "good times" egg is thinner-shelled and develops into a miniature adult soon after it pops through the mother's body wall). They may be transported about on the legs of wading birds or blown away by the wind in the dry debris that was the lake bottom. Thus, far from succumbing to drought, rotifers can effectively migrate away from the hard times. Some have even been collected floating like tiny time capsules in the dust of the upper atmosphere. This has led to the somewhat fanciful suggestion that rotifers were Earth's first space visitors.

The little crustacean *Lovenula* is also a primitive lake herbivore. Not much is known about them except it lives only twenty-two days, feeds mainly on *Spirulina*, and, along with the protozoans and rotifers, makes up an impressive microherbivore biomass of well over 2,000 tonnes in Lake Nakuru. This is roughly equivalent to the weight of the 10,000 wildebeest and zebra on the Athi-Kapiti Plains near Nairobi.

The specialist

Specialisation usually produces a marvel of both design and architecture, with form tightly fitted to a particular function. The lesser flamingo (one of the world's six flamingo species) specialises on the blue-green algae like *Spirulina*. Its long legs allow it to wade and feed in water nearly a metre deep. Frequently algae-rich waters are shallower than this, so a long neck is essential for reaching the surface. A duck, swimming on the surface, can feed on algae and other small floating plants with its head in an upright position. If the flamingo were to keep its head upright, it would need an extra kink in the neck. It solves the problem by feeding with its head upside down.

Flamingoes harvest algae by "grazing" in the top couple of centimetres of water. Inside their bills they have a remarkable filtering mechanism. The upper mandible (*detail right*) is triangular and fits tightly into the lower bill when it is closed. The inner surfaces of both are covered with fine hairy processes, arranged in rows, about forty to the centimetre. The thick and fleshy tongue is confined to a tubular groove in the lower mandible where it moves back and forth like a piston pump. The tongue retracts and sucks water in over the filter hairs. It extends and forces the water out again, erecting the hairs with the pressure and catching the algae in masses along the downy inside of the mandibles. These masses are rolled down the gullet in a continuous stream propelled by the pumping tongue.

A feeding flamingo submerges its bill in the water – upside down – and a pulsing ring of water can be seen booming rapidly out of the

beak, some seventeen strokes a second. The lower mandible, which is uppermost in the feeding position, is cellular and filled with air spaces. It is so light that it will float like a cork if detached from the bird's head. This buoyancy allows flamingoes to feed in choppy water without having continually to use energy in adjusting the height of their heads to compensate for waves.

Thus flamingoes are an extreme example of specialisation in cropping primary production. Since they sieve off only the top layer of blue-greens and do not feed over the entire lake, it is clear that they take only a minute fraction of the algae available. Yet even so, it has been calculated that an average population of 300,000 removes about 180 tonnes of *Spirulina* daily from Lake Nakuru.

An Alice-in-Wonderland debate raged mercifully briefly, over the question "Why does the flamingo stand on one leg?". Hypotheses ranged from the statistical (to halve the chance of being bumped into

by passing ducks or of being blown off both feet by gusts of wind), to the anti-predatory (to confuse predators who are expecting birds with two legs), to the physiological (to ensure only half the amount of blood accumulates in the feet after long periods), to the conventional (for the same reason that most other birds and some humans stand on one leg), to the absurd (to make certain only one foot gets stuck in the mud). In that creative vein, one of our reviewers observed that "if it took both legs off the ground, it would fall over." We can think of nothing to add, except to observe that the reason flamingoes are pink is because of the pigments in their blue-green food source.

Dangers of specialisation

Specialists like the lesser flamingo are gamblers who put most of their survival bets on the abundance of one type of food. When that type is plentyful, the specialists thrive and do far better than other consumers who are not specifically designed for the job. Thus flamingoes on Lake Nakuru have on occasion reached a staggering 1.5 million birds. All is well as long as the food source is present. Periodically, however, the culmination of a chain of external events drastically affects the *Spirulina* population. A long dry period reduces the lake level and consequently increases the alkaline concentration. When it becomes too high for the *Spirulina* to tolerate, they shrivel and die.

The flamingoes then have two choices – to move and look for blue-green algae elsewhere, or to die as well. They make attempts at falling back on an alternate food source, such as the green algae *Clamydomonas* that replaces *Spirulina*. But here specialisation leaves the birds at a disadvantage. The green algae are smaller than the blue-green cyanobacteria, and the flamingoes' precision-built filters let too many escape. Thus they do not get enough to eat, even when the waters are as turbid with green algae as they were with blue-greens a few weeks before. They are forced to change their feeding habits altogether and spend long hours sieving the lakeshore mud for single-celled plants called diatoms. These are a limited food source compared to the profusion of an algal bloom, and can only support a fraction of the algae-hungry flamingoes. In such cases, within a few weeks the flamingoes of Nakuru all disappear – some starve, most migrate.

There are three interesting questions connected with the flamingoes' dilemma: how do they know when to go, how do they know where to go, and where do they in fact go? Doubtless they decide when to go by reacting to their stomachs. There comes a point in the decline of the *Spirulina* when each flamingo is not getting enough. Awareness of this, which we would call hunger, results in a restlessness that leads to the birds flying away from the lake. Any body of water attracts the migrating flamingoes initially, or perhaps they have ancient maps built into their genomes that provide the first compass bearing. In either case, they land and test the blue-green algal pastures or the diatom content of the mud. If sufficient, they stay. If not, the same forces compel them to move on. They disperse to lakes up and down the Rift Valley – north as far as Lake Turkana on the Ethiopian–Kenyan border and beyond to the Ethopian lakes; or south, some authorities hold, as far as Botswana, over 3,000 kilometres away. Iranian flamingoes are regular non-breeding season visitors to the Indian sub-continent.

But it is not all that easy to explain their movements, for within a few weeks of a recurrent blue-green algae bloom in Nakuru a huge number of the birds are back. So the specialist either needs the ability to reproduce very quickly in order to take advantage of gluts of its special fare, or the ability to move and seek out new food sources with tenacity and stamina and an uncanny timing and awareness.

A place to mate

In the warm alkaline waters and abundant food supply of the lakes, another cichlid fish, tilapia (*Tilapia grahami)* breeds all year round. The species is fiercely territorial – but only in the mornings. At sun-up the males prepare to defend the centres of their forty-centimetre-diameter territories (*opposite*). Other males who wander into the territories receive open-mouthed threats that feature the conspicuous white lips. Adjacent territorial males gape across the boundaries and probably bombard each other with invisible water pressure blows in an aquatic equivalent of huffing and puffing. Transient males bounce through the area from one territorial encounter to the next, whereas schools of females and young sweep through the breeding grounds leaving a wake of posturing territory holders, who suddenly switch to behaviour designed to attract gravid females rather than repulse invading males.

At eleven o'clock, they all knock off for lunch, leave the breeding grounds more or less in company and seek out algal grazing commons (*below*). It sounds curiously sporting – a jolly good morning of territorial aggression and a spot of mating, followed by a light but nourishing lunch, and an afternoon of social idling, snacking and dodging pelicans or darters. The next morning the same males will be back in their territories threatening their neighbours.

A place to brood

We saw in the wooded grassland that some animals like the impala defend a space in order to protect a food supply. *Tilapia grahami*'s little territory clearly has some other function, since it is too small to provide enough algal food and is usually in a part of the lake where there is little algae growing, such as in clear water near a spring. The territories then, appear to serve mainly as a meeting and mating place. In Lake Malawi, males of related cichlid species have been observed to stay on the same territory for a year and a half, and they are able to find their way back even though displaced up to two kilometres away.

When the male tilapia is not repelling intruders he spends his time tidying up his "breeding pit" in the centre of his territory (*below left*). These eight-centimetre depressions in the lake floor are carefully excavated by picking up sand particles in the mouth and spitting them out over the rim. We would guess that they are constructed in concentric terraces so that the shadowed relief makes them more conspicuous to passing females.

If a female leaves a school to inspect a pit, the male courts her with an eager side-on display (*below right*) that catches the light, shows her the splendour of his breeding colours, and at the same time points his otherwise threatening mouth in a neutral direction. She is likely to be receptive if she showed interest in the pit in the first place, and mating occurs over the breeding pit. Territorial neighbours look on, but do not interfere. They have learned not to trespass to the centre of the territory where the holder's reaction is most violent.

Tilapia grahami is one of the rare species of fish that is a mouth brooder. Soon after the eggs are laid, the female takes them up in her mouth. It is not known whether egg and sperm meet in the open water or in the female's mouth. In either case, the brief period between laying and picking up is one of potential risk, since other tilapia are cannibalistic on the eggs. Another major function of the territory, then, is to provide a relatively safe venue for the few moments when the eggs are in open water between one end of the female and the other.

When the eggs hatch, the fry stay in the female's mouth until they are about a centimetre long. During the two-week period, the female shows a remarkable restraint and sensitivity, for she feeds all the while without swallowing her offspring – at least not too many of them. The ethologist Konrad Lorenz once observed a mouth-brooding mother of another cichlid species faced with a particularly tempting but large morsel of food. She paused, spat out her fry, gobbled up the food, and took up the young again in a flash.

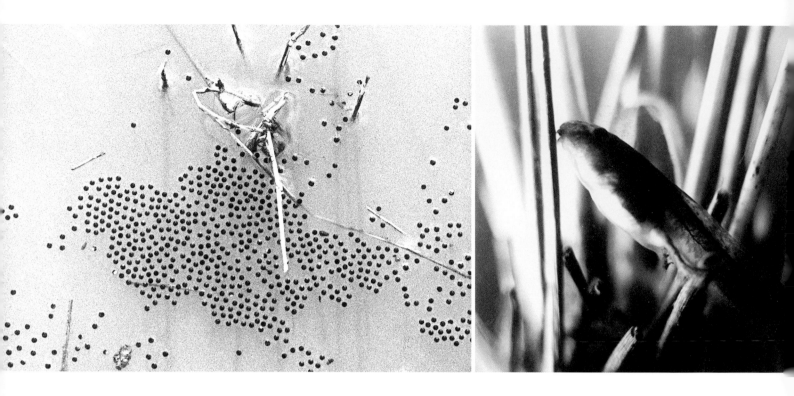

The changing amphibian

The frog is an ambivalent creature, Gollum-like and lowly, yet holding a changeling's portent in its baleful eye. Not only does it live a bit like a fish and a bit like a reptile, but it is also both a herbivore and a carnivore, depending on how old it is. It is a bridger of media, a straddler of trophic levels, a messenger from a wetter world.

One message it seems to be bringing is that something is seriously wrong in its worldwide watery habitats. Numbers are dwindling, whole species disappearing, gross deformities appearing. It is not just because of habitat destruction and loss of wetlands, for even in apparently pristine areas frogs and newts are in trouble. Like us, they are assailed by outside agents: pollutants transported in water, UV from an ozone-depleted atmosphere, and even viral infections (in the amphibians' case, introduced by the exotic-fish trade).

The latest clues point to an infestation by a fungus that is new to science. Perhaps the mystery of global amphibian malaise is solved: fungal spores are common amongst the tiny things, living and dead, that are carried aloft by convective air columns and the wind and scattered to the four corners on upper atmosphere winds. Globalisation takes many forms.

Frog DNA is actually more complicated than ours. It is largely taken up with contingency instructions concerning how to develop under a wide range of temperature conditions, which is how members of this cold-blooded group survive from the tundra to the tropics. The first stage of its metamorphical journey, after emerging from the gelatinous egg, is the schoolchild's friend, the tadpole. Fully aquatic, with gills and a fish-like shape, the tadpole feeds mainly on vegetation and detritus. Through a gradual metamorphosis, legs sprout where before there were none, the tail recedes, lungs develop and the tadpole makes more frequent trips to the surface to gulp air. Until one day, it crawls out of the water and into the next trophic level up, as a carnivorous adult frog (as the hyperolid frog *opposite right*).

In the chronicle of animal evolution there are a few adaptive events of such importance that they literally changed the face of animal life on Earth. Lungs, wings, and the cognitive brain centres of early man were crucial innovations. All these

adaptations have the quality of opening the ecological door to completely new niches, for example, to unexploited food sources. The development of lungs allowed Devonian amphibians 300 million years ago to use oxygen directly from the air. Unlike their fish relatives they could then hunt invertebrate species on land. But the amphibians were and still are bound to return to the water to breed: their spawn must be kept wet to live.

Then, some 50 million years later, perhaps during a period of alternate floods and droughts, another major innovation appeared: an egg which would not dry out even though it suddenly found itself on dry land. A simple but ingenious folding and fusing of an embryonic membrane enclosed the developing embryo in a bag of slightly saline water – the amniotic sac. Adding layers of calcium on the outside ensured the water would not seep out and evaporate before hatching. In this way the early reptiles shook off the bonds of the aquatic environment by means of an egg which contained its own diminutive frog pond within (see p. 197).

This preoccupation with the liquid media of life has led to discussion of a kind of aquatic Gaia hypothesis called "hypersea". The proponents point out that not only are amphibians closely linked to their aqueous medium, but the rest of us are as well. Blood, sweat, tears, eye humours, bile, pre-coital fluid, semen ... virtually all of the fluids we circulate, ooze or spew have a similar chemical composition to that of sea water. The only liquid we can safely inject into our blood stream in quantities, apart from the right type of blood and glucose, is sterile aqueous saline solution. Biochemical analyses of our neural lipids point to the birthplace of the main line of hominids as being not the forest, but the seashore, or perhaps, the saline lakeshore. Furthermore, all other plants and animals have comparable juices. Beyond coincidence and ancient commonalities that required similar sets of amino acids to be washed down and delivered to our energy and growth systems, there is something quite compelling here. As with Gaia, the hypersea hypothesis is rather difficult to test, which does not necessarily make it wrong. We are moved, as with Gaia, to ponder how organism-like properties could evolve in a single system that does no replicate itself as a whole.

The aquatic dinosaur

Only a handful of reptiles in the world are not carnivores. The rest, like the crocodile, need the high protein and energy food that the bodies of other animals provide. Some 150 million years ago, during the "age of reptiles", the earth teemed with several times as many genera as there are today. With a cooling in the climate, the soft swamp vegetation of the Jurassic period diminished and so did the herbivorous reptiles. Although the fall of the reptilian rulers was a complex ecological event, one reason may have been that the jaws and teeth of their herbivore legions could not cope with the evolving and more robust terrestrial vegetation.

Curiously, reptile jaw structure and musculature have never progressed very far past the snapping stage, much less to slicing and grinding. Even today, the crocodile's trap-like jaws are hinged only to open and shut, the teeth designed to grip rather than do any intricate dissection. The toothed trap snaps over the whole fish, or over an exposed part of a large prey item such as a misplaced terrestrial leg. It is held fast, and the body of the crocodile spun around by a corkscrew snap of the massive tail. Chunks of meat, bone and sinew are thus twisted off like pieces of toffee and swallowed whole.

Despite the grisly way of dealing with prey, crocodile mothers are remarkably protective, almost tender, in their care of the young. This parental care, as every schoolchild and western cinema-goer now knows, has been around since the Jurassic period, and has been one of the really astonishing elements of dinosaur behaviour that was

able to be deduced from the fossil evidence from nest sites.

Crocodile eggs are laid in shallow pits scraped in the sand of the shore, and the female spends most of the gestation period in the vicinity of the nest. She must leave to feed, however, and during her brief absences the main threat to crocodile numbers – apart from humans – strikes like an operant from the past. The monitor lizard (*right*) is uncommonly fond of crocodile eggs, and given the chance can wipe out a whole nest in a very short time. The mother's attentiveness not only discourages monitor lizards, but also means that when the little crocodiles emerge she is on hand to escort them across the few dangerous metres from nest to water. Large avian predators such as hawks and marabou storks, lurking like pterodactyls, could eliminate a whole season's progeny as they scramble across the open shore. The mother is an effective deterrent and even continues to guard the young during their first few weeks in the water. The young also share her meals, snapping up bits that fall from her jaws.

This leftover from the age of the dinosaurs represents the last top carnivore that is a truly integrated part of the aquatic African food chains. It can move quickly on land – almost at a gallop, if necessary – to bring down waterside prey. But apart from short dashes, nesting and basking, the crocodile spends its life in the water. It has evolved a tricky biochemical mechanism involving bicarbonate waste products that trigger selective oxygen release by haemoglobin, allowing it to hold its breath

under water for more than an hour. Crocodiles eat in the water; they excrete and die there. Such aquatic fidelity sets them apart from the alien predators of lake produce, who usually die out of water and bequeath their materials to a terrestrial ecosystem. It is also in sharp contrast to the dinosaurs, who after all didn't make it.

One prey – many predators

The most conspicuous predators of lake produce are the two dozen species of fish-eating birds, all of whom may be dependent on one or, at best, a couple of species of fish. Tilapia were introduced into Lake Nakuru in the 1960s and their success provided the basis for a blossoming of the numbers of fish-eating birds. The birds are fussy eaters, plucking morsels of meat out of the algal vegetable soup. Their main tool for the job is the beak, strikingly similar – long, robust, sharp – in birds as different from one another as the kingfisher and the stork. Methods are varied. Kingfishers dive through the surface,

storks wade and stab. Cormorants and darters "fly" underwater in pursuit of fish, and then have to hang their wings out to dry.

In daily life, animals interact with the environment on a one-to-one basis. We see discrete moments in a continual parade of predation – one pied kingfisher eats one tilapia; a little malachite kingfisher (*opposite*) eats a smaller tilapia; one yellow-billed stork (*above*) catches a large tilapia; the red-legged stilt stalks another tilapia; individual fish are sacrificed. Although such interactions are exciting to see, and interesting in their own right, it is the sum total

of such events on the level of the community (and the population for individual species) that determines the nature of a biological system.

Thus these four birds are representatives of four of the many predator populations, which in Lake Nakuru, for example, make a living out of just one tilapia population. The effect on the ecosystem of the one bird–one fish interaction is trivial by itself, as trivial as a human shooting a grouse. As we saw in the wooded grassland, the key to the very existence of a particular predator species is the numbers of prey that are available. Parasites also play an important

role – but only to the extent that they rob the host of its livelihood, directly or indirectly.

A relatively simple ecosystem like the alkaline Rift Valley lake, with several predator species depending on just one prey species, is particularly vulnerable to perturbations. If disease, or a fluctuation in the amount of algae, were to drastically reduce the numbers of tilapia, all species of fish-eaters would be out of the fishing business and would have to look for alternative food sources in that place. It is significant that none of these "fish-eaters" are totally dependent on fish: they all eat insects with gusto. Nonetheless, in a hypothetical fish dearth, the species structure of the bird community would change overnight, because the links in the food web between prey and predator would change and the hunters would have to change their time and motion, as well as look elsewhere in the ecosystem for nourishment.

When we observe several predator species populations feeding from a single prey type, we might think that the predators were necessarily competing. Indeed, overlap on one vital resource is the set stage for competition, but not necessarily the enactment. Competition in this case would only be demonstrated if it were shown, for example, that the kingfishers took enough fish to deprive the storks, and that as a result the number of storks was reduced from what it would have been with no kingfishers around. The individual bird may feel the pinch, but the effect is measured in the population. Indeed, we might intuitively think that competition *between* species for resources is more intense than competition *amongst* members of the same species. In general, it seems to be the reverse. Perhaps that's why we feel charity must begin at home.

One man's fish

Depending how you look at it, the story of Lake Victoria is a tale either of biological vandalisms or of significant management success. Worried biologists quite rightly point to the pre-1950s, when the lake – like other Rift Valley lakes after a mere 15,000 years of existence – harboured thousands of endemic invertebrates and vertebrates. Indeed, it is claimed that Lakes Victoria, Nyasa and Tanzania support the world's richest assemblage of vertebrates per square kilometre in the form of hundreds of species of colourful little fish, most of them perch-like cichlids, belonging to one much-studied sub-family, *Oreochrominae*, the "half-coloured ones". There are probably more species in either Nyasa or Tanzania – over 1,000 in each, it seems – than in the rest of the world combined.

They make a fine art of niche definition: there are so-called mud-biters who eat bottom detritus; then we have algae-scrappers, leaf-choppers, snail-crushers and their cousins the snail-shellers, the plankton-eaters, prawn-catchers, insectivores, and, in Lake Victoria, a large group of some 130 species who prey on other fish. The predators take niche specialisation to absurd extremes: some eat only fins, others pluck out eyes, some feed on the scales on the left sides of their prey, others on the right.

This fish-taxonomist's paradise was violated in 1954 when the hefty and hardy Nile perch was introduced into Lake Victoria to support a planned fishing industry. The perch loved it, and like a good conqueror was successful both in exploiting the food resources of the cichlids and in eating the cichlids themselves. Perch eat a lot:

individuals of 150 kilos have been recorded. Aided and abetted by another famous introduction in the form of St Peter's fish (tilapia) as well as the growing hungry population, some two-thirds of the 300-odd endemic cichlid species became totally extinct within thirty years.

That's the bad news. The hundreds of thousands of Tanzanians, Ugandans and Kenyans who now feed their families and make their livings directly or indirectly from the perch and tilapia, have a somewhat different view of the story. A dependency web of a different sort has flourished, supporting fishermen as well as boat-builders, fish-smokers, salt-grinders, truck-drivers, restaurant-owners and the myriad specialists of the human ecosystem. The thirteen species of cichlid mud-biters were replaced by one species of freshwater prawn that proved to be a favourite of the perch and helps large specimens grow to the size of small goats. The direct loss of biological diversity is less annoying to the stakeholders than the clouds of lakeflies (*chironomids*, see p. 207) that frequently choke the air or the algal blooms that periodically cover the surface – their predators were eaten out decades ago. A small price to pay for a sustained livelihood, some might argue.

In the meanwhile, that particular livelihood is under threat, ironically from another introduction. The water hyacinth, a runaway ornamental from South America, found its way into the lake along the Kagera River from Rwanda and Burundi in 1989. Unlike the native Nile cabbage (*Pistia stratiotes*, *opposite*), if the hyacinth is fed with uncontrolled nutrients flowing in from burgeoning

agriculture and industry in the drainage area, it runs riot. The weed has now virtually encircled the 3,000-kilometre shoreline with a nearly impenetrable thirty-metre mat of floating leaves and aquatic roots. It interferes both biologically and physically with the fishing industry. Sporadic though enthusiastic *harambee* (group efforts) by local communities to root it out by hand proved futile. Then two South American weevils that eat water-hyacinth leaves were released in large numbers around the lake. But they made hardly a dent in the hyacinth. As the search continues for even more ravenous exotic predators to introduce, lake authorities are now eyeing an old favourite in the arsenal of management bludgeons, namely, 2,4-dichlorophenoxyacetic acid, better known since its use in Vietnam as the defoliant "Agent Orange". Some serious lateral thinking about how people make a living in the region is required, before they call for a nuclear strike.

Pouch fishing

The bird whose beak can in fact hold more than its belly can is the most important African fish-eater. Both pelican species found in Africa – the larger white and the pink-backed – are floating fishnets. The sack of membrane slung between the rims of the lower jaw inflates to an enormous ten-litre capacity when dragged under water. How the bird can even swim with it distended and full of water is a mystery. But clearly the system works. Odd bills seem to run in the family: DNA affinity testing reveals that the pelican's cousin is the shoebill stork.

The pink-backed pelican fishes alone: presumably it is able to see and strike at particular fish. Sometimes a fish might leap from the water in an attempt to escape, but the pelican's net has been cast to sweep up the morsel as it falls back to the water. The whites are more abundant than the pink-backed at Nakuru, perhaps because of the limited availability of suitable trees for the smaller and more vulnerable birds to roost in. It is the white pelicans that fish in "flotillas". Up to twenty birds swim along in an oblique formation. At a signal we cannot detect, the line closes smoothly and quickly into a horseshoe whilst the birds dip into the water in perfect unison. Heads come up, the odd fish will be swallowed by one of the flotilla, the line reforms and the birds swim on.

In terms of fish caught per individual pelican, there seems little difference between the flotilla and solitary methods. A diligent researcher has noted that a lone pink-backed made fourteen strikes in ten minutes and caught eight fish; whilst one white pelican of a group made eighty-six sweeps in ten minutes and caught nine. It was observed that lone birds fish mostly in the morning when the waters of the lake are clearer and the glare from an overhead sun is absent. As the day wears on, glare increases and the turbidity of the water builds up as algae are stirred by freshening winds. We can only infer that the flotillas drive fish blindly, partially surround them after a tested time, and then dip the nets where the fish should be. It seems reasonable to suppose that when it is impossible to see below the surface, the flotilla method is more successful. Although each flotilla member clearly spends more energy per fish caught, it probably gets more food than it would fishing alone at that time of day. As is often the case, this sort of

hypothesis is difficult to test, for it is doubtful if a bird could be forced to hunt singly in turbid water so that we might record its success rate. As a tentative demonstration of the hypothesis we might better rely on negative evidence, namely, that single birds are rarely seen fishing when visibility is poor.

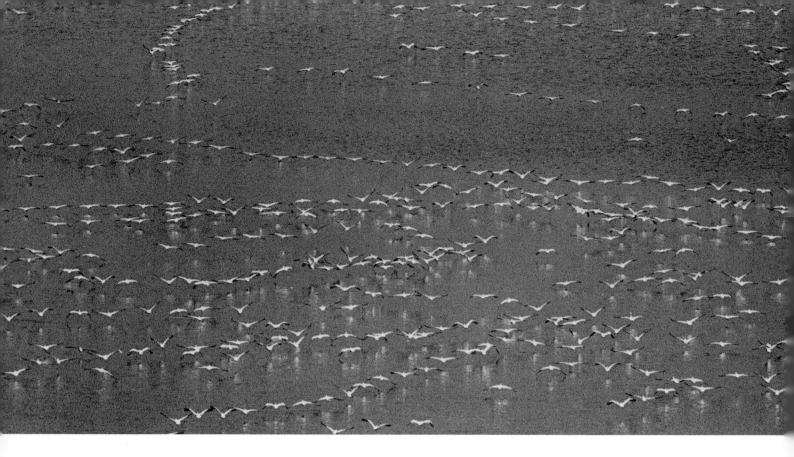

To fly

Flight, like the amniotic egg, changed the nature of animal life on earth. It comprises a set of complex instructions that has not been much revised for aeons. Insects took to the air, probably at first skimming over the Devonian surfaces at least 100 million years before the vertebrates. Inevitably there were hungry Earthbound creatures that chased after the flying morsels. Amongst them were small two-footed reptilian beasts from whom both dinosaurs and birds are descended. When you think about it, most animals fly. This is because most animals are insects, and the vast majority of them fly. And if you just consider warm-blooded vertebrates, there are far more flyers than non-flyers: there are twice as many birds as mammals, and a quarter of mammals are bats.

In the very earliest stages, vertebrate "flight" was little more than a hop, a skip and a jump with the forelimbs outstretched to maintain balance and grab the insect. New evidence from China

links predatory dinosaurs – related to the fearsome velociraptors of the movie *Jurassic Park* – to the famous "first bird" archaeopteryx. The traces of plumes on the fossilised bodies and tails of these flightless runners suggest that feathers were initially for insulation rather than flight. But, as natural selection finds solutions where it can, it is likely that around 140 million years ago, the scaly proto-feathers of sprinting theropods became more prevalent and longer, altering the shape of the forelimb and creating an archetypal wing. Jumps lengthened, airspeed increased, and more insects were caught more efficiently.

The airfoil cross-section of a wing is the key to all flight. Because the curved upper surface of an airfoil is longer in cross-section than the flat lower surface, an air current split by the leading edge must flow faster over the top than along the bottom in order to recombine at the trailing edge. But since it is the same quantity of air

top and bottom, it can only flow faster by "stretching" and becoming thinner. Thinner air weighs less, so consequently there is less pressure on top than below, and the airfoil is literally sucked up into a vacuum of its own making. This wonderfully simple design serves equally well most flying requirements, from those of a thirty-gramme sunbird to that of a 300-tonne Boeing 747.

Gradually the scales on these incipient wings became feathers, and the form was further refined. The reptiles were either able to gain lift after flying prey or enjoy a bit of drag to avoid a crash when pouncing on ground-dwelling fare, or both. The selective advantages were enormous: a whole new world of airborne or fast-running food, the ability to move from food source to food source, and escape from the rapidly evolving mammalian predators.

The wonder of the bird's wing is that it is both wing and propeller, providing lift to keep the bird up and thrust to move it forward. The

inner half of the wing provides the main lift component. The outer half flaps at greater amplitude and by a twisting motion on the flick of the down-stroke creates both lift and thrust. A reverse twist and "feathering" of the flight feathers on the upstroke provides more thrust, but does not reduce the net gain in lift. The basic pattern varies in speed and twisting to suit the particular species' needs. Sunbirds beat fifty times a second, pelicans one and a half; swifts can fly at over 150 kilometres per hour; sunbirds can fly backwards.

The slotted wing tips of birds that soar, like eagles, vultures and pelicans, reduce drag by changing the effect of the wing on the airflow at the tip. These birds can thus glide with a low rate of sink and with greater manoeuvrability than the long thin-winged albatrosses and sailplanes.

That practical guild of birdwatchers – aircraft engineers – has looked carefully at the physics of the familiar V-formation of large, migratory birds, and has revealed the function: energy conservation. Each bird, except for the leader, positions itself in relation to the wing-tip vortex of the bird in front. These vortices are like miniature tornadoes that spin off wing tips. They create so much local turbulence that those of an Airbus can flip over a little Cessna that happens to take off too quickly in the larger plane's wake. Being full-time pilots, the birds are somehow able to ride the eddies and gain additional lift or thrust, or both. On long hauls, older birds may tow younger ones along in the invisible air current. Human test-pilots flying in a very tight bird-like formation were able to reduce fuel consumption by an amazing fifteen per cent.

The wonderful synchrony of bird flocks is also a popular subject for modellers of complex co-ordinated behaviour. One group reckons it has reduced the behaviour of flocks of between ten to a hundred individuals down to a single number: the ratio of the typical body size to the product of the average flying velocity and the time taken for each wing beat. If this is less than one, the group moves in a line, with a highly ordered motion like that of a skein of pelicans moving from lake to lake. If the value is greater than one, individuals move at random within a swarm that stays together but wanders irregularly, like a burst of quelea over a millet field. We leave it to the reader to calculate the number, whilst we watch a flock of flamingoes pyrning and gyring against the morning sun.

The ability to fly, as we have said, is as inborn as the wings themselves. But the art must be perfected through practice. It is always amusing to watch a colony of young birds like pelicans on their maiden flights. Many of them make their first approaches downwind, hit the ground faster than the legs can run, and end up rolling head over heels.

To go or not to go

A classical definition of migration – "the act of moving from one spatial unit to another" – rather understates the spectacle, excitement and often danger of large animal movements; the dry words do, however, capture its universality. At one time or another, everyone migrates, permanently or periodically. The scale may be very local – aphids moving from one leaf to another; international – wildebeeste trekking from the Serengeti to the Maasai Mara (see p. 49); or global – arctic terns flying their 25,000 kilometres pole-to-pole circuit. These marsh terns (*left*, along with gulls) are more conservative than their arctic cousins, and only fly some 5,000 kilometres from North Africa for winter feeding over Rift Valley lakes like Kenya's Lake Nakuru. Observing what animals do when they get to where they are going unambiguously points to the underlying reasons for migration: food and sex. Since one could well have sex "at home", optimising nutrition has to be the prime proximate mover. Since there's no point in eating unless it keeps you hale and hearty for breeding, reproductive success is, as usual, the ultimate driver.

As we might expect, something so ubiquitous has many variations on the theme. "Dispersal" tends to refer to movements away from areas of high density, like the daily flight of pelicans from breeding to feeding grounds (see p. 201); "emigration" indicates movement away from a place never to return; "nomadism" suggests more or less ad hoc wanderings in search of breeding sites or food, such as the fearsome forays of army ants (see p. 282); "eruption" (escapes) or "irruption" (invasions) describe what happens when the proportion of, say seed-eating quelea, and the direction they travel varies greatly from year to year.

Even in the most impressive of migrations, not everyone goes along with the crowd. To a greater or lesser degree most migrations are actually "partial migrations", with some proportion of the population staying at home. This reflects the inevitable constraints to what has been called an "ideal free distribution" in patchy (i.e. most) habitats. If each individual were free to move to any patch without let or hindrance, then ideally each would go to the patch were the payoff is highest: most food, fewest predators, nicest climate, etc. etc. But life, sadly, is not that simple, and the complex all-pervading patterns of animal migration are testimony to the continuous balancing act of weighing the costs and benefits of one survival strategy – staying here – against another – going there.

Winging it

The dragonfly is an aptly named predator, both as an aquatic nymph and an aerial adult. The former looks nothing at all like the latter and specialises in grabbing swimming prey. Large nymphs may even take small fish. At the appropriate moment the nymph crawls out on to a reed stem, splits its skin down the back and steps out a new animal. It takes to the air and spends the rest of its life hawking insects and mating over the lake surface.

The unexpected sight of two dragonflies locked together in the air in an improbable position leads us to wonder how they actually mate. Just before seeking out a female the male injects sperm into a receptacle on the second segment of his elongated abdomen. When he finds a mate he clasps her behind the head with the end of his abdomen. Then, in flight, he drops in front of her, she reaches into his receptacle with the tip of her abdomen and takes up some sperm.

The function of these aerobatics is obscure. We would guess that having mated in this way, the pair can then fly over the lake in tandem with four pairs of wings to pull the female out of a near-stall as she dips into the water to lay an egg.

Dragonflies with thirty-centimetre wing spans were flying about long before the birds evolved. Insect flight is perhaps even more amazing than vertebrate flight since it uses wings that are not modifications of existing appendages. They have developed out of the brittle material that makes up the animals' external skeleton.

The flight mechanism of the dragonfly seems relatively primitive.

The two sets of rigid, rough-surfaced wings move independently, each beating some forty times a second. They are controlled by the same muscles that work the legs. Other muscles pull in the forward component of the wing beats, as well as the twisting necessary not to lose lift on the return strokes. Primitive the basic movements may be, yet the joints, hinges and pulleys involved somehow work together to allow insects to fly. No-one is yet quite certain how the combination results in flight at all, let alone efficient flight. Insect wing muscles convert only about six per cent of the energy they consume into useful mechanical work. The rest generates heat, which means that many insects risk overheating, and have to restrict their activities to cooler times of the day. Conversely, on very cool mornings, some larger insect flyers, like moths, have to vibrate their wing muscles to warm them sufficiently to perform for take-off.

Part of the answer may lie in the peculiarities of wing shape and surface. These create surrounding air vortices that in turn provide an enabling environment for efficient lift and thrust. Another part of the secret in modern insects is a flight muscle that requires no beat-frequency command from the brain. A small mosquito's wings may beat 1,000 times a second – far too fast for nervous impulses to travel down nerves from the brain. The brain message merely switches on the muscle, which then beats at its own inbuilt tonic frequency. Flying insects, therefore, have no idea of how fast their wings are moving, and most fly about their business even when naïve human wingloading equations suggest they should not be able to.

Cues for the courting dance

The cavorting dance of the male yellow-billed stork is the external sign of the onset of breeding. But what triggers the dance? This simple question would take an entire research programme to answer properly. We can always generalise, though. Behavioural acts are set in motion by preceding events that fall into three time scales.

The first is measured in minutes or seconds. Just before we observed the dance, the external world changed in the eyes of the dancer. He perceived a visual or audio stimulus that "moved" him to dance. The signal that set the dance in motion quite likely emanated from a member of the opposite sex.

Secondly, the bird must be somehow ready to send or receive such signals. He must be primed by events that occurred some time before. We now consider a time scale of days or weeks. Breeding seasons are usually linked intimately to ecological events, particularly the availability of food. Somehow the animal receives information from the environment that the optimal time to breed is approaching. It may be a response to a direct improvement in the level of nutrition or to a more subtle signal, like the change in light intensity, temperature, even wind direction and humidity. Furthermore, the leaping and bill clacking of the male may, over the

course of the first few days of the breeding season, lead to an alteration in the female's chemistry. Her attention is attracted at one level by the colour and movement, at another by an inbuilt propensity to recognise that anyone who has the energy to prance about in such a way must be reasonably fit and therefore a potentially good source of genes. All these cues affect specific sites in the brain which, in turn, signal the animal's hormonal system. The last glands in the flow of chemical information are the sex glands. Their secretions cause physical changes, like brightening of plumage and production of eggs, as well as behavioural changes – nest-building, territoriality, courtship and a willingness to mate.

Thirdly, we have the evolutionary time scale, measured in thousands of years. The dance may be tripped by proximal events, such as visual or hormonal signals, but the choreography and indeed the very existence of the dance are products of generations of selective events. Males who danced more attractively, females who responded more readily and discerningly, animals who timed their activities to hatch broods at the best time of year, all were favoured by natural selection. These animals produced more young, all of whom received a genetic legacy that included the dance programme.

The appropriate egg

Since one line of small egg-laying reptiles developed into birds during the Jurassic period, we can state categorically that the egg came before the chicken by at least 100 million years. Of all major evolutionary events, the amniotic egg is one of the most striking – as we have seen, it allowed the vertebrates to conquer the land and is therefore as powerful in function as it is elegant in form.

As the immediate product of courtship amongst birds and most reptiles, eggs are very precious. They are also obviously organisms in a relatively helpless state. Anyone who has played Easter-egg games is aware of the intrinsic strength in the shape of the egg. The shell is a design compromise. It has to provide a watertight defence without being too costly to produce, as well as so strong that the chick cannot eventually hatch. In fact, the inner and outer surfaces of the shell have a different fine structure that makes them easier to break out of than in to. The amniotic membrane and the shell combine to protect the young from the physical environment, but what about the animate environment – particularly predators who relish the concentrated packets of protein and carbohydrates? When the egg's first line of defence – the parent – leaves for reasons of safety or for foraging, most eggs must rely on concealment.

If eggs are secreted in a nest pocket invisible from the outside – a hole in the ground or a tree trunk, or in the foliage of a thick bush, or in a completely enclosed nest like that of a weaver bird – they need no special colour pattern. Equally, eggs protected by formidable parents like ostriches or fish eagles can also afford to be conspicuously white.

However, small species like plovers, which lay their eggs in more open conditions, increase their chances of survival by camouflage. The ground colour of the eggs matches that of the background and a myriad of flecks and spots disrupts the unmistakable egg shape. It is relatively easy for an animal's genes to programme a mechanism to produce a systematic pattern, such as alternate stripes or regular polka dots. But repetitive patterns are more easily learned, remembered and detected by predators. The bird must therefore produce egg patterns that appear irregular. It has to develop a mechanism homologous to an abstract painter in the pigmentation region of its egg-duct. We do not yet know how they achieve this controlled irregularity, but it is tempting to invoke the chaotic mechanics of fractals that seem to be accounting for more and more natural phenomena. A small set of instructions from the genes that oversee development, perhaps like "green wash, a little black pigment, skip, half-black, mix, start over..." initiated under different starting conditions (diet, temperature, the next morning), can produce the studied irregularity of a cloudscape or a coastline.

Design with nature

Weaver birds nests festoon most African trees. Each of the hundred-odd ubiquitous, mainly yellow-hued species, go to impressive lengths in nest-building. Mainly the males put in great efforts harvesting suitable grass or tearing strips of palm-leaf edges, and then follow a programmed sequence of steps to build an impressive array of species-specific nests. Like the birds themselves, all the nests are variations on one theme and are only barely distinguishable to the trained eye. Most start with a basic ring, hung on a branch or slung between two branches. Some are round, other pendulous, some have only one entrance hole underneath or on the side, others have more than one, some are loosely woven, others are tighter, some incorporate thorns, other do not. All provide the same thing: an insulated, near waterproof nesting platform, easily accessible from the air with minimum access along the branch tip from which they hang, like Christmas ornaments.

Weaver nests are what Richard Dawkins dubbed "designoids" – living bodies or their products that are so cunningly put together that they look as though they had been consciously designed. They have not, of course, but have been shaped by behavioural pathways driven by the "magnificently non-random process" of natural selection to create "an almost perfect illusion of design".

The old adage, "there's safety in numbers" has been shown again and again to hold true for flocks and herds. If you are one amongst many, the probability that you will get nabbed by a predator is lower than if you were one amongst few or on your own (unless you had some other trick up your sleeve, like good camouflage).

The corollary to this is that it is safer in the middle of the flock than it is on the edge, where the hyaena first encounters a herd of topi or a Nile perch a school of cichlids. In a colony of nesting weavers the edge-effect will buffer those nearer the centre from a marauding harrier hawk, a weaver nest specialist. Even relatively non-social weavers seem to use this ploy. A male Holub's golden weaver, for example, fills the idle hours whilst his mate is already sitting on eggs by busily building a half dozen or more dummy nests on different fronds of the same Phoenic palm – a virtual colony.

A male vitelline masked weaver (*Ploceus velatus uluensis*) displaying at his nest entrance to any female who cares to pay attention

The inhospitable nursery

Pelican breeding is a sporadic affair, which succeeds only when food is sufficient and suitable sites available. White pelicans are clumsy on land and vulnerable at the nest. They therefore seek out islands, either in the water or surrounded by inhospitable stretches of soda and mud. All these requirements are met only once every few years.

Often the feeding and breeding grounds are not in the same place. The Nakuru pelicans, for instance, breed on Lake Elmenteita, where there are no fish. So each day in the breeding season, they spiral up the columns of warming air which rises above Lake Elmenteita, glide across the ten or so kilometres of intervening hills, and feed at Nakuru. They return in the same leisurely fashion, bringing with them half-digested fish for their young (*below right*). The daily migration costs the pelicans little in energy, since they use the convective air movements for lift, and barely need to flap their wings. Their infidelity to the lake ecosystem that feeds them, however, costs Lake Nakuru tonnes of materials that the pelicans leave deposited on the shores and mud flats of Lake Elementaita.

Pelican chicks start to pester their parents when very young – in fact, whilst still in the egg. A recent study found that if the embryos are too hot or too cold, they cheep persistently inside the egg until an adult does something about it. Once the temperature becomes more equitable, they stop. This is a rare observation of young birds actively manipulating parental behaviour before they have even hatched.

Because of the scarcity of isolated and inaccessible sites, pelicans

are forced to put up with crowded conditions in the breeding colony. During the day, the chicks are left in the blazing sun whilst the parents go off to feed. Although fussy when inside the eggs, the chicks have to be remarkably tolerant to heat stress. Their black colouring (*above top*) would seem to be the worst possible choice for sitting on a shadeless mud flat. Perhaps the advantage of being instantly recognised as a defenceless young bird by the crowd of aggressive adults outweighs thermal disadvantages.

Co-operative breeding

It was an exciting revelation nearly twenty years ago when researchers in Kenya found a subtle pattern in the apparent confusion of white-fronted bee-eaters darting in and out of their riverbank nest holes. Although co-operative breeding had been observed in birds nearly forty years earlier, the Lake Nakuru bee-eater became one of the best-studied examples of its costs and benefits in a colony. Of course, people were beginning to be sensitised by the revolutionary thinking of the emergent social-biologists, who were bold enough to suggest that a co-operating colony may be more than just the sum of its parts and that a function consistent with evolutionary theory could be imputed to altruistic behaviour. Charity inevitably begins at home; it only pays to help those who share some of your genes, but also, tit-for-tat, to help those who help those who share your genes.

The salient feature of co-operative breeding is the presence of family "helpers", who are typically young mature birds of the previous breeding seasons that actively participate in the care and feeding of the young of the year. The longer this pair of northern anteater chats (*Myrmecocichla aethiops*, *right*) was watched, the more numerous they became. After a couple of hours, six different adult birds (two males and four females) were seen to be feeding three nearly fledged chicks in a small annex on the slopes of warthog burrow. Clearly only two were the father and mother of the

chicks and the rest, already in adult plumage, were most likely the young of the previous season. The yearlings lack the experience and social acumen to breed successfully themselves, and, particularly if breeding-site space or food supply is limited, it is an ideal way for the youngsters to spend their time. It takes a bit of a load off mum and dad, and, since it transpires that the helpers are always the sons and daughters or at the very least nephews and nieces of those helped, ensures that more of their genes will survive to replicate again. This seemed like such a good idea; it was a wonder that more birds didn't do it.

As it turns out, many more do – perhaps as many as one-tenth of passerine species. And the more that researchers watch carefully over a span of breeding seasons, the more it seems that co-operative breeding in tropical birds may turn out to be the rule, rather than the exception.

Much work is now going into trying to understand the circumstances and specific functions of co-operative breeding: seasonality, food supply, numbers, predators, nesting sites, climate, disaster... a host of factors are being weighed and sifted. And all the time more and more species are turning up who do it. The little bee-eater (*Merops pusillus*, *opposite*), a close relative of the originally-studied species, was observed to muster helpers after an aerial spraying campaign against tse-tse

fly all but destroyed one of its population. As time goes on, we find such concluding remarks as "...the tendency to breed co-operatively may depend largely on the opportunistic assessment of environmental conditions. We therefore suggest that birds... will opt to breed co-operatively only when conditions are unfavourable for independent breeding." That sounds to us like you do it all the time, except when it's better not to. In other words, we think it *is* the rule – one that strangely went unnoticed for years in one of the most-watched groups on Earth.

The nest and territory

The fish eagle is a curious bird to be catching fish. Apart from small spikes on the bottom of its feet to help grasp slippery prey, this specialist is a hefty black and white eagle. Its striking resemblance to the iconic American bald eagle is hardly surprising, since they are classified in the same genus, along with a European cousin (the white-tailed sea eagle) that bridges the global distribution gap, albeit without the impressive white head. All three are descended from the scavenging kite family as opposed to the nobler true eagles and have modified their attack behaviour to cope with a plentiful and nutritious source of food. The African fish eagle in particular still hunts by stooping from heights. However, the instant of strike has had to be greatly modified. At full stall, with the talons below the water and the extra weight of a large snagged fish, the bird has to take off again before they both sink. This requires incredible timing and enormous strength. Perhaps the need for strength explains why it took an eagle, as opposed to a small hawk or falcon, to master the trick.

In general, eagles are relatively rare animals, who pay the price of being top carnivores by having to divide the terrestrial ecosystem into vast territories, each of which can only provide enough food for a pair of birds and their season's offspring. But the fish eagle's switch from relatively scarce and inaccessible land-living food to an abundant

aquatic fare allows it to live at high densities – near water, of course. Along the shorelines of Kazinga Channel in the Queen Elizabeth National Park, Uganda, there is a "despotic distribution" of nesting fish eagles every 200 metres, and with each nest goes a portion of the lake. They spend much more time engaged in territorial display and defence than their terrestrial cousins, simply because their territories are far smaller and they thus encounter their neighbours more often. When not delivering fresh fish to their one or two chicks, they guard their fishing grounds, either by chasing out other eagles or by uttering their beautiful and mournful call from a shoreline perch.

When the chicks fledge, they spend several weeks sitting around in their parents' territory being fed by both adults. What befalls them thereafter is the fate of many children from a territorial home. The parents' area will not support four adult birds, so the young eventually leave, with considerable encouragement from the adults, when they begin to feed themselves from their parents' fishing grounds. They are literally chased along the shore, from territory to territory, until they end up in less favourable occupied areas with the others of the year. The strong survive the ordeal, and when an old territory holder dies, its place is immediately taken by one of the young outcasts.

To eat and be eaten

In a few drops of water from the bottom of the lake we see minute red threads. They squirm to escape the unaccustomed light. They are chironomids, or lakefly larvae, who wiggle through the lake-bottom ooze feeding on dead matter that drifts down from the upper layers of the water. Their niche is that of decomposer. In this state their fate is frequently to provide carnivorous fish and beetles with something like twenty tonnes of meat a day from Lake Nakuru. But the survivors turn into free-floating pupae which, when ready, rise to the surface of the lake until, with uncanny timing, the adults in one part of the lake, now transformed into flies, take to the air together. From a distance they look like a swirling column of smoke emerging from the water at sunset. Indeed, they have caused short-lived fire alerts. Closer, there is a high-pitched whine of wings as thousands of midges whirl about looking for a mate. Closer still, they are a choking nuisance. Their prevalence has significantly increased over the past twenty years with the changes in the lake fish complex. Once in the air, they again become a feast, this time for aerial predators like swifts and flycatchers, and even people who gather them up and press them into nutritious cakes. We are frequently puzzled by the "extravagance of nature", and ask: Why lakeflies? What is the purpose of the dense cloud of insects? The question is wrongly put. Where food becomes available – lake detritus, for example – some organism will inevitably evolve the wherewithal to migrate in to eat it. By using lake offal and providing predators with another source of food, lakeflies speed up the flow of materials through the lake ecosystem. The spectacle of midges moving materials may distract us momentarily from the simple fact that their "reason for being" is merely to produce more lakefly DNA.

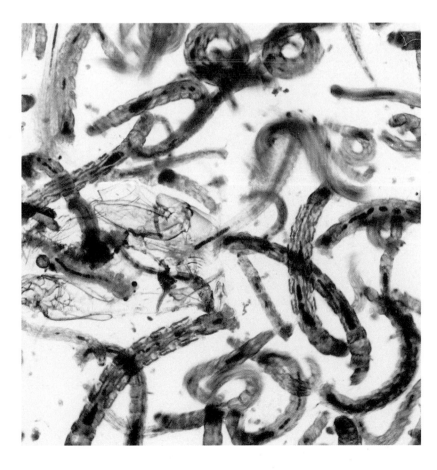

The adaptable omnivore

There are some designs that have been used in the animal world for millions of years. They have persisted because they work so well. The outer casings of bugs, beetles, tortoises (see p. 102) and crustaceans, for example, are elegant in their functional simplicity. Smooth, hard, light and tough, impervious to most enemies, streamlined yet roomy – the domed carapace is an unquestionably beautiful shape. At one of the roots of beauty is an implicit congratulation on surviving thus far.

The corixid bug is an aquatic dome-wearer. As a typical "true bug", its young are nymphs – miniature versions of the adult – unlike beetle larvae that resemble maggots.

Corixid bugs are omnivorous – another successful and persisting trait. When primary productivity is low, they can easily switch to a diet of herbivores. When the herbivores succumb to a lack of vegetation, the bugs can feed happily on their dead bodies until the primary productivity recovers.

The protective shell is eventually breached in death. The contents of a tiny isopod crustacean (*Lovenula*) spill into the water and mingle with a swirl of microscopic decomposers (*below*). These are the penultimate step in the aquatic food chain, followed only by the bacteria who return organic molecules and disorganised minerals to the water.

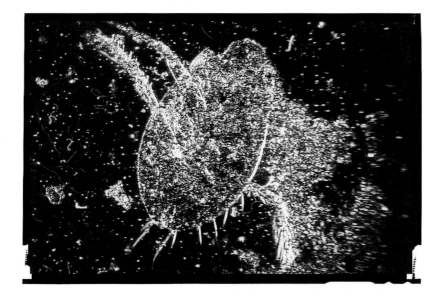

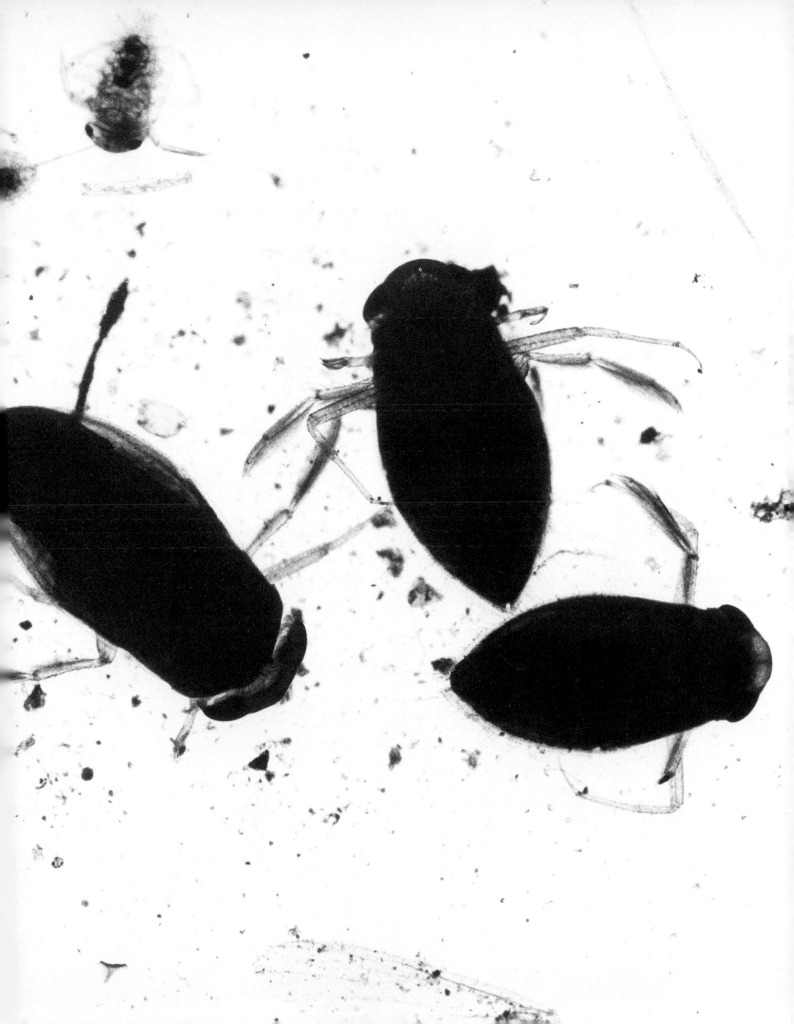

Endpiece

In every ecological system there is the portent of change. The term "balance of nature" does not describe the state of even a natural ecosystem; it reflects rather what we would like to see mirrored there, it echoes our hope that we can find neat laws to govern the system, a number to sum it all up. The so-called balance shifts continuously, like the image in a kaleidoscope. In our investigations of the natural world we have to freeze its dynamic ebb and flow as a "momentary stay against confusion". But no sooner have we fixed the image than the scene has changed, imperceptibly or dramatically – in nature it really does not matter which. Sooner or later lakes will dry up, but that is no cause for concern; for in their place grasslands will appear.

Forests

The essential forest

There is probably no such thing as the "forest primeval". Climate change, storms, fires, little consumers like insects and big consumers like people have been working over and through and under them since their beginnings. Almost everywhere we dig in forests for minerals or lost cities we find charcoal – evidence that fire or people or both have been there before. Those very stresses contribute to the incredible biological diversity amongst forest plants and animals (see p. 218). Deep green, cool, apparently immutable, the tropical forest has become an icon of the stability and equilibrium of nature. The fact is it may be as changeable as grassland, albeit over more time and less space (see p. 31).

Some 30,000 years ago, in a cooler, wetter period, forest covered most of equatorial Africa. The occurrence today of the same species of plants and animals in forests or remnant patches now separated by hundreds of kilometres of semi-arid bushed grassland is compelling evidence of former continuity. A drier spell from about 25,000 to 12,000 years ago reduced the extent of the East African forests, which also accounts for the paucity of both plant and animal species there compared with tropical forests elsewhere in the world. Not all species could survive the dry period.

Once established, a forest contributes to the climate and water conservation that sustain it. Leaves break the fall of rain, and even the most torrential rain drips from leaf to leaf to the floor, seeps through layers of humus and percolates into the soil. Much water is used where it falls: the

canopy awning that keeps out the sun slows the evaporation of soil moisture. Moreover, minute particles, exhaled, as it were, from millions upon millions of living and decaying leaves, rise to the upper air layers. Atmospheric water adheres to the particles as ice and eventually falls back to the forest again as rain (see p. 25). It is possible, then, that forests may even increase a region's rainfall by actually seeding the clouds above them.

The forests' ability to increase rainfall on the one hand and help water seep into the soil on the other makes them vital to all neighbouring ecosystems. The flow of a grassland spring or the level of a particular lake, indeed the water table and soil moisture of a whole ecosystem, may be directly linked with the water catchment of the nearest forest. Such connectivity suggests that the custodians of landscapes and planners of landuse must take a wide view when forming their plans and plotting their utilisation.

Forest soils are frequently dark red, acidic from the decay of plant material, incredibly fertile as long as the nutrients used by the trees are recycled. They are, however, unforgiving if abused. Should the forest be indiscriminately cleared, and a season's rain allowed to pound down directly on the soil, the soluble nutrients are quickly leached away – the next dry season will produce a brick-hard layer formed by the baked oxides of aluminium and iron. It leaves sterile land that could take a thousand years to remulch.

Mount Kenya's changing face

The path of water

Life's solvent, water, determines precisely where the forests grow; and the manner in which it is present determines the type of forest formed. There are three main types: montane, groundwater and coastal. All are products of local geography and climate. In each case these two factors have combined to increase the amount of water available to plants. If the rainfall is greater than about a hundred centimetres a year, one of the most serious constraints to the growth of large trees is relaxed.

Trace the path of water from the sky, to the mountains, through the land to the sea: in tropical Africa wherever water passes regularly, or otherwise accumulates in the soil, you will usually find a forest. On a vegetation map or dry-season satellite image of East Africa, for instance, forests are but a few threads and patches of deep green in amongst the ninety per cent burnt yellow that represents the dry grasslands.

Rainfall potential may be more or less constant throughout the land, but where geographical sculpting has created a mountain to elevate and cool air masses, more rain will fall, and a forest will clothe the mountain slopes – a montane forest. Where groundwater is constant all year round – near a spring at the foot of a Rift Valley wall, at a swamp edge, or along the banks of a perennial river – the moisture requirement of large trees is met, and a groundwater forest results. Or, where wet monsoon winds meet the equatorial coast, heat up, rise and then cool to the point at which they cannot hold their moisture more than twenty miles inland, rain combines

with sun to produce an archetypal jungle – the coastal forest. Between these patches are what the old African hands fondly referred to as "miles and miles of bloody Africa" – bushed and wooded grassland, too dry for forests or rain-fed agriculture.

The forest types, then, are determined by a combination of moisture and altitude, and within the three broad groupings we hear such distinctions as highlands lowland, moist montane, dry montane, moist evergreen, moist semi-deciduous and so on. Although classifying a forest by the kinds of

trees growing in it is very difficult, occasionally pure stands of one or two species make classification a bit easier – African olive, cedar, yellow wood (*Podocarpis*), *Brachylaena-Croton*, *Cynometra* and *Hagenia*, for example, are frequently encountered in discrete patches. These specific zones are the result of subtle differences in moisture and altitude within the forest.

Strength in diversity

Fragmentation is the watchword, some say the epitaph of forests. Fragments have edges, and these are eagerly nibbled away by a hungry and needy human population. A shrinking fragment presents an exponentially diminishing edge to an exponentially growing population. It requires a certain minimum motherload of seed-producers to maintain the key characteristic and secret to success of the forest ecosystem – species diversity. Just at what fragment size forest diversity starts to be irrevocably lost is not generally known. Field estimates are very difficult to obtain, but seem to vary from some four to one hundred hectares for specialised forest communities.

Each African tropical forest tends to be composed of distinct combinations of tree species. Beyond discovering amazing numbers of species, surveys reveal interesting patterns. For example, as the sample size increases, so do the numbers of species encountered. Would the numbers increase indefinitely? Certainly not. In fact, if we calculate the species density, it appears that the larger the sample area, the smaller the number of species per unit area. The numbers are still impressive, but the diminishing density with increasing sample size suggests that forest trees tend to live clumped in particular species associations. Even so, it is very difficult to tell which part of which forest we happen to be in. We are surrounded by a bewildering array of trees all looking distressingly similar. So much alike are the leaf shape and growth forms of most forest trees that only an expert able to reach a flower can specifically identify them.

This astonishing diversity of tree species within a stone's throw seems to fly in the face of conventional views of ecological niches: surely living conditions must be identical for trees in the same half-hectare? Does each have an ecological niche to itself, or are there just a few niches, each shared by a variety of tree species? This question points up the forest paradox of a diversity of species but a convergence of form: many different types that all look and live alike.

A tempting explanation seems to lie once again with the lowly parasite. Perhaps the trees – almost like a co-operating community – are reducing the chances of any particular pathogen taking hold in the neighbourhood by presenting it with a confounding array of different potential hosts. The pathogen cannot adapt to all, and so does not take hold very ferociously on any. Most farmers are familiar with similar mechanisms in so-called "herd immunity". There is no need to catch and inoculate each and every beast. Having a fair number of them immune greatly diminishes chances of the disease spreading through the herd. In a forest, a pathogen may fix for a while on a common species, but that species, being just one out of a great many, quickly becomes a minority leaving the evil agent high and dry. We may record diversity as a characteristic of the forest tree community as a whole. On closer inspection, it appears to be the result of an anti-parasite trick played by all the members of the forest ecosystem to increase the survival of each.

In our time scale the forest looms as a climax form, a classical endpoint of tropical plant succession. The

apparent permanence of the forest reflects only the brevity of the human life span. In our eyes, a forest is always a forest. Surely only a major climatic change could overcome the stability of the forests, unlike in the grasslands where minor and quite local effects turn bushed grassland to woodland in one decade. Or so it used to be. Today something odd appears to be happening in the world's tropical forests. Across four continents, trees are living faster and dying younger. A likely cause is carbon dioxide "fertilisation" arising from industrial emissions that inject an extra "fix" of carbon dioxide into the atmosphere creating more fast-growing, soft-tissued plants releasing even more carbon dioxide leading to greater greenhouse warming, and so on. This is just one of those little facts of the modern world that, if taken to a likely conclusion, could change life on Earth as we know it today.

The indigenous Nandi fame tree (*Spathodea campanulata, above*)

A fading fossil

Long before grass and herbs, sunlight was being trapped by primitive rooted plants that got along without the advanced technology of flowers and encased seeds. Some like ferns (see p. 239) and club mosses relied on a moist surrounding to transport spores. Others develped cones to hold and protect embryos. There are numerous remnants of cone-bearing dinosaur fodder around today: horsetails and the ubiquitous group of gymnosperms that includes evergreen pines and spruces in the northern hemisphere, araucarias and so-called screw pines in southern forests and coastal zones respectively. But the cycads or sago palms carry both the mystery of "the past and the lure of rarity". Today there are some 160 species occurring in the forests and grasslands of all southern continents – a reminder of the Permian period when there was just one southern supercontinent, Pangaea.

Around 250 million years of existence have resulted in a conservatism of lifestyle and simplicity of form and process. The bulbous heart of the plant, the corm, has its shallow roots in a sandy, well-drained soil. Seasonal crowns of spiky pinnate leaves sprout out of the corm. At long, apparently irregular intervals, male and female plants each produce unisex cones from the midst of the whorl of protective leaves. When the cones are ripe the plants alter their metabolism and increase the cone temperature by as much as 5 degrees C. Warming encourages the oozing of juices and wafting of odours irresistible to particular species of weevils. These willing messengers nose about, feed on fluid and pollen and in the

process carry pollen from male to female cones. Cycad sex pre-dates seeds as well as flowers. Seeds are designed to remain encased and dormant, with growth and development in check until favourable circumstances prevail. The seeds, like the adults, are particularly fire-resistant, and this allows them to survive the inevitable end-of-dry-season wildfires (like the *Encephalartos sp.* shown here). The fertilised cycad ova are in fact embryos, alive and growing immediately after the weevils finish their work.

Many African botanists aspire to immortality by having new cycad species named after them. And every couple of years, there is a happy botanist who manages to see for the first time minute features in the male or female cones of a specimen collected on the slopes of a remote granitic hill. Undoubtedly

uncontrolled collecting is taking its toll of cycads, but their disappearance from many parts of their former range is believed to be the impact of habitat modification on the beetle pollinator rather than directly on the basically robust plant. Despite the cycad's nearly complete imperviousness to wildfires, geriatric stands of all male or all female plants are now being found across eastern and southern Africa, with no viable future in sight.

Strange giants

If we venture out of the forest's upper edge, somewhere between 3,000 and 4,000 metres, depending on the mountain, we find a weird display of endemic plants, ancient descendants of forest and lowland stock pioneers that are now confined to specific moorland habitats. The price they seem to have paid for venturing into a harsher environment was to become monstrous. In contrast to bending over to observe the familiar ragworts, those troublesome weeds that pollute the dairy farmer's pasture with alkaloid poisons or the friendly little bellflowers familiar as bedding plants to all gardeners, on the African mountain moorlands we are obliged to gaze upwards at the towering top-heavy cabbages of a giant groundsel (*Dendrosenecio sp.*, *opposite*) or the four-metre floral spike of a giant lobelia (*Lobelia sp.*).

Each of the handful of montane species in these very distinct groups has evolved similar mechanisms to deal with the common high-altitude problems of water loss from intense solar radiation and tissue damage from freezing night-time temperatures. The oversized rosettes or "nightbuds" on the groundsels and some of the lobelias (*above*) are leaf arrangements that insulate the "delicate primordia", as botanists are wont to describe

the soft growing and reproducing bits in the plant's heart. Layered sheaths of persistent dead leaves augment the cork-layered stems to insulate and seal off internal tissues that store and conduct water. The living leaves of the groundsels and the bracts of the lobelias are typically light green and shiny to reflect, and hairy to insulate.

They even behave the same. At night, they both "close" their leaves inwards to protect the centre. On a frosty morning after a cold, clear night, the internal temperature of a giant groundsel can be 5 degrees C

warmer than the surrounding air. The lobelias have the additional trick of secreting an aqueous liquid at the base of the fleshy leaves. Dissolved salts and sugars probably account for the liquid's viscosity. When the plant closes up for the night, there is some ten centimetres of this "antifreeze" pooled and trapped in the rosette. Only the top centimetre or so will freeze on a really cold night, and the lower layers stay relatively warm.

People and forests

It is unfortunate for both elephants and people that they like to gather in the same places, where there is perennial water, lots of vegetation for food and shelter and an equitable temperature. Those places are often forests. One scenario has our pre-human ancestors leaving the trees and creeping out of the forest to hunt abundant game meat on the hoof, 7 to 10 million years ago when savannas were replacing forests in Africa. This helped accelerate the development of a Big Brain to better avoid predators and, paradoxically, get along socially and make war. With the typical restlessness of opportunistic omnivores, some then moved back into the cool, rich "green mansions". There they could, amongst other things, put their newfound agricultural skills to even more productive ends, including supplementing the rather carbohydrate-poor fare found in forests. In conventional wisdom, this sets the stage for classic pillaging of natural resources, and we have all seen the images of ravaged forests until we grow weary.

The fact is that there are a number of peoples around the world who apparently live in perfect harmony in forests and have done so for millennia, extracting whole livelihoods without destruction. Invariably the noticeable conversion and displacement of plant and animal species takes place when demands for wood, minerals or agricultural land arise from sources well away from the forest edge, even beyond the boundaries of the sovereign states in which the forests happen to be. Every forest on Earth now seems to have a common set of concerned parties: those people

who live in it, those who live around it, and those who live far away who wish either to consume it or preserve it. These people all have an opinion of what to do with the forest, ranging from chopping it down completely, through selectively using its resource to leaving it completely untouched.

There is no simple formula – certainly not one that can be applied across the board. Cutting clearings and replacing them by plantations may not affect the hydrological regime, but certainly upsets one array of species diversity (namely, forest species); colonisers may be quite diverse. Partial clearing has been shown to increase animal species richness in some taxa, but provides inroads for illegal activities. Total *laissez faire* may be good for plants and animals, but is of less help to the surrounding human stakeholders. It is quite inconceivable that in any one situation a balance could not be struck, were it not for

human greed for forest products, which seems to be proportional to the distance from the forest itself. As a respected expert on the human population question observed, there are three possible strategies for a solution: a bigger pie, fewer forks, better manners. The first two are unlikely bets. How sad that the only hope lies in the last and most hopeless option.

Mbuti pigmies in the Ituri forest of the Democratic Republic of Congo (*above*) and the conversion of an Okavango riverine forest tree into a dugout (*opposite*)

Trees

In the grasslands, we continually scan horizontal lines: the acacia tops, the cheetah's line of chase, the unbroken horizon. In the forest, the axis rotates to the vertical and our eyes are compelled upwards.

Trees are the dominant features, their enormous growth engendered by an abundance of water. In the apparent peace of the forest there is a ponderous race upward to reach the light in order to produce what the water in the earth below makes possible. This silent, slow, yet fierce, competition requires the structure of the trunk to support a crown far above the forest floor, and, ideally, above its competing neighbours. In the wet of the forest, the growing season is almost continuous, and prodigious production goes into the woody structural elements.

This one fact – massive trunks supporting relatively small bunches of leaves – determines, more than any other, what the forest ecosystem is like. Because so much material is tied up in tree trunks, the atom of phosphorus that passed through the wooded grassland from the plant back to the soil in a few weeks is likely in the forests to get stuck in a tree for decades. When there is talk of global "carbon sequestering", eyes turn to forests. Energy and materials flow much more slowly in the forest than in the grassland. Therefore although the standing crop of the forest is perhaps ten times that of the grassland, the annual production of edible greenstuff is only twice as great – even less if the grasslands have had a good year.

The food-producing requirements of a forest tree demand that water be pumped from below ground to the leaves, perhaps fifty metres above. But how? The principle force comes from the properties of water itself, particularly the difference in energy potentials between the water in a cell that has the compounds of metabolism like sugars dissolved in it and water outside the cell that is slightly "purer". The process of osmosis insists that the water outside will try to move through the cell wall in a blind attempt to dilute the inside water and equalise the chemical concentrations on both sides. The marvellous design of the cell walls indeed allows some passage, but the essentially rigid celluloid structure prevents complete equalisation. Thus the pressure inside the cells is greater than in the surrounding tissue, and this differential effectively creates an unbroken column of "frustrated" water, with a differential pressure, higher below than at the top. On a sunny day, with photosynthesis churning out sugars, and water being evaporated from the leaves and sucked in through the roots, that difference can be between ten and twenty atmospheres. If you had to support such a water column in the palm of your hand you would need to push upward with a tonne of force. Water is a remarkably cohesive substance, and each molecule drags another up with it. This pressure gradient affects the entire tree, and at midday, when photosynthesis and transpiration are at their peaks, it is actually possible to measure a decrease in the diameter of the trunk as a little water from each cell is forced up the column.

When next caught hugging a tree, say you are testing this notion.

Tree layers

New technologies to probe and move about in forest canopies are revealing that there is a staggering number of plants – particularly parasites and epiphytes – and animals – invertebrates, mainly – that only live attached to trees high above the Earth. Their offal drifts down to the forest floor, but much of their material and energy is circulated above ground.

With the trees hoarding so much material or keeping it aloft, the pyramid of life in the forest becomes distinctly bottom-heavy. There are myriad forest micro-habitats, apparently providing for almost endless diversity and richness. Waterbuck and other large ungulates do find a niche, but with the bulk of the available forest green matter in the form of leaves above their heads, it is not surprising that there are proportionally fewer of them than in the grassland. The majority of the forest animals – herbivores and carnivores alike – are insects, birds and small mammals. A large part of the processing of the primary production is left to the decomposers in the soil litter, who receive their nourishment direct from the continual rain of falling canopy leaves.

The canopy is what makes the forest a forest. You can tell that you are in a "forest" and not just a particularly thick woodland, if when you look up you see at least one-tenth of the sky is blocked out by trees greater than five metres tall. A typical forest canopy is stratified into three layers. The top layer is composed of emergents with buttressed trunks that rise unbranched fifty metres until out of sight. In the second layer the tree crowns are bushier to make

up for the shadows cast by the top layer. In the third, about ten metres above ground, the crowns are often pyramidal, since sunlight reaches them at an oblique angle, slipping between the taller trees just before and after midday.

Though lower trees get less sun than those in the upper storey, they lose about half as much water from evaporation – a nice balance. But, in the shade on the floor of a mature forest getting enough sunlight becomes crucial: the light intensity is only one-hundredth of that which falls on top. Plants on the floor only survive by virtue of a few minutes each day in the form of sunflecks. Many shrubs have evolved broad flat leaves that make the most of these vital moments of pure sunlight.

All the trees have similar problems, such as getting enough sun from above ground and nutrients from below, or producing a leaf that is efficient both in catching light and rolling with the punch of a tropical downpour. They live together in an environment that has relatively constant temperature and growth. Thus, evolutionary experiments are many, but take the form of species that differ by just a little.

A niche, we have said, is the way as well as the place in which a species makes its living. If two species begin to do the same thing in the same place, one of them should eventually evolve a trick to get more nourishment and reproduce more quickly – to the eventual exclusion of the other. But events between trees occur slowly, and tree reproduction is a lengthy process. Thus not only does it take a very long time for one tree species to "notice" the effects of another,

but also centuries may pass before it is seen to do anything about it. So evolution, or the divergence of form, in forest trees occurs exceedingly slowly; which is why they appear to share the same niche at the same time. Moreover, we have seen above that there might be good reasons for them to "appear" to be one species, namely to befuddle parasites (see p. 218).

Leaves

The similarity of form in the forest is not limited to the big-tree vertical structure. Closer to, we are struck by the similarity of the leaves as well, elongated, tapering, ten to twenty centimetres long, dark green with a waxy shining surface – once you have seen one you have seen virtually all of them. Such conservatism can only be born of a common need.

The shape of the archetypal forest leaf is one that spills off heavy rain most effectively without sacrificing size; and the size is most likely a nice compromise of an area large enough to maximise available sunlight, but not so large that it shades the lower leaves of the same tree. The shining leaf surface is produced by wax glands in the leaf epidermis, and apart from providing a sun- and waterproof coating that controls evaporation, it may also be a filter to reduce the amount of harmful ultra-violet radiation reaching the food-making cells. Finally, when we look up at the canopy in the morning or afternoon, we notice that many leaves are shining, reflecting light downwards from part of their curled surface. Perhaps the waxy layer is also a reflective device, designed to share sunlight with the leaves lower down.

Trees, of course, do not eat in the sense that animals do; but like all organisms they need some form of food to sustain their growth. Like all plants they use water, carbon dioxide, nutrients from the soil, and sunlight to energise the food-production factories in their leaves.

The simple equation of photosynthesis – carbon dioxide plus water plus sunlight in the presence of chlorophyll produces oxygen and sugars – is a metaphor for a complex biochemical process. The green pigment chlorophyll is the key. It exists in discrete packages called chloroplasts in green cells. The impact of light on a chloroplast releases an electron that creates an instant of chemical instability. High-energy chemical bonds are shifted, and atoms are borrowed from the molecules of carbon dioxide and water. When equilibrium is re-established in the plant cell a thousandth of a second later, we find a molecule of sugar and one of oxygen – a transmutation worthy of a philosopher's stone.

A current hypothesis suggests that chloroplasts once existed on their own, similar to the numerous forms of bacteria which are capable of making their own food. During the course of green-plant evolution, these bacteria-like beasts found a niche in plant tissues and now exist in symbiotic relationship with the plants: the chloroplast enjoys an ideal chemical environment in the leaf; the plant uses the chloroplast as the crucial link in the photosynthesis chain.

Food-making takes place in a layer of cells sandwiched between the upper- and lower-leaf epidermis. The sugar enters the plant's vascular system to nourish the cells or to be stored as starch. The oxygen not used by the plant is exhaled through trap-door cells in the leaf surface.

The rest of the plant is solely designed to get the leaves to the light and allow the plant to live out of water. The trunk, branches and twigs of a tree encase and support the circulatory system. Internal vessels, made of special elongated cells, take water and minerals

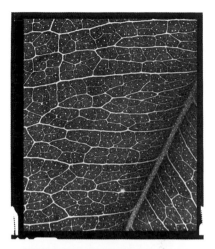

from the ground to leaves; more peripheral vessels take sugars and waste products away from them.

Giant grass

The quality of the environment changes so rapidly up on a mountain slope – temperature drops one degree C for every hundred metres, moisture increases, the sun is fiercer in the thinner air – that the boundaries of tolerance for various species are abrupt. We step literally from one vegetation zone to another as we climb.

Vegetation changes in the grasslands produce a mosaic effect; on a mountain slope we find belts of vegetation which gird the peaks. One such belt occurs between 2,000 and 3,000 metres on tropical mountains like the Aberdares in Kenya where a long season of almost continuous cloud produces enough moisture to support bamboo (*opposite*). Kilimanjaro is one of the driest mountains in East Africa, being totally exposed to desiccating winds which leave most of their moisture miles behind at the coast. Consequently there is no bamboo zone on Kilimanjaro.

Like many forest plants, bamboo is gigantic in proportions, with stems over ten metres high, and ten centimetres wide. This is not so remarkable perhaps, compared with some of the forest trees, but impressive for a stalk of grass, which is what bamboo actually is: a grass that has established itself as a ubiquitous forest species with an if-you-cannot-beat-them-join-them lifestyle. Perhaps it is an evolutionary response to the strictures that the forest environment places on orthodox grass species.

When we said there is relatively little grass in the forest we were, of course, referring to the grasses that ungulates can eat. Bamboo, though grass and enjoyed by Sykes monkey (*top left*), elephants,

buffaloes and virtually every herbivore that can reach the leaves or find a shoot, does not make an appreciable difference to the size of the large ungulate populations in the forest. It does, however, mean a great deal to the quarter of the world's population that makes some use of it for building materials and livestock fodder, as well as to the rather smaller fraternity that feeds the leaves to giant pandas.

Bamboo grows to maturity, flowers just once and then dies, like a disproportionate annual grass. But what the annual does in one short year can take the bamboo thirty or more. Just what sets the bamboo's flowering and seeding cycle is not known. The only real clue is that it runs in a geometric series – bamboo plants flower every fifteen, thirty, sixty or 120 years. It is probably not a general response to climatic changes, since different stands in the same forest may have different periods to their flowering calendar. Entire

stands flower together no matter what stage of growth any one plant is in – although you must look closely to see the minute half-centimetre-long trumpets (*top right*). Once flowering is over, the entire stand dies together, stems split and fall (*above*), leaving room for forest shrubs to proliferate for a while and also leaving behind a carpet of seeds to start the next bamboo cycle.

Decomposing plants

The moisture and heat of the forest environment, the decay and slow turnover of forest materials allow a host of lower-class plant citizens to suck a living from the offal of the higher plants. Mosses and liverworts, lichens and fungi all share with the ferns the two-stage sexual–asexual reproductive strategy, the ability to propagate by budding, and the dependence on large amounts of water. They spread their spores and fertilised seeds on the wind, or drop a part of themselves that then grows, or simply creep into most of the darker, wetter parts of the forest.

Mosses are the familiar lush cushions of green carpeting damp stones and filling moist crevices. Liverworts, though everywhere in the forest, are hardly ever seen;

and if seen, pass unrecognised. They are simpler in structure than mosses but they are also capable of photosynthesis.

The ubiquitous Spanish moss (*right*) festooned over forest trees in the wetter areas is actually a lichen. So are the patches – often circular – of yellow, orange and brown clinging to riverside rocks (*above*). They are composed of a fungus related to yeast, and an alga. These two very different types of plant live together in a symbiotic relationship. The alga is single-celled, capable of photosynthesis and so provides the partnership with food. The fungus provides anchorage, carbon dioxide and water. Lichens are the most widely distributed plants in the world, from the arctic to the

desert, and are usually the first pioneers on unclaimed rocks. They start to change rocks to soil and in fact have been measured to speed up chemical weathering by a hundred times. The forest species have a relatively easy life and contribute substantially to the return of materials to the soil.

A fungus (*opposite top*) is devoid of chlorophyll, and so cannot manufacture its own food like the green plants. But undeterred by this fact, the fungi make a living in a number of other ways. Some, as we have seen, are symbiotic. Others are either parasitic or saprophytic – the former types deriving nourishment from the juices of living organisms, the latter from dead. Still other forms are predatory; they grow quickly

around or into tiny organisms and actually eat them up. Fungi vary in form from the undifferentiated mass of protoplasm called slime moulds to the relatively well-organised mushrooms.

The simplicity, perhaps even inadequacy, of our pyramid metaphor is demonstrated very clearly in the forest ecosystem, where some plants consume other plants and many are decomposers – where, in fact, ninety per cent of the primary production never reaches the herbivores, the second trophic level. Instead it falls directly to a host of both animal and vegetable decomposers on the forest floor – worms, moulds, fungi and bacteria – who thus short-circuit the conventional food chain. Although unprogrammed and unplanned, this effectively is the

forest's way of "feeding itself", for when the decay is complete, the elements are back in the soil again – around the roots of the tree that last fixed them in the canopy leaves.

With decomposers in effect performing the functions of both herbivores and carnivores in moving most of the materials along the forest food chain, it is not surprising that as much energy is tied up in them as there is in the more conventional and conspicuous consumers such as large mammals. Of course, the forest-floor decomposers do speed up the turnover of materials, but they use a lot of energy in the process. This fact, together with the trees' hoarding of materials in the form of wood, impoverishes the lot of other consumers in a forest ecosystem.

Dependence on others

The apparent serenity of a mature forest belies the fierce and constant struggle between trees for light at the canopy level and for nutrients at the root level. The trees also have to vie for the attention of animals on whom their reproductive success depends. When a plant flowers, the blossom must provide colour or odour to attract, and nectar to reward the animals who act as couriers for fertilisation. Plants cannot move, but animals make up for this immobility by transporting the male pollen to the female ovarian receptacle.

The problem does not end with pollination. In most cases ripe seeds would have little chance of growing if they fell into their parents' shade. Their chances of germination and growth are far better if they are dispersed, for then the probability increases that they will land on a temporarily vacant spot, such as a break in the canopy where a tree has fallen. Wind dispersal cannot work as well in the shelter of the forest as it does in the open grasslands. The only other agent is an animal. But animals need to be persuaded or tricked into doing the job – hence the majority of forest trees package their seeds in an edible casing like a nut or fruit. The massive *Vitex*, the ubiquitous *Chrysophyllum*, the figs and the African olives, all provide monkeys, trogons, hornbills, bats and bush-babies with nourishing treats. The seeds are generally impervious to digestion and are excreted or simply spat out whole, hopefully in a place where competition is less keen.

The seedlings of most forest trees are remarkably tolerant of shade and shoot up extremely fast, perhaps like the etiolated potato in the cellar. This adaptation demands a drastic difference in the chemistry of the seedlings. When they reach their place in the canopy they settle down to spread and grow as much as their neighbours will let them for the rest of their lives – which may be two human lifetimes.

One way to avoid competition in becoming established on the shaded, root-filled ground is to set seed well above ground. Numerous species of orchid (like *Rangaeris amaniensis*, *opposite*), lichen and most figs drape themselves on other trees. They take water directly from the moisture in the air through specially thin-walled aerial roots. Orchids have a particular dependence on fungi. They have tiny seeds comprising an embryo wrapped in a thin skin. They contain no food store to provide for germination and growth of the young plant. The embryos get the nutrients they need from a fungus, and each species of orchid has this special relationship with a particular fungus. Considering that orchids are the most numerous of flowering plants – in excess of 25,000 species worldwide – there must also be a comparable number of fungus species to support them. Co-operation pays.

Strangling fig tress lure animals to their tasty fruit. The sticky seeds are passed out in due course or fall from fur or feathers into the crotch of an established tree. The fig seedling begins life benignly enough, just using the host tree for a place to perch. Once established though, the fig roots grow quickly down and around the host's stem. And thus begins an act of parasitism which may last a hundred years. Figs, particularly the "strangling fig", are relatively fast-growing:

before very many decades have passed there is more fig than host. Inexorably the host tree is choked to death; finally it succumbs, having given support and its place in the canopy to the fig. Despite or perhaps because of its acquisitively successful characteristics, this particular species is sacred to the Kikuyu people in Kenya. They will never fell a mugumu tree and use it as the main prop when exhorting N'gai – God – to make it rain. An interesting role model.

Figs do not have the last word when it comes to parasitism. They typically host three ecologically distinct groups of wasps: those that pollinate the fig flowers, those that do not but are parasitic on fig tissue, and those that are parasitic on some of the fig parasites (so-called parasitoids). It may sound contrived, but the story does not stop there. There is a fungus that disperses spores designed to attach to insects. When a spore of the fungus lands on an insect, it germinates, sending a tube through the cuticle. The fungus follows through the tube, grows inside the insect, and eventually kills it simply by clogging up the circulatory system. We have not discovered what parasitises the fungus, but suspect there must be something, for as every ecology teacher reminds us: "Big fleas have little fleas upon their back to bite 'em, and little fleas have lesser fleas, and so ad infinitum."

Sexual and asexual

When we see the forest light filtering through the leaves of tree ferns, do we not at once recall that "the sporophyte of all pteridophytes is, at maturity, independent of the gametophyte"? Perhaps not, for the oddity of fern reproduction usually lies forgotten in our early textbooks and is overshadowed by the proud advertisement of flowering plants.

Similar giant fern-like plants, over ten metres tall, were the first colonisers of the land 500 million years ago when most animal life still squirmed about in the water. The ferns (pteridophytes) are indeed anachronisms, but not out of place in the forest, a realm of vegetative extravagance, gigantism, rapid growth, exotic shapes and smells. In that earlier time when plants had no animals to rely on as couriers in the reproductive cycle, ferns were dominant. They were successful as the worldwide distribution of the common bracken testifies. Primeval African tree ferns (*opposite*) persist in forests – a statement about their success and the constancy of the forest environment over time.

Reproduction is a two-staged affair, an alternation between the sexual and the asexual. The undersides of the leaves of the "adult" fern (the sporophyte, *right bottom*) are lined with special spore-producing capsules that release millions of asexual spores. "Asexual", because they are viable without the union of male and female elements, and are, therefore, genetically identical to the parent sporophyte. The spores fall on a suitable surface like a moist ball of elephant dung, and grow into tiny "plants" called gametophytes. These live on the juices of decay and the effluent of death and hence

belong to a class of decomposers called saprophytes. Each gametophyte is a hermaphrodite: it sports both a male and a female organ. The male part matures first, a safeguard against self-fertilisation, releasing microscopic male cells which literally swim off through the surface moisture. Like a plant version of sperm, they seek out the female parts of another gametophyte (*below*), which will already have matured. The fertilised female part then grows into another "adult" fern. And so it has gone on, for as long as there has been moisture enough

to provide the medium of transport for the tail-wiggling male cells.

The asexual half of the fern's reproductive effort is a process that allows for no change in form, none of the experimental reassortment of the characteristics of male and female parents. This mechanical conservatism slows down the possible rate of evolution of the ferns, and, along with a constant forest environment and the apparent distastefulness of ferns to herbivores, has left us with tree ferns not much different from those the dinosaurs brushed past.

Flowers

A flower is a plant's window to the world, its antenna, its satellite dish. Most of the crucial information the plant sends and receives goes and comes through the flower. When the time is ripe, the plant puts extension effort beyond its own metabolic business: it puts on a pretty face. This is perhaps fanciful, but how else does the plant effectively invite a host of co-operators to lend a hand in sending and receiving vital messages of reproduction? Small wonder we are able to make a billion-dollar business of using flowers for sending messages of love.

Animals confine embryonic development to a limited period early on in life, but plants never stop developing. Throughout their lives they keep groups of dividing cells – apical meristems – ticking over at the tips of their shoots and roots. As the plant grows, the domed meristems push steadily upwards by adding new cells to the layers beneath. At intervals bulges appear on the edges of the dome. These grow into either leaves or more meristems, the beginnings of new branches. This rolling, recursive production of meristems, branches and leaves is punctuated by the development of the flower organs. Typically these are nestled in a series of whorled concentric rings. The first lines are the sepals, the leaf-like structures that encircle and protect the petals. The petals in turn ring the pollen-producing stamens. And at the heart of the flower arrangement nestle the carpels with ovules that become seed when pollinated. As in animals, the plants have special homeotic genes that act like "shop stewards" to oversee the timing and sequence of such

development. The mechanism is becoming better understood – the sequential development of the flower parts has been likened to playing "chords" of gene switches – but how the sequence is switched on and off, and how the chords are held for just the right length of time is still obscure.

It has been found that some plants make their flowers bigger and more colourful through re-cycling "junk DNA" that has served its purpose in other phases of development and is now just hanging around cluttering up chromosomes. Bigger flowers, it has been shown, are more attractive to pollinators.

The aim, of course, is to get the pollen from the male bits of the plant (the anthers on the stamen) to the "egg" in the female parts (carpel and pistil). This sounds straightforward enough and it usually involves a distance of only a few millimetres or less. But bridging that gap has led flowering plants to invent more forms and tricks to accomplish that one task than any other functional entity, except perhaps the sex organs of insects. A legion of invertebrates, birds and mammals are lured, guided,

tricked or trapped into the job. They usually get something for their effort, such as a meal of pollen or nectar. Many orchids, on the other hand, "deliberately" short-change their avian pollinators by providing a diluted but tantalising taste of nectar. This encourages the bird to look for another treat nearby and thereby encourages cross-fertilisation.

Once fertilised, the flower transforms into a device to disperse the ripening seed by as many ways as you can think up: by gravity; by explosion; by wind or water; on the backs, in the fur, on the feet or in the guts of another host of co-operators, who willy-nilly collect the information for the plant's next generation and deliver it abroad. Not just a pretty face.

Left to right: desert rose (*Adenium obesum*); *Lobelia keniensis* (see p. 221); *Tephrosia hostii*; *Scadoxus multiflorus* (opposite)

The longest-living tree?

Like a squat prehistoric monster, the baobab tree grows as easily in the coastal forest where we see it here as it does in the semi-arid grasslands below 1,300 metres. Its enormous bulk of soft wood holds moisture like a huge sponge and presents a relatively small surface area to the desiccating sun. Legend has it that God, in a fit of anger because the baobab could not decide in which habitat to settle down, threw the tree over His shoulder. It landed on its crown and has grown, roots upward, ever since. Seven of the world's nine species landed on the island of Madagascar. One species, *Adansonia digitata*, stands sentinel throughout mainland Africa.

This strange tree seems to be threatened only by the very large and the very small. Elephants are well known to gouge large chunks from the sides of baobabs, particularly during droughts, to the point of apparently killing large numbers of trees in areas like Tsavo West National Park in Kenya. One heavily scooped-out tree in Taragire Park in Tanzania struck a blow for the other side when it suddenly collapsed, breaking the back of the bull elephant who was dozing in its shade (*right*). At the other end of the scale, baobabs in the northern Transvaal, weakened perhaps after a decade of drought, are enduring attacks from a fungus that leave the trunks of these national monuments shrivelled, dark and dull, as if burnt, covered with black scars and lesions.

Perhaps just as legendary as its origins, although more widely accepted by scientists, is the contention that the baobab attains an age to match its proportions.

Carbon-dating has shown that large baobabs in Kenya, some with a girth of twenty metres, are more than 1,000 years old. Portuguese cannon balls 400 years old are embedded in baobabs lining the approach to Kilindini harbour in Mombasa. Clearly the one we see here growing through the wall of the Arab-African city Gedi in the remnants of the Kenyan coastal forest must have been seeded in the seventeenth century contempoaneous with the abandonment of such settlements in the face the southern advance of the Galla from Somalia.

But a characteristic of the tree's growth form suggests an alternate hypothesis to us. Out of the top portion of a mature baobab, we observe two to four main "turrets" which within a surprisingly short distance subdivide into smaller branches. Follow the lines of the "turrets" down and they appear to cap major portions of the trunk. Is it possible that several seeds germinate simultaneously out of the twelve-centimetre pod, or from the spot where an animal has spat them out? If so, then several seedlings would grow cheek by jowl, eventually touch, and being soft and fast-growing, fuse into one disproportionately wide stem. A look at a younger baobab strengthens this idea, for the trunk subdivisions are even more apparent.

The hypothesis, if true, in no way lessens the magnificence of a baobab which, for all the diverse life it supports in its branches, is rather like a one-tree ecosystem. Our wonder should be as great for a 200-year-old tree of such proportions as it is for one 2,000 years old.

Holes in the canopy

Suddenly, from the dark of the forest, we stumble into a blaze of light, a large hole in the forest canopy – a clearing. From the air we can see them as light spots regularly spaced in the dark green blanket covering the mountainside. Occasionally they are created by one or more large trees toppling over from age or a local windstorm. More often, they coincide with slight depressions in the ground that subtly impede drainage in the otherwise sloping topography. The soils of the clearings accumulate silt and nutrients and are therefore somewhat different from the surrounding forest. Frequently there is a water hole in the centre, slightly saline in flavour. This attracts large herbivores such as rhinos and elephants who help keep the clearing clear.

Being holes, the clearings have edges called ecotones. These are zones of rapid gradation from the conservatism of the trees in the forest to that of the grass in the glade. The edge-effect is usually one of richness, fast growth, diversity and a high degree of attraction for species endemic to both sides of the edge. Thus the forest meets the grassland not only at the periphery, but deep inside as well. One of our reviewers suggested that natural treefalls might provide a useful pattern for selective logging – reduce impact and increase diversity all at one fell swoop.

Animals from the grasslands

With open grassy glades and perennial water, it is not surprising some large herbivores from the grasslands also live in the forests. Buffaloes, rhinos and elephants all make use of the ecotones, open patches, and the lower vegetation layers within the forest. It is estimated that fully one-third of Africa's elephants are forest-dwellers. Their social patterns appear to be more or less the same as those of their wooded grassland cousins, except at maturity the females, as well as the young males, leave the family unit. As we have seen in the grasslands, buffaloes and elephants are mainly grazers, so since only a small proportion of the plant biomass in the forest consists of grass, these animals form a relatively insignificant part of the total biomass of forest consumers.

The forest provides retreats and hiding places, but puts certain demands on its inhabitants, which can be seen by comparing forest and grassland populations. The forest buffaloes and elephants are noticeably smaller in stature, perhaps from a combination of less food to go around and the disadvantages of outsized proportions in the tangle of the forest edge. The relatively weak bosses of the buffaloes and the slender tusks of the elephants compared to their grassland conspecifics say much for the protection – from man in particular – which the darkness of the forest offers.

In the wooded grasslands we pointed out the activities and constraints involved in the flow of materials through the system. The same general principles – such as competition and social organisation geared to food supply, predation and anti-predation – also apply to forest species. Rather than labour the general points, we will touch on them, but concentrate more on specifics, and on how some particular problems are solved. To do this, we have to shift perspective a little, to get closer and go upwards.

The indigenous inhabitants

Of all large mammals, least is known certainly about the indigenous forest species. Such gaps in our knowledge stem from the very inaccessibility that allows beasts like the giant forest hog (*below*) to thrive. These prosper by specialising on the glades' produce and by hiding in the nearby forest. Not long ago they were abundant and large groups grazed their way across the year-round grass production of the glades of the forests of the Aberdares range in Kenya. Now they are virtually gone, probably eaten out by a population burst of lions

in the early 1980s. African swine fever is also a threat in a round-about way: as carriers, they are the target of eradication campaigns mounted by neighbouring domestic pig farmers.

Similarly the lifestyles of other forest ungulates such as bongos (*opposite*), bushbucks, sunis and duikers, remain a scientific mystery. They are doubly inaccessible in the vastness of the forest by being shy and widely dispersed. In the absence of any important grass cover, they appear to browse mainly on shrubs or fruit fallen on the

forest floor. Their numbers are presumably limited by their food supply. Pairs of Harvey's duiker chase each other back and forth from a territorial boundary in the middle of the night. The eyes are relatively large for maximum resolution in the reduced forest light. Their pelage is dark, often spotted or streaked with white, which enhances the effect of camouflage on the sunflecked forest floor.

Ecologists tend to think of habitat selection by animals in terms of the forces that keep them from being freely and evenly distributed every-

where. There are at least three things that push or pull antelopes into a patchy distribution. First, a particular habitat may provide adequate amounts of the right food and therefore be chosen to minimise the cost of obtaining resources. Next, an animal may end up in a place because it is hemmed in, as it were, through competition with other species or between invisible barriers of temperature and moisture. This is a kind of negative selection. Finally, living in one place as opposed to another may help them avoid predation by providing escape routes and cover, or through association with other species who enhance safety through distraction of predators, additional early warning, or active protection. All of the above are likely to influence forest ungulates.

We might wonder how such apparently frail creatures can survive predation. Their appearance is deceptive. They are like coiled springs which at the least disturbance release in a surprising burst of energy. When alarmed they disappear in a flash into the foliage so quickly that they seem to vanish. With their stoop-backed posture duikers can run straight through the thickest vegetation with unbelievable speed. It is even difficult for a human to restrain a twenty-kilo duiker. An attempt by a predator to bite the neck of such a struggling packet of muscle could mean a needle-sharp horn in the eye.

The indigenous forest ungulates are impressive, but relatively unimportant in the canopied ecosystem. This is not an excuse for our lack of knowledge, but a deduction from the observation that they account for only a fraction of the materials moving around in the forest.

A leaf-eating monkey

The deficit of primary production on the ground and abundance aloft creates a herbivore niche that requires special skills to exploit. Ungulates are earthbound, and the price, as we have seen, is relatively low numbers in the forest. But monkeys are more mobile. They move up and down as quickly and effortlessly as they move back and forth. The black and white colobus monkey is a daring and agile climber who feeds on canopy leaves. Perhaps its gentle disposition is connected with its entirely vegetarian diet. Its close relative, the vervet of the wooded grasslands, is a successful opportunistic feeder and an unpredictable and mischievous beast at close quarters.

The colobus travels through canopy pastures by jumping fearful distances, with its long fur flared out like a cape. The fur may actually have an aerodynamic quality that slows the downward speed of long descents. The hand has lost the thumb, presumably a modification that makes hooking on to passing branches easier. The missing thumb gave the colobus its name, for the Greek root of the word means "mutilated".

Colobus monkeys live in troops of usually less than ten, led by a male. They move about constantly within one stretch of forest and are probably territorial in order to protect the troop's feeding grounds from the depredations of other groups. The males utter a ferocious, guttural roar, which is presumably designed to advertise the troop's presence and to intimidate neighbouring troops.

Not a great deal is known about interactions between groups, although in other species it has

been observed that interactions are relatively peaceable when the main food species are widely distributed, as leaves certainly are. There are less than ten species of primates (not counting several sub-species) in East African forests, which is relatively few compared with other tropical realms. Comparative studies have shown that the smaller the area of tropical forest and the lower the rainfall, the fewer primate species occur. Both factors could be at work in the relatively small forest patches that exist apart from the Congo Basin.

The function of the black and white coat is obscure. Possibly it serves as an unambiguous signal to keep the animals orientated to one another when moving quickly through the canopy. They are so conspicuous, even from an aircraft, that it is difficult to imagine that the colour is camouflage, say, to the African crowned eagle that specialises on colobuses. Of course, the monkeys may behave differently

to an eagle than to an aircraft, and immobile in the canopy a black and white animal may be difficult to see.

The colobus has a fermentative gut to break down the cellulose of the green foodstuffs. This causes what seems to be constant indigestion and waves of belches rich with hydrogen sulphide gas. These are offensive to human observers but they are delivered so deliberately and lovingly when facing a troop member that they may serve as a bizarre form of social signal.

With such an apparently rich food supply in the forest canopy, it is may seem strange that colobuses and indeed other primate leaf-eaters are not more abundant. The leaves of many tree species are rich in tannins and high in cellulose, bitter to taste and tough to break down. Only a few vertebrate herbivores have both the guts and agility to tackle the canopy food niche.

Mouths and numbers

The bushbuck feeds on the leaves of shrubs. Since the bulk of the forest primary productivity is in the trees above, so are most of the forest herbivores. In terms of movement of materials and energy flow, the really important primary consumers are the invertebrates, the little spineless animals.

Most of them are small, inconspicuous, short-lived but with a high metabolism. Their front-ends are of a very particular design because the edible things in their world are larger than they are; the weevil sucks nourishment from a leaf that the bushbuck bites off whole.

We might be surprised that insects do not grossly overpopulate the forest, for their potential rate of increase is astonishing. Suppose one female weevil, weighing three grammes, produces a conservative twenty offspring. Say one half are female, each of which matures in a fortnight and produce another ten females. The sixteenth generation alone, that is, only the weevils that hatched in the eighth month, would weigh more than the world biomass of tropical forest plants – some 10,000 million tonnes. Happily, this potential is never realised: it is rare to see an area over-eaten by insects on a large scale in an undisturbed forest. Somehow the number of insects is regulated.

Virtually all populations – from weevils to wildebeest – grow in a similar manner: slow at initial low densities, faster as the animals get into the swing of things, and then at higher densities slowing down to the point of stopping increase or even diminishing. The interesting question is what puts the damper on unbridled growth. The mechanism of population regulation is complex enough to study in a simple system and virtually impossible to tackle fully in the diversity of a forest ecosystem; but there are guidelines. Two general forms of mechanism could be operating, either separately or in concert: control from within the population itself or control from without by some external agent.

Internal regulation can operate through adverse effects that increase as the population size increases. For example, the more animals that are eating a limited food supply, the less there is for each animal to eat and the lower the chance that each gets enough. The point at which the food per insect reaches the danger level must be near the point where the trees are being rapidly defoliated.

Insects have parasites, like virtually every other form of life, so another "density-dependent" process might be a disproportionate increase in the numbers of these parasites as the insect population grows. This kind of restraint has been observed in temperate climes but has not yet been demonstrated in tropical forests, though we might expect it to operate there too.

External regulation on the other hand, can work through environmental changes that make conditions temporarily unfavourable to the population growth. This is a crucial factor in the seasonal grasslands, but unlikely to be very important in the comparatively stable forest environment.

Insects are small and vulnerable targets to a large number of predators, thus predation is a very plausible check on insect population growth. The fact that insects have evolved a colourful and startling array of anti-predator adaptations demonstrates that predators are a very real danger to them.

Finally, it is possible that the plants themselves effectively limit the insects' food supply by being distasteful, or even poisonous. Substances have been found in some plants that seem to play no role in the plants' metabolism, such as toxic wastes that the plant "deliberately" retains. But then if this were the only governor on insect populations, we would expect to find starving insect herbivores, or else a mosaic of healthy distasteful plants and defoliated benign species.

Unusual outbreaks sometimes give us a clue. In Kenya in early 1998 there was a plague of the so-called "Nairobi-eye", a primitive and exceedingly noxious little black and red blister beetle (*Cantharidae*) that causes acid-burns on the skin if squashed. Within a two-week period, patches of forest floor and outdoor lights were teeming with them. They arrived hard on the heels of an unseasonably prolonged rainfall event, probably associated with "El Niño", in which the short and long rains merged and ten times the normal rain fell. Clearly Nairobi-eyes like it cool and wet and their numbers are normally kept under control by the very dry periods that punctuate the wet.

Obviously a combination of such factors keeps insects in check; exactly what those combinations are is often very hard to deduce. Yet they clearly work since we are generally free of Nairobi-eyes and insects do not in fact eat their potential weight in forests.

Meloid beetle feeding on a flower

Super bee

Word is out: the proverbial busy bee only works 3.5 hours a day; the rest of the time, she loafs, or, more euphemistically, "patrols". However, as if to make up for that blow to conventional wisdom, it now appears that the integrated workings and production of a beehive are greater than the sum of its parts, the individual bees. In fact, "patrolling" is probably a mechanism designed to expose the individual to the tenor of the hive, to gather vital information on the collective state of the colony so that her next bout of activity – feeding young, cleaning cells, shaping comb, eating pollen, removing the dead, foraging – can be most efficiently tailored to the collective need.

The smooth functioning of any complex system depends upon its various parts getting the correct information at the right time and place. The colony members do share and have access to an astonishing array of signals and cues. Between themselves, they shake, waggle and buzz, they tap each other, cross antennae, puff and smear phero-mones. The famous "waggle dance" of the returning worker is a highly evolved signal that informs hive mates of the distance and direction to a food source. The state of the hive itself presents a host of passive cues. It echoes the physical degree of completion of a section of comb; the chemical state of the queen; the thermal deviation of the central brood chamber from the optimum temperature of 34 to 36 degrees C; and even the nutritional level of the hive, as measured by the number of seconds a returning forager has to wait before a food-storer (the younger workers that specialise in converting nectar to honey) wiggles up to collect her load.

The hive is literally abuzz with information exchange. Not only that,

but it has the added advantage of decentralised control, namely, it can respond more quickly to short-term local stresses than is possible in a centralised command system. If a part of the hive warms up or a predator invades, there is no waiting for the alarm to reach command control and the appropriate instruction to return through channels from a supervisor. Each bee "knows" hive policy, and reacts immediately: fanning to cool, contracting flight muscles to warm, or stinging to repel. We are reminded of the vertebrate autonomous response: if we stick our finger into a flame, a peripheral loop in our nervous system contracts the necessary muscles to snatch the hand back before the brain's central processor even registers and forms the "ouch".

By virtue of their integrated functioning, colonies of social insects – bees, fungus-growing termites (see p. 78) and safari ants

in particular – have been dubbed "superorganisms", that is, groups of individual organisms that together behave in ways that resemble a single organism, for example, in choosing a nest site, collecting food, brood-rearing, hive air-conditioning, and colony defence. There is considerable debate over the reality of the concept. Is it a metaphor for an astonishing product of natural selection, or is it a real thing? Or something in between? E.O. Wilson has said that "its usefulness is that it describes something intermediate between fully integrated, unmistakable organisms on one side and a group of loosely organised, interacting organisms on the other." With the kind of consilient jump of which professor Wilson is fond, we might observe that many human organisations have superorganism qualities. The buzz of interactions at, say, a meeting of the United Nations Environment Programme Governing Council seems as chaotic as, well, a beehive. Yet individual predilections and group allegiances apart, all of the parts are ostensibly working towards a common goal.

Classic natural selection may appear to fall short of accounting for the thousands of sterile female worker bees that organise and sacrifice themselves for the greater good, like so many white blood cells tackling infection or red blood cells carrying nourishment for the rest. Of course, given just one queen in a hive, the workers are effectively all sisters and are defending and feeding their mother as well as their younger sisters and brothers. That may explain the apparent altruism, but not the organisation.

A school of thought is emerging that suggests that the functional organisation and self-regulation that characterises superorganisms may be viewed in the context of complexity theory which attempts to account for the apparently spontaneous emergence of order and pattern from the internal dynamics, design and structural constraints of enigmatic systems like weather, the stock market and ecosystems. Traditional evolutionary biology explains order in nature as the sole outcome of adaptation through natural selection; complexity theory suggests that some of this order emerges from within the system itself, often serendipitous solutions to a current need, with natural selection doing the fine tuning.

Complexity is admittedly a very difficult notion to get the mind around. It is so, well...complex. Mathematical modellers throw up their hands and admit that they do not have a calculus to deal with it. It is why we continue to have books like this, and, happily, why we have honey.

Niches

The invertebrates occupy a staggering number and variety of niches in the forest: a whole world of micro-habitats of which we are largely ignorant. The number of species is virtually uncounted: considered estimates range from 3 to over 30 million, of which most have not even been found, leave alone named. Known ratios suggest that most species, like the weevil, are probably beetles, since beetles account for nearly half the 1.8 million named species of animals on Earth. This fact led the evolutionist J.B.S. Haldane's now legendary response to a cleric who asked him what characteristics a biologist would attribute to the Creator: "an inordinate fondness for beetles". It seems He is quite

attached as well to slugs and snails, since gastropods make up the next most species-rich group with an estimated 50,000 species.

The weevil (*Curculionidae, opposite, top*) and the milkweed bug (*Hemiptera, opposite, bottom left*) pierce and suck juices from a leaf, whereas the meloid beetle (see p. 252) bites pieces from the leaf or flower's edge. Some invertebrates like termites and their little gut helpers (see p. 78) eat wood, living or dead; others like the millipede (*Diplopoda, opposite, below centre*) root around chewing up decomposing leaves. Some, like snails (*above, left*) and slugs (*opposite, below right*), scrape the surface cells off plants. There are those that inhabit the heads of

specific flowers; some eat the petals, others the pollen, and both help perform the invaluable function of pollination. Butterflies and moths such as the Sphingid (*above, right*) feed exclusively on nectar. Variations on the plant-eating theme are legion, augmented by the fact that the vast majority of the eaters can fly, so any part of any plant from the ground up is fair game.

The creation of new species and the fading of old ones are continuing processes and have been since the beginnings of life. It is sobering to think that since ninety-nine per cent of all species that ever existed are now extinct, most, perhaps millions of the current species will disappear before we have ever had a chance to meet them.

The flying fruit-eaters

Birds, of course, seem to us more at home in the treetops than do mammals. But birds that eat predominantly vegetable matter are in the minority. The high rate of metabolism associated with the physiology of frequent flight is only satisfied by a high-energy, high-protein diet. Very few birds eat leaves, and the forest herbivore birds only eat plant produce rich in carbohydrates. Hornbills, trogons and parrots eat fruits and seeds, sunbirds drink floral nectar. The herbivore–plant relationship is advantageous to both forest birds and trees, and both go to adaptive lengths to bridge the trophic gap. We might almost view the trees' response as a pro – as opposed to anti – predation adaptation. Fruits have evolved to be visually attractive to the birds that serve as seed dispersers. Reds, oranges, and yellows are favourite advertising colours. Flowers, too, are gaudily painted in reds, and even shaped and arranged for ease of insertion of the nectar-probe bill of the sunbirds, who drink and pollinate at the same time.

The bills of the fruit-eaters are heavy and sharp-edged for slicing fruit and cracking nuts, as well as useful tools for dealing with an occasional insect attack. The silvery-cheeked hornbill's enormous casque on top of the beak is something of a mystery. It is a honeycomb structure, incredibly light for its size. The casque is certainly used in the bill-clacking courtship ritual, and it may help serve as a sound-amplifying megaphone to enhance vocalisations through the dense canopy. On the other hand, it may simply give rigidity and additional strength to the bill for attacking particularly robust fruits.

At the time of year when young are in the nest the food supply may become critical: consequently this is when most of the herbivore bird species jump a trophic level and begin to catch insects and small vertebrates. This may hark back to the habits of their dinosaur ancestors or simply be the consequence of the availability of protein, especially to augment the diet of the growing broods. The birds' ultimate dependence on the reproductive cycles of the trees makes them indispensable to the forest ecosystem on the one hand, but limits their numbers on the other. There are always some fruit or flowers in season in the canopy, but in amounts that are only a fraction of the total plant production.

Call of the wild

What is the mere chattering of monkeys or squawking of birds to human ears may be structured and meaningful to other animals. Bird song has been known for hundreds of years to carry meanings such as "this is the edge of my territory, keep back", or "feed me" and other rather simple messages. Sometimes the species language-barrier is bridged, for example, when the oxpecker takes to the wing with its characteristic buzz, one can be sure that the rhino from which it took off knows something is up.

Pitch carries meaning. Even the first time you listen to a group of primates you can get the message from the tone. High and strident implies fear and defensiveness in a reactive animal. Low and rumbling conveys menace and threat from a position of dominance. In our minds, such differences have come to be associated with female and male characteristics, to the point that management advisers urge their women clients to speak a few notes lower in order to carry home a point. But that is surely just physiological baggage taken to extremes by drill sergeants. A shriek from a baboon troop is probably being uttered by a subordinate

male being seen off by one of his elders and betters, male or female.

Recent work on monkey vocalisation has revealed new dimensions to their communication: they have a vocabulary. It has been shown that vervet monkeys, and presumably their close relatives, such as Sykes and other *Cercopithicines*, utter specific calls when they spot particular kinds of predators. There is, for example, one call for terrestrial predators like leopards, another for avian predators like eagles, and yet a third for snakes like pythons. We can debate about whether or not

they have the conscious intent to warn their fellows, but the effect is positive and dramatic. Listeners will respond immediately in the appropriate way, for example, by dashing for the nearest tree after the leopard alarm, looking up or jumping out of trees after the eagle expletive, scanning the ground after the snake shout. Do the reactors simply see the alarmers and respond to their body language? It seems not: researchers have controlled for visual signals by playing back the alarm calls in the absence of excited actors. The reactions are the same.

The ubiquitous butterfly

We often need something to jar us out of lazy habits of looking at things. Butterflies, particularly dull little brown ones like the ubiquitous bushbrowns, are nearly as common but far less noticed than houseflies, simply because they are less annoying. They flutter around innocuously near the forest floor, often in the company of more colourful species, like the equally common "sulphurs" (*Pieridae*, *right*). If asked, we probably would not remember them after a walk in the forest, just part of the background. Innocuousness is, of course, part of the trick of avoiding being noticed and possibly eaten.

But the butterflies must go about their business finding others of the same species to mate with and then finding the correct food plant on which to lay eggs. So they chase about in the sunlight, often along predictable flight paths and corridors that are preferred because of micro-qualities, such as a bit more shelter from the winds, a bit more filtering down through the canopy, a few more examples of a favourite food plant in the neighbourhood.

Watch what happens when the sun goes behind a cloud. All the butterflies seem suddenly to disappear, grounding themselves with wings folded back till the sun comes out again. This is in part to conserve vital flying energy that

is more quickly dissipated from the large wing surface in cool air: even a degree or so can make a difference. With the re-emergence of the sun, they take off again, mingling and dancing about, reducing their chances of getting hawked by a passing bird by being just one of the crowd.

The poisonous caterpillar

The monarch butterfly has been poisoned, but with the skill of an alchemist has turned the deed to its own advantage. The food plants of the monarch larva are various members of a poisonous family of "milkweed" herbs and creepers. To discourage herbivore attacks, the milkweeds have evolved the production and retention of cardiac glycosides in their veins. The monarch, however, has countered by evolving immunity to these heart poisons. Since the monarch is the only herbivore known to eat milkweeds (with the exception of one of the ever-present beetles, see p. 256), the plant has not found it necessary to make another move in the evolutionary game.

Not only is the monarch immune to the poison, but it goes so far as to incorporate the chemical into its own tissues, making it a potentially fatal meal for its predators. Once a naive bird has tried a monarch caterpillar, it never forgets how ill it was: in small doses the poison acts as a powerful emetic. Nor does it forget the specially designed colour pattern of the larva, which instantly changes from a bright attractive object to a warningly coloured one.

Some species of butterfly caterpillar have been observed to enlist the anti-predation assistance of ants. The caterpillars perform a kind of tap-dance with their legs, drumming a vibrating tune on the plant's branches that attracts the ants initially. The ants hang around, feeding on proteins and sugars that the caterpillars secrete. In return, the ants vigorously keep parasitic wasps at bay, preventing them from laying their eggs on the caterpillar's back. Whilst watching monarch larvae,

we noticed another trick. When the caterpillar grows large enough to stop scraping the epidermal cells off the surface of the leaf and to start gnawing away at the edge, it begins to cut into the larger veins of the leaf. This releases a stream of the sticky latex-like "milk".

A mouthful of the material causes obvious discomfort, both chemical and mechanical. So, before starting a meal, the larva crawls deliberately to the leaf stem and spends considerable time pinching the stem with its mandibles. This seems to cut off the leaf's circulation and the flow of noxious latex without cutting off the leaf. The larva then returns to the leaf proper and consumes the whole thing, veins and all.

Metamorphosis and mimicry

The larva has but two functions in the butterfly lifecycle – to eat and to grow. And grow it does, to some 2,000 to 3,000 times its birth weight. It will even eat butterfly eggs, which is why just one or two are laid on a single food plant. Only at night or when it is shedding one of its five skins does it pause. It reaches its full five centimetres in only two weeks, a vulnerable time for a soft worm, even a distasteful one like the monarch larva. It is best to get over this period quickly. We have come to view the phenomenon of complete metamorphosis with the acceptance we afford to a stage conjurer. But consider it again; the larva, a bag of materials, nearly blind, almost senseless, clumsy and thick-legged, sheds its skin a last time and with a wave of the wand is a pupa hanging on the leaf. Inside the pupa the most incredible reorganisation of cells takes place. All parts change size, shape and colour. Mandibles and legs vanish, proboscis and wings appear. In a couple of weeks, another pass of the wand and a butterfly pops out.

Of course, the larva must go into the metamorphosis with everything set up beforehand. The miracle is rigged by the chemistry of the genes, with some guidance from the homeotic "stage manager" genes. Simple skin cells, which look uniform to us, have messages encoded in their nuclei that they will become wing, antenna or proboscis. Trip the switch with a dose of growth hormones and the cells change and grow, like a beautiful and organised cancer.

The larva that disappears during the complete metamorphosis not only passes the materials and the blueprint to the butterfly, but, in the case of the monarch, a dose

of cardiac poison as well. The adult is as emetic as the larva; its colours just as striking. Unlike more furtive tasty species, the monarch flies a lazy cocksure pace around the forest edge and through the clearings, as though it knows its warning colour pattern has been learned by most potential predators, mainly birds. Obviously a few monarchs have to be sacrificed to teach the birds a lesson, but the nett benefit to the butterfly population is ninety per cent immunity from predation. If there were more milkweeds, the skies would be orange with monarchs, as it is during the migration of the North American variety.

So successful is the warning colouration of the monarch butterfly

that other species – tasteful, non-poisonous ones, like females of the Flying Handkerchief butterfly (*Papilio dardanus*) – have found it advantageous to mimic the monarch. Even a small patch of orange will make an initiated bird feel uneasy or at least check its attack long enough for the incipient mimic to escape. A survival advantage of only a few per cent is all that is necessary to favour and fix an adaptation in the population. Over many generations, through "predator selection", which is really a rejection of anything monarch-like, the resemblance is perfected. At this point only an entomologist or a butterfly can distinguish between the model and the mimic.

A small family gallery selected from an African butterfly mimicry complex that involves tens of species and at least nine sub-families. At the top is the male Flying Handkerchief. Both he and his multi-coloured females like the three in the right-hand column are relatively tasty to predators. The females gain a protective advantage for themselves and their eggs by copying to a remarkable degree the colour patterns of various distasteful species in the monarch's sub-family Danainae (left-hand column, top to bottom, *Amauris navius*, *Danaus chrysippus* and *Amauris echeria*). At this point, only an entomologist or a butterfly can distinguish the model from the mimic.

CARNIVORES PURSUIT OF FOOD

Hunters in the air

The majority of forest carnivores are birds. The reason is found one level down in the pyramid of life: most of the forest herbivores are insects – ideal bird food. Compare that to the grasslands, where there exists an impressive array of large mammal herbivores, far better fare for big fierce mammals. Birds of prey are relatively rare in any habitat because of the difficulties in getting at small scurrying mammals from the air. Consequently many eagles, such as the Tawny (*opposite*), are territorial and vigorously defend their hunting grounds and food supply from intruders. Specialised bird-of-prey equipment, such as a large and strong bill, makes them efficient killers, and indeed the bulk of their food comprises rodents. To a lesser extent they also take smaller birds, hatchling tortoises, snakes, lizards and carrion. Their sheer size and equipment reduces the availability of very small prey, the most numerous type, because their retreats are physically inaccessible. Thus, the majority of the birds in the forest, like the long-tailed fiscal (*Lanius cabanisi, above*) are smaller insectivores because energy is available to them mainly in the form of insects. Although the proportion of bird species that eat insects is the same in the forests and the grasslands – about sixty per cent – the diversity of species is far greater in the forest. Forests only cover about one per cent of Africa south of the Sahara, yet thirty per cent of the 1,500-odd species of African birds live in forests. This is a direct result of the richness of the insect fauna, which, as we have seen, is in turn a function of the richness of forest canopy vegetation.

Catching insects is a full-time occupation, and birds use a lot of energy in flying around to get enough food for energy and growth. They would seem to be flying in vicious circles if it were not for the fact that part of each meal contributes to body maintenance and reproduction. Although there is always the edge of competition between species, there are periods of truce when so-called feeding parties of several species of insectivorous bird move as a group through the foliage. There is probably a distinct advantage in having a group of like-minded "beaters" flushing insects from all quarters. Presumably, this occurs only when there are enough insects to go around. There are also other advantages to being one of a crowd: more eyes to see and warn about danger, and more potential targets – apart from yourself – should danger strike.

The burden on the adult bird is increased several-fold when there are young to feed. It spends the whole day rushing back and forth in a flurry of finding food and stuffing it into the irresistible gaping beaks of the nestlings. During the nesting period an adult bird may lose almost as much weight as the young bird gains. Invariably, the avian hunters hold and defend territories against both members of the same species and others to ensure that there is an adequate food supply in the neighbourhood of the nest. Although the territory subtends a patch of ground – roughly circular if other territory holders surround it – it also reaches upwards, an invisible no-fly zone extending into the canopy. The camaraderie of the feeding-party is put on hold till breeding is over.

CARNIVORES PURSUIT OF FOOD

A golden-rumped killer

There are few mammalian predators to be seen in the forest. Bats may be heard twittering at night and with luck the golden-rumped elephant shrew may be heard in daytime, rustling through the leaf litter of the coastal forest with its curious long-legged gait, in constant search of its invertebrate food. The gilded hindquarters provide a striking contrast to its burnished chestnut coat. Bites and scars have been found on the rump suggesting the conspicuous patch is designed to divert attacks.

It is large for a shrew, some fifteen centimetres long, which is just one reason why it is not a true shrew. No-one seems to be quite sure what it is. It may be related to the tree shrews, which are not shrews either, but arboreal insectivores that appear to be the precursors of primates. The golden-rumped elephant shrew may even have fairly close herbivore ancestors: some scientists have ventured the suggestion of an affinity with rabbits, and recent blood-protein mapping has linked it with aardvarks and, yes, even elephants. Whatever it may turn out to be for the palaeo-taxonomists, for our purpose it is a small forest carnivore who spends eighty per cent of the day nosing through fallen leaves catching and eating a weight of insects, worms, millipedes and snails equivalent to its own.

Elephant shrews do not follow rules. There is one called the "energy budget rule" that states that if an animal's daily energy budget is negative it should behave in a risk-prone manner. Put another way, if it's hungry, it will take chances. Laboratory experiments with elephant shrews have shown that they continue to be careful even when hungry. The experimenters conclude that "a risk-averse response to reward-size variance is expected, because an elephant shrew may not reliably perceive those circumstances under which risk-prone behaviour should be adopted". In other words, the shrews appear daft since they do not conform to the rule. Maybe it's just a silly rule.

Daft or not, elephant shrews seem to make do: of the thirty-three species and sub-species that have been described, only six forest-dwelling ones are threatened. Adult females of the short-snouted elephant shrew in Zimbabwe are able to rear five to six litters each year – an impressive annual production of 8.3 young per female. In general, they exhibit conservatism expected of one so primitive, as well as unique social systems. A male and female golden-rumped share a territory on the forest floor of from 1.5 to 2 hectares. Apart from primates, there are very few monogamous mammals. Although the elephant shrews form a pair in the sense that they stay together for several years in the same home range, they almost entirely ignore each other except for occasional bouts of mating. During these, the female is almost totally indifferent and barely stops searching for food during the act. The male chases off intruding males, the female chases off females, but both tolerate invaders of the opposite sex. The first impression is one of happy domestic territorial co-operation – a charitable interpretation for a totally "affectionless arrangement" that ensures each member of the pair gets enough food for itself.

Surprise

The wealth of flying insects in the forests puts a premium on hunters that can take food either in the air, or quickly in the brief instants when the insects alight. The tongue of the Kikuyu three-horned chameleon (*Chamaeleo jacksonii, opposite*) clearly takes the insect completely by surprise. The alternative tactic – taken by other lizards – would be for the chameleon to rush and snap. But insects are fast and have good eyesight. A hungry beast the size of a chameleon would have little chance of sneaking up on its prey. So the chameleon forsakes speed of movement. It moves slowly along branches with a quaint rocking motion that has the rhythm of a leaf swaying in the wind. As it moves, special pigment cells – black and green mainly – just under its skin, expand and contract to produce effects that imitate the colours that the eyes see and the brain interprets. The turreted eyes swivel about independently taking in colour and looking for prey in an almost total sphere of vision. When one eye sights a prey item, the other sweeps parallel to fix the object in a binocular stare. Prey suitability, distance and angle are judged in an instant. A small bone flicks the tongue clear of the jaws, as seen with the high casqued chameleon (*Chamaeleo hoehneli, right, top and middle*) and with an hydraulic surge in the blink of an eye it inflates forward (*right*), like a child's party toy. Pressure is released, the tongue snaps back and the meal is finished in less than a second.

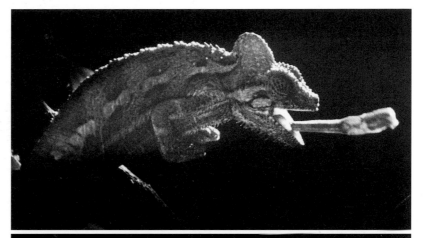

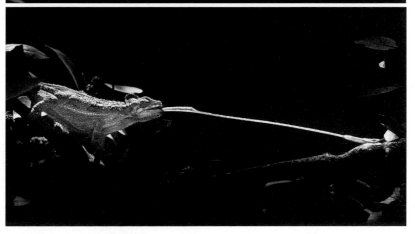

Speed and precision

The precision of the motor control and complex design of our body, sensory and nervous systems are taken for granted by us because we live by them. Consider a forest hunter like the praying mantis (*Manitae*). It catches insects by snatching them out of the air, a feat at which we have only moderate success. The mantis must receive instantaneous information about the insect's position, distance and speed relative to itself. It must process the information, come to a decision, and strike with its elongated forelegs before the insect is gone. Large compound eyes set wide on the head identify that the object is prey and provide the optical data necessary to feed into the distance equation. Unlike most invertebrates, the mantis' head can turn on its thorax. The tilt of the head excites sensory hairs on the neck that signal information about the angle of the prey away from the axis of the mantis' body. The forelegs are cued to the same angle and fired off before the distance parameter changes to a useless value.

It is not surprising if this description uses a jargon echoing that of the control system of a computer operation, for the simile is not far off what must really happen in the animal. The hardware of body and nervous system is designed by natural selection and programmed with a set of genetic code instructions that allow the mantis to catch an insect the very first time it tries. But it is not a flexible system; the mantis cannot do much else as well as it catches insects.

The trapper

Some carnivores go out and hunt their food; others set traps for it. Sheet-web spiders (*right*) build horizontal nets, trampolines of silk, and then wait for insects to fly or fall into them. These spiders are nocturnal for two good reasons – in daylight prey would see the closely woven sheets, and larger predators would see the waiting spider. At the least untoward vibration, which the spider feels with its feet, it rushes out and pounces on the object that caused the disturbance. The chase and kill that follow the moth's arrival are as dramatic as any lion kill. The moth is larger than the predator but at a disadvantage in the tangle of the web. The spider feints and rushes at the thrashing prey, trying to inject an immobilising poison and loop some more strands of silk around the moth. If the moth does not manage to struggle free it is wrapped up and set upon immediately, with the spider quietly sucking out its body fluids.

The orb spider's web (*opposite*) is a marvel of construction and design. It can be thought of as a low-cost (in terms of materials) extension of the hunter – like nets for catching butterflies or fish. We take for granted the technology that goes into the development of the nylon and the weaving machinery for our nets, but consider the work of the spider. She – usually it is the adult females that make the specta-cular orbs – follows an evolutionarily determined sequence that reads like the instructions for assembling an aeroplane in the garage.

Extrude silk type A (you have six types in the kit), flatten end and apply silk type B (the sticky sort). Float on breeze like a kite until it crosses the space to be covered by

the web. When it catches on the other side, Bridge A is in place. Then, catch hold of Bridge A, extrude a bit of type C silk and attach to original side. Next, pull yourself along Bridge A, eating it (to get it out of the way and to re-cycle its materials) and extrude silk type C behind you in generous quantities across the span. Anchor at far side. Bridge B is thus in place, being slightly longer than the original, now eaten one. Move to middle of Bridge B, which should sag under your weight like a V. Fix a fresh thread to the point of the V and let yourself down to the ground, playing out the new line. Fix at bottom. Move to the centre of the resultant Y of silk and...

The instructions go on: two-dozen main spokes are added from the centre of the Y, then a scaffolding of non-sticky silk is put in place across the spokes from the centre to strengthen the orb and provide a platform for adding the finer sticky cross members, the ones that are designed with little built-in "reels" to play out just enough to snag but

not bounce back the impacting fly. All this takes an hour, instead of the 1,000-plus necessary to put an aeroplane kit together. She does it right the first time she tries, and she repeats it every evening.

Because the forest carnivores are mainly small, most of them crawl a thin line between the eater and the eaten. Birds love spiders, so the web-builder must hide off to the side of her web or sit camouflaged in the middle. Some spiders sneak up on other spiders by twanging their victim's webs in imitation of a trapped insect and then creeping forward as the vibration dies down. It has never been measured, but we would guess that forest carnivores eat almost as many of each other as they do of herbivores. The shrike eats the chameleon who ate the mantis, who ate the spider, who ate the herbivore moth. These horizontal food chains may contribute to the conservatism of the forest by slowing down the trophic flow of materials through the ecosystem, but they certainly find some circuitous routes.

The hunter

The hunting spider's technique (*opposite*) of getting food is less passive than its cousin's sheet-web trap. It prowls about the forest floor at night looking for prey with a bank of half-a-dozen sensitive eyes. These eyes are relatively simple in structure and so several of them are needed to get enough information for an accurate charge in dim light.

Even such formidable beasts are at a temporary disadvantage during the reproductive period. The drain on energy and vitality is severe when producing offspring. The act of giving birth, egg-laying or nest-building slows down an animal's movement, fixes it momentarily in space and increases an enemy's chance of making a successful strike. But the effort and risk are obviously unavoidable. The female Lycosid spider encumbers herself for an appreciable portion of her lifetime, lovingly carrying her egg mass under her abdomen. In this way she can carry on her mobile strategy of hunting whilst protecting her egg case. When threatened, she tucks it up under her, and anyone who wishes to take it will have to deal with her first.

The semi-aquatic spider (*above*) in the genus *Thalassius* (family *Pisauridae*), which we found in a pond near the Karua Forest outside of Nairobi and appears to be new to science, seems to be as comfortable in the water as on land. When startled, it simply dove and sat on the bottom. It appeared so at ease under the surface, that we suspect it hunts there too.

The eyes have it

"Let there be light" is one of the most profound utterances of all time, even allowing for the credentials of the imputed source. Not only does it poetically throw the switch of the power plant for life on earth, but it turns on the stage lights as well. Yet the visible light that illuminates most of our lives is only a tiny sliver of radiation in the huge range from gamma rays to radio waves. If the electromagnetic spectrum were this book, the slice of "our" light would be lost in the gutter between the pages.

Light, or more precisely, energy bouncing around in the form of packets called photons at wavelengths between 300 and 700 nanometres (billionths of a metre), is the most pervasive information media life has, particularly when different life forms communicate actively or passively among themselves. The messages have been flying back and forth every second of every day since the world began. From simple ones like night-to-day, to more complex ones like "ah, there's something to eat/mate with/run from" or Bach's *Musicalische Opfer* lit up from little pits on the surface of a compact disc. With all that inexhaustible light energy penetrating as far as it can, small wonder eyes evolved to record and brains to interpret what it was revealing.

Eyes have evolved independently at least forty and probably as many a sixty times in animals since the switch was first thrown. The compound eye in vertebrates and squids is usually taken as the classic example of parallel evolution through remote selection and differential survival of small

improvements over very long periods of time. The alternative or at best complementary view of complexity-theory holds that eyes are the products of "high-probability spatial transformations of developing tissues". It argues that there is something about the very nature of tissues, defined by molecular lattice structures of carbon, the forces on growing materials, gravity, photon intensity and what-have-you that limits and shapes the envelope of the possible of what can emerge. Thus the form and structure of end-product, in this case a highly complex device like the vertebrate eye, is already inherent in the qualities of its simple building blocks.

Or so it might seem. Elegant arguments have been woven and computer models built to demonstrate rather convincingly that small, incremental advantageous mutations could have been passed on from generation to generation to produce body parts and behaviours as complex as you can imagine, and in timespans that makes sense given what we know about the age of fossils. Thus, 300,000 iterations of a computer model might seem like a lot of steps and a long time, but if the hypothetical beast were to improve through selection its visual equipment little by little each generation, and say it were to breed once a year, we would have a span of the order of 300 millennia. That's still only 0.01 per cent of the time real animals have had to come up with complicated compound eyes since primitive animals started slipping through Silurian seas needing to find food and avoid predators.

An army of hunters

The most effective and thorough carnivore hunter in the forest is a colony of *siafu* (*Dorylus*, *above*), the so-called safari ant (also known as the army or driver ant). Every three or four weeks, a dreadful horde of hundreds of thousands of ants pours out of the ground, from a nest some four metres below the surface. Conventional wisdom asserts there is heightened *siafu* activity just before the rains. The real trigger may be a high proportion of worker pupae in the brood, which in turn may be linked to season. E.O. Wilson has suggested that an ant colony functions like a "virtual stomach", since workers

constantly exchange their stomach contents and therefore "know" how hungry the colony is as a whole. With a large hatching just around the corner, there is clearly a need for a well-stocked larder. With some 20 million mouths to feed, rains or no, a collective hunger must motivate them to march.

The direction of the nomadic foray is probably random, since the range of their potential prey is so wide. Any animal of any size, living or freshly dead, which is in the ants' path is quickly set upon, pinned down, sliced up and carried off in tiny pieces back to the nest. Even elephants have been driven

to madness by a trunkful of *siafu*, and there are numerous stories of sleeping babies or penned cows being overwhelmed and killed. Soon there is two-way traffic along the trail, with workers scurrying between rows of alert soldiers – thousands of individuals who are individually worthless, expendable. Soldiers attack against absurd odds: we pluck them off our legs leaving the heads biting us.

It is perhaps the mechanical nature of their predation, their totally unemotional, unreasoning, unqualified instinctive lifestyle that humans find disturbing. We admire the lion, love the bee

and hate the ant. What is it that hardens our reaction to this other superorganism?

The movements are very quick. Even though the foraging front only moves at some twenty metres per hour, everyone seems to be running, and there is continual scurrying back and forth as the vanguard advance a bit and then retreat to be replaced by others from behind. A pheromone trail is marked out by the moving front, which is then followed slavishly and enhanced by those behind. Ants meet head on, pause to touch antennae in instant identification, then rush on. Logs are overrun without pause;

ants cling together to form bridges over small streams in a twinkling; prey items such as grasshoppers are set upon and dispatched with assembly-line efficiency (*right*). Why the hurry? Perhaps the question is too human to apply to ants. We tend to judge events by our own criteria, and therein lies the "inhuman" quality we ascribe to small animals like *siafu*. One foraging hunt of these ants may take a worker's lifetime. That is a long time to an ant, and there are always new mouths to feed.

Honey hunters

What we share with the ratel is an occasionally mean disposition and fondness for honey. The ratel is also called "honey badger". It is known as the most ferocious, fearless animal in the bush, and it is not uncommon for it to attack against absurd odds – for example, trying to bring down a Landrover by going for its tyres. It has a gentler side however, and responds obediently to the displays of a vaguely flycatcher-like bird called, appropriately enough, the greater honeyguide (even its scientific name, *Indicator indicator*, makes sense). Once the honeyguide catches the ratel's attention, it moves from tree to tree, chattering and tail-twisting until it leads the willing instrument of its plan to a beehive. The honeyguide then waits impatiently whilst

the ratel digs out the bees. When the beast has had its fill of honey, wax and larvae, the bird swoops in to pick up the remaining honey-coated grubs.

Humans make similar use of honeyguides who do not seem to mind if it is a human or a ratel that follows them. They do require their reward: legend has it that if the honey hunter does not leave enough for the honeyguide, the next person will be led to a sleeping rhino.

Skilled honey hunters handle the bees with almost trance-like calmness. The African bees are not in general the ravening killers of Grade-B movies, but they are far less tranquil then their long-selected northern hemisphere cousins. Usually a puff of smoke – dried giraffe droppings are best –

is all that is required to fool the bees into a fire drill in which they fill their bellies as a prelude to bailing out. This is what makes them drowsy and tractable – not being overcome by smoke.

The guild of African honeyhunters is an ancient and proud one; members have had their craft handed down from their forebears. Since they cannot eat all the honey they gather or husband in hollow-log hives, they sell or trade most or the joint produce. Honeyhunters thus probably embody at one and the same time the earliest domesticators of wildlife as well as the most ancient entrepreneur group in human society.

Ancient messages?

The arrangement of the carnivore's front-end, as we have seen, is to expedite dealing with mobile meat. The serval cat's threat display (*right top*) is not directed at its prey – there is no time for that – but at other cats or larger animals threatening it: a reminder that teeth could be used for fighting or self-defence if a critical distance is breached. It is designed as a signal of intent, but it might just be a bluff: fear and aggression are often finely balanced in an agonistic encounter. The evolution of animal displays invariably makes use of existing body parts. If those parts enhance the message of the display, so much the better. It's the effect that counts.

Receiving and sending signals is the essence of communication. If the two organisms engaged in the exchange happen to speak the same language or have evolved a mutually-understandable code, then the process is relatively straightforward. But if no "language" is available, a certain amount of "mind-reading" is necessary to predict what might happen next. If we encounter an unknown dog, we would do well to take account of any information we can about its motivational state before trying to pet it. A rival dog would probably go through the same process, but with a somewhat better grasp of "dog language".

We recoil from the serval's threat or from a column of *siafu*, yet we reach out to touch a butterfly. Many of us shudder at a snake, yet when young happily stick our fingers into a wall socket. A young vervet monkey we once knew was totally uninterested when we introduced a shy tortoise to the compound: just another rock. After a while, the tortoise gained courage and started to come out of its shell. When the head and tail became clearly visible, the monkey screamed and fled, presumably at the "snake in the rock"? Is there an absolute quality about the aspects of herbivores and carnivores that leads us to consider the duiker, colobus or butterfly beautiful and the hunting spider, leopard or white-lipped herald snake (*below right*) fearsome? Or does our response to members of these different trophic levels stem from a time when we were functionally closer to them – when the herbivore was vital to us as food and the carnivore potentially fatal, or, at best, painful? "Snake deities" are afforded transcendental meanings as well as patently obvious symbolism in the oldest identified animist cults. And it is no coincidence that the largest snake – the rock python – and one of the most deadly – the Gabon adder (*opposite*) – are those most frequently represented in African art.

The qualities of the attractive and the fearsome, or of beauty and ugliness, have been described by poets, but the meanings of the words may have roots reaching deep into our origins and biological selves. Indeed beauty seems to be more than in just the eye of the beholder; it springs from symmetry that in turn is an outward sign of genetic fitness. Similarly, being a lusty singer or good dancer, even having a sense of humour, are primeval signals of the character of a worthy mate. One of our unique qualities is the ability simultaneously to experience the thrill, and to analyse the components, of the natural world. Is this inherited

from our distant forefathers, whose survival must have depended to a large extent upon their learning to pause and apply a measure of classical, analytical reasoning and perhaps see beyond the face of things at times when the animal in them urged uncontrolled flight, or unbridled attack?

Reluctant pairs

The propensity to live singly and scattered is a common behavioural trait of camouflaged animals. If a predator detects and eats a tasty prey, it looks around the immediate area for more of the same, bearing a "searching image" of the prey in mind. We, too, know that it is easier to find an object if we have a mental picture of what it looks like. If the predator finds no other objects that match the searching image, it gives up and looks for something else. If the prey are scattered, the chance is greater that the predator will give up the search before it finds the next prey.

Just before the rains, chameleons forsake their spatial conservatism and begin to wander about. Immobility and living far from your neighbours is an important adjunct to camouflage colouration, but there is no point in avoiding predation if the chance to reproduce is lost. And there is little chance of finding a mate by staying in the same bush. So once a year they have to risk detection, like a recluse going to a ball.

The innate aversion to getting too close to another chameleon is usually overcome by the male's initiative. He unceremoniously pounces on the female and holds her forcibly whilst they mate. After the act they quickly part company.

Amongst insects, birds and reptiles, birth takes place most frequently from eggs. But eggs require care or careful hiding to avoid the season's output being eaten at one go. Staying in one place and caring for a nestful of eggs is a potentially dangerous and complicated business. It is best left to animals like birds who are capable of the complex behavioural patterns needed to

build, tend and defend a nest, as well as agile enough to fly suddenly away should it be necessary.

The bearded chameleon avoids the eggs-in-one-basket dilemma by being one of the few reptiles to bear its young alive (*above*). The young chameleons are effectively hidden right through gestation by the mother's remarkable camouflage. The energy cost to the female chameleon is probably not much more than it would be to produce eggs.

The young, twenty-six of them in this case, are dropped in a perfunctory way in the space of as many minutes. The female takes no notice of them as they wriggle from the amniotic sac that cushions their fall. They are fully developed and will

flick their tongues at the first insects they ever see, even before they are completely dry. Each goes its own way immediately, totally independent from the moment of birth.

Parasite in the nest

There are birds that shirk the parental duty and let others raise their young. Obviously only a few species can enjoy this rather extravagant lifestyle. The red-chested cuckoo is a classic nest parasite. With the cunning and stealth of an illicit oologist, the cuckoo has to identify birds who are nesting and then locate their nest. The wandering female watches for a diligent parent like the robinchat to leave the nest, perhaps to feed or to collect some nest material. Sometimes a male cuckoo will brazenly advertise its presence with the characteristic "it-will-rain..." call. This is thought to be a distraction to invite mobbing by the defence-minded nesting birds in the neighbourhood. The robinchat boldly chases the cuckoo, not because the chat knows about nest parasitism but because it considers most large birds to be potential predators of eggs or young.

Given a few unguarded moments, the female cuckoo slips in, removes a host bird's egg, lays one of her own and retreats before the chat returns. This in itself is a feat, since the timing of getting the egg out is critical. The cuckoo egg is larger than the robinchat's but this does not bother the sitting bird. Indeed, eggs are extremely compelling objects for broody birds, and large eggs even more so.

The host bird begins incubating. Cuckoo eggs usually hatch first and the interloper chick immediately sets about ejecting the rest of the eggs from the nest. Even if the host and cuckoo eggs hatch more or less simultaneously, the larger cuckoo is typically much more persistent in begging for food. It eats more, grows faster and is stronger than the host chicks, so it soon

succeeds in pushing them over the rim of the nest to oblivion. The grim drama then borders on farce as harassed parents frantically fly about catching an endless supply of insects to stuff into their indolent and ever-demanding foster chick: it eventually outweighs them both.

But it's not always like that, and sometimes the cuckoo fails. In the sequence shown here the cuckoo was late – its egg hatched five days after the host bird's, by which time the larger robinchat was able to demand four times as many meals per day as the parasite. Thus the final infamy of the cuckoo was thwarted; try though it might it could not muster strength enough for its innate trick of heaving the host chick from the nest. Perhaps the energy it used in trying cost it its life, for it died before the

robinchat young was fully fledged. No natural mechanism is perfect; success is a quality to be measured in terms of the probable rather than the absolute; and, sometimes the good guys simply win.

Endpiece

We inevitably return to the decomposers;
to one of the most successful organisms
on Earth – the ubiquitous fly. Amongst the
tens of thousands of fly species, such as
the *Calliphorid*, we find herbivores and
carnivores, predators and parasites, but
the vast majority thrive because of death.
It is curious that our reaction to decomposers is one of revulsion, for the world
would indeed be a revolting place without
them, piled to the sky with dead organisms.
They would not smell, since without
bacteria there would be no putrefaction
but the world would be terribly still, lifeless and ecosystems would have no fuel.

  With the concerted efforts of millions
of decomposers from vultures to flies to
bacteria, an entire elephant corpse,
except the bones, will be returned to the
soil in a few months. Thus the ecosystem's
store of exchangeable resources is
replenished without relying on the long-
term contribution of heaving mantel and
dissolving mountains. The decomposers,
then, are not only the link between the
organic and the inorganic, they are also
the bridge between death and life, which
makes new life possible. Next time
you kill a fly remember that, in the end,
it and the Earth will get their own back.

Annexes

ENDNOTES

The references to additional reading given in this endnote section are by no means exhaustive. They are of three sorts: general books or monographs on a particular subject or species; review articles and analyses; and peer-reviewed scientific papers. These three types, taken in reverse order, mark the general path of science information development and promulgation. Scientific papers present research results. They follow the usual rules of peer-review and replicability and are steeped in an implied deep history of conceptual development. Review papers generally summarise a corpus of scientific work (or debate) on a particular topic and provide a timely, sometimes short-lived synthesis. Compendia are often aimed at a more general readership than the other two, and, like this book, try to assemble a large amount of complex information within a simple framework.

The middle group in our list below usually comprises feature articles from the *New Scientist*. These invariably present a balanced view of an issue as well as pointers to the work of the various protagonists in the debate (if there is one) and to useful websites. For the general reader, as well as the specialist who wishes to venture from time to time out of his or her particular corridor, the *New Scientist* is excellent value. Its CD-rom version contains all past issues since 1989 with a powerful search engine: a wonderful information tool, although sadly priced more for libraries than individuals. The world wide web site ‹http://www.newscientist.com› is a good browse. Another information resource that we have not included is the exceptional library of wildlife films and videos coming out of East Africa, notably those of Alan Root, Simon Trevor, the BBC Natural History Unit and Martyn Colbeck.

FURTHER READING

Throughout the book, we will come back to the Serengeti as the archetypal African ecosystem. Apart from a host of scientific literature that comes from research there as well as the neighbouring Ngorongoro crater in Tanzania and the Maasai Mara in Kenya, the reader may wish to delve into two excellent sequential compendia that deal with the whole fabric of the Serengeti: Sinclair and Norton-Griffiths (1979) and Sinclair and Arcese (1995).

page 8

Bateson (1979)

The brave attempt at costing the services provided by the world's ecosystems is found in Costanza, d'Arge et al. (1997).

page 9–11

The behavioural ecologist's bibles, old and new testament, are: Krebs and Davies (1884) and Krebs and Davies (1993).

Two excellent accounts of life: the historical Fortey (1997) and the philosophical Capra (1996). Any one of Richard Dawkins' excellent books tells us how natural selection works.

Odum's text (1959) is a classic, redone recently (1997) with a social facelift. See also Begon et al. (1996) for a comprehensive textbook.

William Blake was certainly unware that he was marvelling at the outcome of natural selection in his poem "The Tyger" in the *Songs of Experience* (Keynes 1927):

> *Tyger! Tyger! burning bright*
> *In the forests of the night*
> *What immortal hand or eye*
> *Could frame thy fearful symmetry?*

Photosynthesis is explained in a host of texts: the *New Scientist Inside Science* version (Woodward 1989) is very clear and accessible.

page 12

See Begon et al. (1996) pp. 735–6 on the "10% law".

page 13

See Krebs and Davies (1993) on "inclusive fitness".

On the side of natural selection, there is no more articulate champion than Richard Dawkins, for example in *Climbing Mount Improbable* (1996) and *Unweaving the Rainbow* (1998). The proponents of order "emerging" somehow from within the system, however, make very good reading if not a compelling case; for example, Cohen and Stewart (1994), Kauffman (1995), and Goodwin (1995). On a piece of high ground somewhere in-between, leaning markedly towards the natural selection side is E.O. Wilson, who in *Consilience* (1998) argues with weight for a kind of unified field theory to bring ethics, economics and the social sciences into a total ecological framework.

John Casti of the Sante Fe Institute made the public admission in the *New Scientist*, namely that "...mathematically speaking, we are stuck...We have no good mathematical framework within which to probe the properties of complex, adaptive systems." (1996). See also his book *Complexification* (1995).

The last word in the introduction is that of Robert Frost from an essay — "The Figure a Poem Makes" — that introduced his complete works at the time (1961). He could have been talking about science rather than poetry:

> *"...It begins in delight, it inclines to the impulse, it assumes direction with the first line laid down, it runs a course of lucky events, and ends in a clarification of life – not necessarily a great clarification, such as sects and cults are founded on, but in a momentary stay against confusion."*

The resonance between poetry and science seems perfectly natural to Wilson, who reckons that the "...dominating influence that spawned the arts was the need to impose order on the confusion caused by intelligence".

GRASSLANDS

page 19, Geology and climate

UNEP/GEMS (1992); Hays et al. (1976); Nyamweru (1980); Kirschvink (1997) Stephen Jay Gould (1990) and Richard Dawkins (1998) provide differing views of "punctuated equilibrium"

page 20, Learning to cope

Quote from William Shakespeare *Macbeth*, Act 1, Scene 7. On the impact of climate change see: IPCC (1996); Gribbin (1990); Glantz (1998); Mullis (1998); Parry (1991)

page 23, Sum of the parts

Klomp and Green (1996); Capra (1996)

page 24, Setting the stage

Peter Usher (personal communication); Endo (1995); Schnell and Vali (1972); Hamilton and Lenton (1998); Hunt (1998)

page 27, The solar constant

Robert Herrick, "To the Virgins, to Make Much of Time"; Vervij and Schoenmackers (1997); Tinsley (1998); Caniggia (1991)

page 29, Grass

Some estimates put the appearance of grass at 25 million years ago, in the Miocene (Ridley 1996); others put it earlier, towards the end of the Cretaceous (Cohen and Stewart 1994).

See Begon et al. (1996) for a discussion of the continuing usefulness of the concept of "R and K selection"

Ibrahim and Kabuye (1987)

page 31, Grasslands

Lind and Morrison (1974); Pratt et al. (1977); Frank and McNaughton (1991); McNaughton and Banyikwa (1995)

pages 32–3, Prolific pastures

There are two great compendia of studies over time of the Serengeti, one of the greatest surviving ecosystems on earth: Sinclair and Norton-Griffiths (1979) and Sinclair and Arcese (1995).

One UNEP-commissioned study (Long, Jones et al. 1992) indicates that tropical grasslands turn far more carbon dioxide into carbohydrates than anyone suspected, equalling — or even exceeding — the productivity of tropical rainforests

page 35, A tree for all seasons
Tolkien (1954–55); Van Hoven (1991); Brace (1996)

page 39, Fire
Levine (1992)

pages 40–41, Animal furniture
Desmond Vesey-FitzGerald, personal communication, and in various publications, e.g. Vesey-FitzGerald (1969)

page 45, Animal feeding
Kangwana (1996)

page 49, Migration
Sinclair and Norton-Griffiths (1979); Sinclair and Arcese (1995)

page 61, Blood relatives
Von Goethe, J.W. (1808, 1832) *Faust*

pages 66–7, Solitude
Wilson (1975); Hinde (1972)

page 69, The family
Kingdon (1979); Macdonald (1984)

page 71, The harem
Krebs and Davies (1993)

page 72, The matriarchy
References to genomic imprintes are: Keverne et al. (1996); Surani (1991); Ohlsson et al. (1995); and to elephants in: Kangwana (1996); Moss (1988; 1992); Moss and Poole (1983); Lee (1987); Poole (1995); Poole and Moss (1990); Payne (1998)

John Donne, *The Progress of the Soul* (Stanza 39):

Natures great master-peece, an Elephant,
The onely harmlesse great thing; the giant
Of beasts; who thought, no more had gone, to make one wise
But to be just, and thankfull, loth to offend,
(Yet nature hath given him no knees to bend)
Himselfe he up-props, on himselfe relies,
And foe to none, suspects no enemies,
Still sleeping stood; vex't not his fantasie
Blacke dreames; like an unbent bow, carelesly
His sinewy Proboscis did remisly lie.

page 74, Herds and troops
The buffalo "voting" was described by Prins (1987). The general African buffalo story is well told by Sinclair (1977).

page 77, One good turn
Strum (1987); Dunbar (1988)

page 78, The underground society
Wilson (1975)

page 87, Common grounds
Estes (1991); Gosling et al. (1987)

page 88, Courtship ritual
Andersson (1982)

page 90, A time to mate
Leuthold (1977)

pages 92–93, Females choose
Lee (1991); Lee and Moss (1995)

page 95, A deliquescent nest
Hedges (1983) is a general guide to East African reptiles and amphibians.

Great grey tree frog (*Chiromantis petersi*)

Check out the Declining Amphibian Populations Task Force, Department of Biology, The Open University, Milton Keynes, MK7 6AA (t.r.halliday@open.ac.uk) and reports such as that of Speare et al. (1997) and Anderson (1998)

page 96, Husbandry at the nest
Bertram (1979); Brown et al. (1982)

page 98, The economy of numbers
An introduction to the concept of "metapopulation" is found in Hanski and Gilpin (1991)

page 106, Speed for flight
The "Red Queen effect" was apparently first coined by Van Valen (1973); see Dawkins (1986)

page 109, Weapons to fight
Kingdon (1982); Macdonald (1984)

page 110, Behavioural flukes
Holmes (1993); Wills (1996; 1996); Ridley (1993). See also the host of possibilities in *The Ants* (Hoeldobler and Wilson 1990)

page 113, The design of the hunter
Schaller (1974); Hanby and Bygot (1984); Jackman and Scott (1982); Surani (1991); Macdonald (1984); Kitchener (1991); Crawford and Marsh (1989); Hanby et al. (1993)

page 115, The solitary hunter
FitzGibbon and Fanshawe (1989); Lewin (1995)

page 119, Competition between species
See FitzGibbon (1993) for a number of references to her work on cheetah food selection.

page 122 Competition with species
Scheel and Packer (1993)

page 124, A hierarchy of strength
West (1999)

page 127, Winners and losers
Lewis (1997); Harder, Kenter (1995); Roelke, Munson et al. (1996)

page 130, The cooperative clan
Kruuk (1972)

page 131, The competitive clan
Hofer and East (1993); Frank, Holekamp et al. (1993)

page 137, The co-operative imperative
Gorman and Mills (1997); Scott (1991)

page 138, A hierarchy of respect
Davies (1996)

page 141, The nimble opportunists
Macdonald (1984); Vanvalkenburgh and Wayne (1994)

page 142, The omnivorous opportunist
Skotness (1996)

page 144, Seizing an opportunity
Van Lawick-Goodal and Van Lawick-Goodal (1966)

page 147, Dependence on death
Brown, Urban et al. (1982); Houston (1979); Hertel (1994); Kruuk (1967)

LAKES AND RIVERS

page 155, The movement of water
Ives (1996); Dunne and Leopold (1978); Ball (1998)

page 157, The accumulation of water
Bergeron (1996)

page 158 Flood and drought
Western and Van Praet (1973); Davidson (1992); Pearce (1990)

page 163, "Slime city"
We have blatantly borrowed the heading from Coghlan's (1996) *New Scientist* article on biofilms. The enthusiast should not miss the Biofilm Club's website at <http://www.cf.ac.uk/biofilm_club>.

McHarg (1971)

page 165, The microscopic algae
Kleiner (1996)

page 166, Enriching the water
Oosthuizen and Davies (1994)

page 167, The micro-grazers
Concar (1996); Kizito and Nauwerck (1995)

page 170, The specialist
Brown (1973); Brown, Urban et al. (1982)

The great one-legged flamingo debate began with a question by Kathy Marthan in the 27 July 1991 issue of the *New Scientist* (131(1779)) and raged on into the 17 August issue (131(1782)).

page 172, Dangers of specialisation
Behrouzi (1992)

page 176, A place to brood
Nelson (1994); Koning (1992); Seehausen (1996); Turner (1997)

pages 178–9, The changing amphibian
Anderson (1998); McMenamin and McMenamin (1994)

page 181, The aquatic dinosaur
Graham and Beard (1973); Ross (1988); Gardom and Milner (1992); Fastovsky and Weishampel (1995)

page 185, One mans' fish
Trudge (1990); Leveque (1995); Commonwealth-Secretariat (1979); Pearce (1998)

pages 186–7, Pouch fishing
Nightengale (1974); Brown, Urban et al. (1982); Hoyo, Elliot et al. (1993)

pages 188–9, To fly
Richard Dawkins (1996) gives an elegant account of the evolution of flight; Qiang, Currie et al. (1998); http://www.dinofest.org/china/index1.html Campbell and Lack (1985); Yogeshwar (1998); Shimoyama and Hayakawa (1996)

page 191, Migration
Baker (1978); Krebs and Davies (1993)

page 193, Winging it
Heinrich (1992)

page 199, Design with nature
Dawkins (1996); Zimmerman, Turner et al. (1996)

page 201, The inhospitable nursery
Evans (1990)

ENDNOTES

page 203, Co-operative breeding

Emlen (1884); Wilson (1975)

Douthwaite (1986)

Although the term (in English) "helpers at the nest" was first coined by Skutch (1961), the relatively recent emergence of general awareness of the phenomenon is illustrated by the fact that a "New" Dictionary of Birds of the time (Landsborough-Thomson 1964) did not even contain the headwords "helpers" or "communal breeding" unlike the 1985 model (Campbell and Lack 1985). See also Bennun (1995); Plessis, Siegfield et al. (1995)

pages 204–5, The nest and territory

Tarboton, Pickford et al. (1989); Fretwell (1972)

FORESTS

page 215, The essential forest

Pearce (1996); Schnell and Vali (1972); Lind and Morrison (1974)

page 218, Strength in diversity

Heywood and Watson (1992)

page 221, A fading fossil

Goode (1989)

page 223, Strange giants

Hedberg (1964); Lind and Morrison (1974); Reader (1982)

page 225, People and forests

Boesch (1990); Reader (1997); Cohen (1995)

page 226, Trees

Wigley (1994); Woodward (1989)

page 228, Tree layers

Lind and Morrison (1974)

page 231, Leaves

Emsley (1993)

page 236, Dependence on others

Pridgeon (1992); Perera (1884); Odum (1959) quotes Henger (1938) on fleas, but the rhyme was probably around for a while before then.

page 239, Sexual and asexual

Camus, Jermy et al. (1990); Niklas (1996)

page 240, Flowers

Parcy Nilsson et al. (1998); Holmes (1995); Coen and Carpenter (1992); Costich and Meagher (1996); Ackerman (1994)

page 243, The longest-living tree?

Wilson (1989); Noad and Birnie (1989); Kirkman (1975)

page 245, Holes in the canopy

C. FitzGibbon, personal communication

pages 248–9, The indigenous inhabitants

Kingdon (1979); Macdonald (1984); Mduma and Sinclair (1994)

page 250, A leaf-eating monkey

Kingdon (1971)

page 253, Mouths and numbers

Begon, Mortimer et al. (1996)

pages 254–5, Super bee

Seeley (1989); Lewin (1996); Cohen and Stewart (1994)

page 260, Call of the wild

Seyfarth, Cheney et al. (1980); Cheney and Seyfarth (1990)

page 264, The poisonous caterpillar

Brower (1970); Brower, Seiber et al. (1982); DeVries (1990)

page 266, Metamorphosis and mimicry

Bates (1892); Brower (1957); Wolpert (1992); Brower and Jones (1965); Larsen (1991)

page 268, Hunters in the air

Brown, Urban et al. (1982)

page 270, A golden-rumped killer

FitzGibbon (1995); Galen Rathbun (personal communication); Lewin (1998); Lawes and Perrin (1995)

page 274, Speed and precision

Rilling, Mittelstaedt et al. (1959)

page 276, The trapper

The description of the orb spider's web making steps is an imperfect condensation of Richard Dawkins' (1996) excellent rendering of Vollrath's classic work, e.g Vollrath (1992)

page 280, The eyes have it

Richard Dawkins (1996) also provides a tour de force account of the evolution of the eye. In his excellent compendium of the view of complexity-theory thinkers, Roger Lewin (1992) quotes Brian Goodwin on the evolution of the eye. In the spirit of the on-going debate on the relative importance of natural selection versus "emergence" in making life forms, Dawkins might dub the opening quotation an example of "bad poetic science" (Dawkins 1998)

pages 282–3, An army of hunters

On the coffee table or as a definitive reference, *The Ants* by Hoeldobler and Wilson (1990) cannot be beaten

page 286, Ancient messages?

Stamp-Dawkins (1986); Krebs and Dawkins (1984); Roberts (1995); Anon. (1997); Concar (1995)

page 289, Reluctant pairs

McFarland (1981)

page 291, Parasite in the nest

Campbell and Lack (1985)

Anon, (1997). "Birds do it, bees do it . . ." *Economist*. 344: 69-71.

Ackerman, J. (1994). "Orchids short-change pollinators." *Biotropica* 26: 44.

Anderson, I. (1998). "A great leap forward." *New Scientist* 158(2140): 4–5.

Andersson, M. (1982). "Sexual selection, natural selection and quality advertisement." Biological Journal of the Linnean Society 17: 375–393.

Baker, R.R. (1978). *The Evolutionary Ecology of Animal Migration*. London, Hodder & Stoughton.

Ball, P. (1998). "Supercool water." *New Scientist* 159(2145): 30-32.

Bates, H.W. (1892). *The Naturalist on the River Amazons* (reprint of the 1863 unabridged edition). London, John Murray.

Bateson, G. (1979). *Man and Nature: A Necessary Unity*. New York, Dutton.

Begon, M., J.L. Harper, et al. (1996). *Ecology: Individuals, Populations and Communities*. Oxford, Blackwell Science Ltd.

Begon, M., M. Mortimer, et al. (1996). *Population Ecology: A Unified Study of Animals and Plants*. Oxford, Blackwell Science Ltd.

Behrouzi, R.-B. (1992). "On the movements of the Greater Flamingo, *Phoenicopterus ruber*, in Iran." Zoology In The Middle East 6(0): 21–27.

Bennun, L. (1995). The social life of the Social Weaver. *Kenya Birds*. 4: 44–52.

Bergeron, L. (1996). Focus on Rift Valley Lakes. *Swara*. 19: 20–27.

Bertram, B. (1979). "Ostriches recognize their own eggs and discard others." *Nature* 279: 233–234.

Boesch, C. (1990). "First hunters of the forest: Did early man learn to hunt on the plains of Africa or before he left the forests?" *New Scientist* 126(1717).

Brace, M. (1996). "Grassroots research." *Independent on Sunday*. London: 54.

Brower, J.V.Z. (1957). "Experimental studies of mimicry in some North American butterflies." *Nature* 180: 144.

Brower, L. P. (1970). Plant poisons in a terrestrial foodchain and implications for mimicry theory. *Biochemical Coevolution*. K.L. Chambers. Corvallis, Oregon State University Press: 69–82.

Brower, L.P. and M.A. Jones (1965). "Precourtship interactions of wing and abdominal sex glands in male Danaus butterflies." Proc. Roy. Ent. Soc. Lond. 40: 147–151.

Brower, L.P., J.N. Seiber, et al. (1982). "Plant-determined variation in the cardenolide content, thin-layer chromatography profiles, and emetic potency of monarch butterflies, *Danaus plexippus*, reared on the milkweed, *Asclepias eriocarpa*, in California, USA." *Journal of Chemical Ecology* 8(3): 579–634.

Brown, L. (1973). *The Mystery of the Flamingo*. Nairobi, East African Publishing House.

Brown, L.H., E.K. Urban, et al. (1982). *The Birds of Africa*. London, Academic Press.

Campbell, B. and E. Lack, Eds. (1985). *A Dictionary of Birds*. Carlton, T. & A.D. Poyser.

Camus, J.M., A.C. Jermy, et al. (1990). *A World of Ferns*. London, Natural History Museum Publications.

Caniggia, M. and C. Scala (1991). "Sunspots and hip fractures." *Chronobiologia* 18(1): 1-8.

Capra, F. (1996). *The Web of Life*. New York,

Anchor/Doubleday.

Casti, J. (1995). *Complexification*. London, Abacus.

Casti, J. (1996). "What if . . ." *New Scientist* 151(2040).

Cheney, D.L. and R.M. Seyfarth (1990). *How Monkeys See the World: Inside the Mind of Another Species*. Chicago, University of Chicago Press.

Coen, E. and R. Carpenter (1992). "The power behind the flower: What makes a plant flower?" *New Scientist* 134(1818).

Coghlan, A. (1996). "Slime city." *New Scientist* 151(2045).

Cohen, J. and I. Stewart (1994). *The Collapse of Chaos*. New York, Penguin.

Cohen, J.E. (1995). *How Many People Can the Earth Support?*, W.W. Norton.

Commonwealth-Secretariat (1979). *Management of Water Hyacinth*. First Review Meeting on the Management of Water Hyacinth, Papua New Guinea, Commonweath Science Council.

Concar, D. (1995). "Sex & the symmetrical body." *New Scientist* 146(1974).

Concar, D. (1996). "Sisters are doing it for themselves." *New Scientist* 151(2043).

Costanza, R., R. d'Arge, et al. (1997). "The value of the World's ecosystem services and natural capital." *Nature* 387(6230).

Costich, D. and T. Meagher (1996). "Junk DNA & flowers." *Proceedings of the Royal Society* B 263: 1455.

Crawford, M. and D. Marsh (1989). *The Driving Force: Food, Evolution and The Future*. New York, HarperCollins.

Davidson, G. (1992). "Icy prospects for a warmer world." *New Scientist* 135(1833).

Davies, S. (1996). "Stressed out." *New Scientist* 152(2060).

Dawkins, R. (1986). *Blind Watchmaker*. New York, W.W. Norton.

Dawkins, R. (1996). *Climbing Mount Improbable*. London, Viking Press.

Dawkins, R. (1998). *Unweaving the Rainbow: Science, Delusion and the Appetite for Wonder*. London, Penguin.

DeVries, P. (1990). "Caterpillars tapdancing." *Science* 248: 1104.

Douthwaite, R.J. (1986), "Effects of drift sprays of Endosulfan, applied for tsetse-fly control on breeding Little Bee-eaters in Somalia", *Environmental Pollution* (ser. A) 41:11–22.

Dunbar, R.I.M. (1988). *Primate Social Systems*. London, Chapman and Hall.

Dunne, T. and L.B. Leopold (1978). *Water in Development Planning*. San Francisco, W.H. Freeman.

Emlen, S.T. (1884). Cooperative breeding in birds and mammals. *Behavioural Ecology: An Evolutionary Approach*. J.R. Krebs and N.B. Davies. Oxford, Blackwell Science: 305–339.

Emsley, J. (1993). Photochemistry. *New Scientist*. 137.

Endo, S. (1995). "Japan's ancient trees whisper their secrets." *New Scientist* 146(1977).

Estes, R.E. (1991). *The Behaviour Guide to African Mammals*. Halfway House, RSA, Russel Friedman.

Evans, R.M. (1990). "Vocal regulation of temperature by avian embryos: A laboratory study with pipped eggs of the American white

pelican." *Animal Behaviour* 40(5): 969–979.

Fastovsky, D.E. and D.B. Weishampel (1995). *The Evolution and Extinction of the Dinosaurs*, Cambridge University Press.

FitzGibbon, C.D. (1995). "Comparative Ecology Of 2 Elephant-Shrew Species In a Kenyan Coastal Forest." *Mammal Review* 25(1–2): 19–30.

FitzGibbon, C.D. and J.H. Fanshawe (1989). "The condition and age of Thomson's gazelles killed by cheetahs and wild dogs." *J. Zool* (London) 218: 99–107.

FitzGibbon, C.D. and J. Lazarus (1993). Antipredator behaviour of Serengeti ungulates: Individual differences and population consequences. *Serengeti II: Research and management for ecosystem conservation*. A.E.R. Sinclair and P. Arcese. Chicago, University of Chicago Press: 274–296.

Fortey, R. (1997). *Life: An Unauthorised Biography*. London, HarperCollins.

Frank, D.A. and S.J. McNaughton (1991). "Stability increases with diversity in plant communities: empirical evidence from the 1988 Yellowstone drought " Oikos(62): 360-362.

Frank, L. G., K. E. Holekamp, et al. (1993). Dominance, demography and reproductive success of female Spotted Hyenas. Serengeti II: Research and management for ecosystem conservation. A.E.R. Sinclair and P. Arcese. Chicago, University of Chicago Press: 364-384.

Fretwell, S. D. (1972). *Populations in a Seasonal Environment*. Princeton, Princeton University Press.

Frost, R. (1961). *The Complete Poems of Robert Frost*. New York, Hold, Rinehart and Winston.

Gardom, T. and A. Milner (1992). *The Natural History Museum Book of Dinosaurs*. London, Virgin Books.

Glantz, M.H. (1998). *El Nino, La Nina. Our Planet*, UNEP. 9: 27–28.

Goode, D. (1989). *Cycads of Africa*. Capetown, Struik Winchester.

Goodwin, B. (1995). *How the Leopard Changed its Spots*, Phoenix.

Gorman, M. and M. Mills (1997). *Conservation Biology* 11(1397).

Gosling, L., M. Petrie, and M.E. Rainey (1987). "Lekking in topi: a high-cost specialist strategy." Animal Behaviour 35: 616–618.

Gould, S.J. (1990). *Wonderful Life: the Burgess Shale and the Nature of History*. New York, Norton.

Graham, A. and P. Beard (1973). *Eyelids of Morning: the Mingled Destinies of Crocodiles and Men*. Greenwich, Connecticut, New York Graphic Society Ltd.

Gribbin, J. (1990). *Hothouse Earth*. London, Black Swan.

Hamilton, W.D. and T.M. Lenton (1998). "Spora and Gaia: How microbes fly with their clouds." *Ethology, Ecology and Evolution* 10(1): 1–16.

Hanby, J.P. and J.D. Bygott (1984). *Lions Share: The Story of a Serengeti Pride*. Boston, Houghton Mifflin.

Hanby, J.P., J.D. Bygott, et al. (1993). Ecology, demography and behaviour of lions in two contrasting habitats: Ngorongoro Crater and the Serengeti Plains. *Serengeti II: Research and management for ecosystem conservation*. A.E.R. Sinclair and P. Arcese. Chicago, University of Chicago Press: 315–331.

BIBLIOGRAPHY

Hanski, I. and M. Gilpin (1991). "Metapopulation dynamics: brief history and conceptual domain." *Biological Journal of the Linnean Society* 42: 3–16.

Harder, T.C., M. Kenter, et al. (1995). "Phylogenetic evidence of canine distemper virus in Serengeti's lions." *Vaccine* 13(6): 521–523.

Hays, J.D., J. Imbrie, et al. (1976). "Variations in the Earth's orbit: pacemaker of the ice ages." *Science* 194(4270, 10/12/76).

Hedberg, O. (1964). "Features of Afroalpine plant ecology." *Acta Phytogeographica Suecica* 49: 1–411.

Hedges, N. G. (1983). *Reptiles and Amphibians of East Africa.* Nairobi, Kenya Literature Bureau.

Heinrich, B. (1992). *The Hot-Blooded Insects: Strategies and Mechanisms of Thermoregulation.* London, Springer-Verlag.

Henger, R. (1938). *Big Fleas Have Little Fleas, or Who's Who among the Protozoa,* Williams & Wilkins Co.

Hertel, F. (1994). "Diversity in body size and feeding morphology within past and present vulture assemblages." *Ecology* 75(4): 1074–8.

Heywood, V. and R. Watson, Eds. (1992). *Global Biodiversity Assessment.* Cambridge, Cambridge University Press.

Hinde, R. A., Ed. (1972). *Non-Verbal Communication. Cambridge,* Cambridge University Press.

Hoeldobler, B. and E.O. Wilson (1990). *The Ants. Cambridge, Mass,* Belknap Press/Harvard University Press.

Hofer, H. and M. East (1993). Population dynamics, population size and the commuting system of Serengeti Spotted Hyenas. *Serengeti II: Research and management for ecosystem conservation.* A.E.R. Sinclair and P. Arcese. Chicago, University of Chicago Press: 332-363.

Holmes, B. (1993). "Evolution's neglected superstars." *New Scientist* 140(1898).

Holmes, B. (1995). "Message in a genome?" *New Scientist* 147(1990).

Houston, D.C. (1979). The adaptations of scavengers. *Serengeti: Dynamics of an Ecosystem.* A.R.E. Sinclair and M. Norton-Griffiths. Chicago, University of Chicago Press: 263–286.

Hoyo, J.D., A. Elliot, et al., Eds. (1993). *Handbook of the Birds of the World.* Lynx.

Hunt, L. (1998). "Send in the clouds." *New Scientist* 158(2136).

Ibrahim, K.M. and C.H.S. Kabuye (1987), *An Illustrated Manual of Kenya Grasses,* Rome, FAO.

IPCC, Ed. (1996). *Climate Change 1995. Impacts, Adaptations and Mitigation of Climate Change: Scientific-Technical Analysis.* Contribution of Working Group II to the Second Assessment Report of the Intergovernmental Panel on Climate Change. Cambridge, Cambridge University Press.

Ives, J.D. (1996). *Glacial Lake Outburst Floods and Risk Engineering in the Himalaya. Kathmandu, Nepal,* ICIMOD – International Centre for Integrated Mountain Development.

Jackman, B. and J. Scott (1982). *The Marsh Lions: The Story of an African Pride.* London, Macmillan.

Kangwana, K. (1996). *Studying Elephants.* Nairobi, African Wildlife Foundation.

Kauffman, S. (1995). *At Home in the Universe.* New York, Oxford University Press.

Keverne, E.B., F. Martel, et al. (1996). "Primate brain evolution: genetic and functional considerations." *Proceedings of the Royal Society London B* 262: 689.

Keynes, G., Ed. (1927). Poetry and Prose of William Blake. London, Nonesuch Library.

Kingdon, J. (1971). *East African Mammals* Vol. I. London, Academic Press.

Kingdon, J. (1979). *East African Mammals Vol. IIIB: Large Mammals.* London, Academic Press.

Kingdon, J. (1982). *East African Mammals Vol. IIIC: Bovids.* London, Academic Press.

Kirkman, J. (1975). *Gedi.* Nairobi, National Museums of Kenya.

Kirschvink, J.L., R.L. Ripperdan, et al. (1997). "Evidence for a Large-Scale Reorganization of Early Cambrian Continental Masses by Inertial Interchange True Polar Wander." *Science* 277(5325): 541–545.

Kitchener, A. (1991). *The Natural History of the Wild Cats.* London, Christopher Helm/A & C Black.

Kizito, Y.S. and A. Nauwerck (1995). "Temporal and Vertical-Distribution Of Planktonic Rotifers In a Meromictic Crater Lake, Lake Nyahirya (Western Uganda)." *Hydrobiologia* 313: 303–312.

Kleiner, K. (1996). "One small step for a tomato." *New Scientist* 150(2025).

Klomp, N.I. and D.G. Green (1996). "Complexity and connectivity in ecosystems." *Complexity International* 1996(3).

Koning, A. (1992). *Cichlids and all the other fishes of Lake Malawi.* Waterlooville, Portsmouth, TFH Publications.

Krebs, J.R. and N.B. Davies (1884). *Behavioural Ecology: An Evolutionary Approach.* Oxford, Blackwell Science.

Krebs, J.R. and N.B. Davies (1993). *Behavioural Ecology: An Evolutionary Approach.* Oxford, Blackwell Science.

Krebs, J.R. and R. Dawkins (1884). *Animal signals: Mind-reading and manipulation. Behavioural Ecology: An Evolutionary Approach.* J.R. Krebs and N.B. Davies. Oxford, Blackwell Science: 380–402.

Kruuk, H. (1967). "Competition for food between vultures in East Africa." *Ardea* 55: 172–193.

Kruuk, H. (1972). *The Spotted Hyena: A study of predation and social behavior.* Chicago.

Landsborough-Thomson, A., Ed. (1964). *A New Dictionary of Birds.* London, Nelson.

Larsen, T.B. (1991). *The Butterflies of Kenya and their Natural History.* Oxford, Oxford University Press.

Lawes, M.J. and M.R. Perrin (1995). "Risk Sensitive Foraging Behavior Of the Round-Eared Elephant Shrew (Macroscelides Proboscideus)." *Behavioral Ecology and Sociobiology* 37(1): 31–37.

Lee, P.C. (1987). "Allomothering among African elephants." *Animal Behaviour* 35: 278-291.

Lee, P.C. (1991). *Reproduction. The Illustrated Encyclopedia of Elephants.* London, Salamander: 48-63.

Lee, P.C. and C.J. Moss (1995). "Statural growth in known-age African elephants (*Loxodonta africana*)." *Journal of Zoology,* London 236: 29–41.

Leuthold, W. (1977). *African Ungulates: A comparative reveiw of their ethology and behavioural ecology.* Berlin, Springer Verlag.

Leveque, C. (1995). "Role and Consequences of Fish Diversity in the Functioning of African Fresh-Water Ecosystems — a Review." *Aquatic Living Resources* 8(1): 59–78.

Levine, J.S. (1992). *Global Biomass Burning: Atmospheric, Climatic and Biospheric Implications.* Boston, MIT Press.

Lewin, R. (1992). *Complexity: Life at the Edge of Chaos.* New York, Collier/Macmillan.

Lewin, R. (1995). "Are we smart enough to save this bird?" *New Scientist* 14(2003).

Lewin, R. (1996). "All for one one for all." *New Scientist* 152(2060).

Lewin, R. (1998). "Family feuds." *New Scientist* 157(2118).

Lewis, M.E. (1997). "Carnivoran paleoguilds of Africa: Implications for hominid food procurement strategies." *Journal Of Human Evolution* 32(2-3): 257-288.

Lind, E.M. and M.E.S. Morrison (1974). *East African Vegetation.* London, Longman.

Long, S.P., M.B. Jones, et al., Eds. (1992). *Primary Productivity of Grass Ecosystems.* London, Chapman & Hall, UNEP.

Macdonald, D. (1984). *The Encyclopaedia of Mammals — I.* London, Sydney, George Allen & Unwin.

Macdonald, D. (1984). *The Encyclopaedia of Mammals — II.* London, Sydney, George Allen & Unwin.

McFarland, D., Ed. (1981). *The Oxford Companion to Animal Behaviour.* Oxford, Oxford University Press.

McHarg, I.L. (1971). *Design with Nature.* Garden City, New York, Doubleday/Natural History Press

McMenamin, M. and D. McMenamin (1994). *Hypersea: Life on Land.* New York, Columbia University Press.

McNaughton, S.J. and F.F. Banyikwa (1995). Plant Communities and Herbivory. *Serengeti II: Dynamics, Management and Conservation of an Ecosystem.* A.R.E. Sinclair and P. Arcese. Chicago, University of Chicago Press: 49–70.

Mduma, S.A.R. and A.R.E. Sinclair (1994). "The Function Of Habitat Selection By Oribi In Serengeti, Tanzania." *African Journal Of Ecology* 32(1): 16–29.

Moss, C. (1988). *Elephant Memories: Thirteen Years in the Life of an Elephant Family.* New York:, William Morrow.

Moss, C. (1992). *Echo of the Elephants.* London, BBC Books.

Moss, C.J. and J.H. Poole (1983). Relationships and social structure of African elephants. *Primate Social Relationships: An Integrated Approach.* R.A. Hinde. Oxford, Blackwell Scientific Publications: 315–325.

Mullis, K. (1998). *Dancing Naked in the Mind Field.* New York, Pantheon Books.

Nelson, J.S. (1994). *Fishes of the World.* New York, John Wiley & Sons.

Nightengale, D. (1974). "Ecology and Behaviour". Department of Zoology. Nairobi, University of Nairobi.

Niklas, K. (1996). *The Evolutionary Biology of Plants.* Chicago, University of Chicago Press.

Noad, T. and A. Birnie (1989). *Trees of Kenya.* Nairobi, Noad & Birnie.

Nyamweru, C. (1980). *Rifts and Volcanoes.* Nairobi, Thomas Nelson and Sons.

Odum, E. (1959). *Fundamentals of Ecology.*

Philadelphia, W.B. Saunders.

Odum, E. (1997). *Ecology: A Bridge Between Science and Society*. Sunderland, Massachusetts, Macmillan.

Ohlsson, R., K. Hall, et al., Eds. (1995). *Genomic Imprinting: causes and consequences*. Cambridge, Cambridge University Press.

Oosthuizen, J.H. and R.W. Davies (1994). "The biology and adaptations of the hippopotamus leech Placobdelloides jaegerskioeldi (Glossiphoniidae) to its host." *Canadian Journal of Zoology* 72(3): 418–422.

Parcy, F., O. Nilsson, et al. (1998). "A genetic framework for floral patterning." *Nature* 395: 561–566.

Parry, M. (1991). *Climate Change and World Agriculture*. London, Earthscan.

Payne, K. (1998). *Silent Thunder*. New York: Simon & Schuster.

Pearce, F. (1990). "High and dry in the global greenhouse." *New Scientist* 128(1742).

Pearce, F. (1996). "Built to last". *Independent on Sunday*. London: 52–3.

Pearce, F. (1998). "All-out war on the alien invader." *New Scientist* 158(2135): 31–38.

Perera, J. (1884). "Plague of fungus could limit locusts." *New Scientist* 141(1916).

Plessis, M.A.D., W.R. Siegfield, et al. (1995). "Ecological and life-history correlates of cooperative breeding in South African birds." *Oecologia* 102: 180–188.

Poole, J. (1995). *Growing up with Elephants*. New York, Hyperion.

Poole, J.H. and C.J. Moss (1990). "Elephant mate searching: group dynamics and vocal and olfactory communication." *Symp. Zoological Society London* 61: 111–125.

Pratt, D.J. and M.D. Gwynne, Eds. (1977). *Rangeland Management and Ecology in East Africa*. London, Hodder & Stoughton.

Pridgeon, A. (1992). *The Illustrated Encyclopedia of Orchids*. Sidney, Kevin Weldon.

Prins, H.H.T. (1987). The Buffalo of Manyara: The individual in the context of herd life in a seasonal environment of East Africa. *Gedragsbiologie Zoologisch Laboratorium*. Groningen, University of Groningen: 283.

Qiang, J., P.J. Currie, et al. (1998). "Two feathered dinosaurs from northeastern China." *Nature* 394(162).

Reader, J. (1982). *Kilimanjaro*. New York, Universe Books.

Reader, J. (1997). *Africa: A Biography of the Continent*. New York, Alfred J. Knopf.

Ridley, M. (1993). "Is sex good for anything?" *New Scientist* 140(1902).

Ridley, M. (1996). *The Origins of Virtue*, Viking.

Rilling, S.H., H. Mittelstaedt, et al. (1959). "Prey recognition in the praying mantis." *Behaviour* 14: 164–184.

Roberts, A.F. (1995). *Animals in African Art: From the Familiar to the Marvelous*. New York, Museum of Modern Art.

Roelke, P.-M.E., L. Munson, et al. (1996). "A canine distemper virus epidemic in Serengeti lions (Panthera leo)." *Nature* 379(6564): 441–445.

Ross, C.A., Ed. (1988). *Crocodiles and Alligators: an Illustrated Encyclopedic Survey*. Merehurst Press.

Schaller, G.B. (1974). *Golden Shadows, Flying Hooves*. London, Collins.

Scheel, D. and C. Packer (1993). Variation in predation by lions: tracking a movable feast. *Serengeti II: Research and management for ecosystem conservation*. A.E.R. Sinclair and P. Arcese. Chicago, University of Chicago Press: 299–314.

Schnell, R.C. (1974). "Biogenic sources of atmospheric ice nucleic." Laramie, Wyoming, Department of Atmospheric Resources, University of Wyoming.

Schnell, R.C. and G. Vali (1972). "Atmospheric ice nuclei from decomposing vegetation." *Nature* 236: 163–5.

Scott, J. (1991). *Painted Wolves: Wild dogs of the Serengeti-Mara*. London, Hamish Hamilton.

Seehausen, O. (1996). *Lake Victoria Rock Cichlids, Verduijn Cichlids*.

Seeley, T.D. (1989). "The honey bee colony as a superorganism." *American Scientist* 77: 546–553.

Seyfarth, R.M., D.L. Cheney, et al. (1980). "Vervet monkey alarm calls: semantic communication in a free-ranging primate." *Animal Behaviour* 28(1070–94).

Shimoyama, N. and Y. Hayakawa (1996). "Flocking and flying." *Physical Review Letters* 76: 3870.

Sinclair, A.R.E. (1977). *The African Buffalo: A study of resource limitation of populations*. Chicago, University of Chicago Press.

Sinclair, A.R.E. and P. Arcese, Eds. (1995). *Serengeti II: Dynamics, Management and Conservation of an Ecosystem*. Chicago, University of Chicago Press.

Sinclair, A.R.E. and M. Norton-Griffiths, Eds. (1979). *Serengeti: Dynamics of an Ecosystem*. Chicago, University of Chicago Press.

Skotness, P., Ed. (1996). *Miscast: Negotiating the Presence of the Bushmen*. Cape Town, University of Cape Town Press.

Skutch, A.F. (1961). "Helpers among birds." *Condor* 63: 198–226.

Speare, R., L. Berger, et al. (1997). "Pathology of mucormycosis of cane toads in Australia." *Journal of Wildlife Diseases* 33(1): 105–111.

Stamp-Dawkins, M. (1986). *Unravelling Animal Behaviour*. Harlow, Longman.

Strum, S.C. (1987). *Almost Human: A journey into the world of Baboons*. London, Elm Tree Books.

Surani, M.A. (1991). "Influence of genome imprinting on gene expression, phenotypic variations and development." *Human Reproduction* 6(1): 45–51.

Tarboton, W., P. Pickford, et al. (1989). *African Birds of Prey*. Ithica, Cornell Univeristy Press.

Tinsley, B. (1998). [sunspots]. AAAS

Tolkien, J.R.R. (1954-55). *The Lord of the Rings*.

Trudge, C. (1990). "Underwater, out of mind:." *New Scientist* 128(1741).

Turner, G. (1997). "Small fry go big time." *New Scientist* 155(2093).

UNEP/GEMS (1992). *The El Nino Phenomenon*. Nairobi, UNEP.

Van Hoven, W. (1991). "Mortalities in Kudu (Tragelaphus strepsiceros) populations related to chemical defense in trees." *Journal of African Zoology* 105(2): 141–146.

Van Lawick-Goodal, J. and H. Van Lawick-Goodal (1966). "Use of tools by the Egyptian Vulture Neophron percnopterus." *Nature* 212: 1468–1469.

Van Valen, L. (1973). "A new evolutionary law." *Evolutionary Theory* 1: 1–30.

Vanvalkenburgh, B. and R.K. Wayne (1994). "Shape Divergence Associated With Size Convergence In Sympatric East- African Jackals." *Ecology* 75(6): 1567–1581.

Vervij, W. and B. Schoenmackers (1997). Sunspots: welcome addition to greenhouse theory. *Change*, RIVM. 39.

Vesey-FitzGerald, D.F. (1969). "Utilization of the habitat by buffalo in Lake Manyara National Park." *East African Wildlife Journal*, 7: 131–145.

Vollrath, F. (1992). "Spider web and silks." *Scientific American* 266: 70–76.

West, G.B., J.H. Brown and B.J. Enquist (1997), "A general model for the origin of allometric scaling lows in biology", *Science*, 276:122–6

West, Peytar (1999), Personal Communication

Western, D. and C. Van Praet (1973). "Cyclical changes in the habitat and climate of an East African ecosystem." *Nature* 241: 104–106.

Wigley, T.M.I., Ed. (1994). *The Carbon Cycle*. Cambridge, Cambridge University Press.

Wills, C. (1996). *Plagues: Their Origin, History and Future*. London, HarperCollins.

Wills, C. (1996). "Safety in diversity." *New Scientist* 149(2022): 38–42.

Wilson, E.O. (1975). *Sociobiology: the New Synthesis*. Cambridge, MA, Belknap Press/Harvard University Press.

Wilson, E.O. (1998). *Consilience: the Unity of Knowledge*. New York, Knopf.

Wilson, J. (1989). *Lemurs of the Lost World*. Harrap/Impact.

Wolpert, L. (1992). "The shape of things to come: How does a fertilised egg know how to develop into a human being?" *New Scientist* 134(1827).

Woodward, I. (1989). "Plants, Water and Climate." *New Scientist* 121.

Yogeshwar, R. (1998). "Why the tip of the wing is bent." *Lufthansa Magazine*. 98: 70.

Zimmerman, D.A., D.A. Turner, et al. (1996). *Birds of Kenya and Northern Tanzania*. Halfway House, RSA, Russel Friedman.

INDEX

INDEX

AKNOWLEDGEMENTS

We should like to thank Cristina Boelcke, Clare FitzGibbon and Mike Norton-Griffiths for taking the time to read and comment thoughtfully on the entire draft manuscript. In agreeing to write the foreword, Richard Dawkins naturally found himself somewhat snared into having a close look at the text; as a result, he provided many insightful comments and corrections. Any subsequent errors or omissions cannot be blamed on these friends and colleagues, but to us not paying sufficient attention. Others have been very helpful in a number of ways: reading and commenting on parts of the text, straightening us out on points of fact, helping with identifications or logistics. They are: George Amtete, Leon Bennun, David Campbell, John Fanshawe, Peter Fera, Claire FitzGibbon, Ian Gordon, Clive Hambler, Hans Herren, Hilary Kahoro, Maarten Labeeuw, Paul Mackenzie, K.A McLuckie, Cynthia Moss, Patrick Kamau Nderi, Mike Norton-Griffiths, Joyce Poole, Phyllis Lee, George Robertson, Suresh Raina, Hezy Shoshani, Peter Usher, Luc de Vos, Eliud Wanakuta and Peyton West. We thank them all for their contributions.

We want to say a special word of thanks to the Rockerfeller Foundation, in particular the directors and administrators of the Bellagio Study and Conference Center: Pasquale Pesce, Gianna Celli, Susan Garfield and their staff. We were awarded a residency fellowship to spend a month in that wonderful place in the Spring of 1998 in the humbling company of once-in-a-lifetime syzygys of scholars in order to finish the re-organisation and writing of this book. One day, in the Villa Serbelloni library, we found the proceedings of a series of Bellagio conferences organised by C.H. Waddington in the late 1960s, "Towards a Theoretical Biology". Some of the intractable questions raised then still linger on (see p. 13); we know we haven't answered them, but hope we have contributed to the quest and helped shed a bit more light.

"The lyricism and biological insight of Harvey Croze's words are matched by the very same quality of John Reader's stunning photographs"
RICHARD DAWKINS

"Explains as no other book has ever done, precisely how those laws of ecology work ... elegantly told and magnificently photographed"
BRIAN JACKMAN *Sunday Times*

Whatever the outward appearance, nothing seen in nature is an entirely random occurrence. Each blade of grass, each grazing gazelle, stalking lion and soaring vulture is obeying a natural law within the complex web of life. These relationships form pyramids or patterns repeated a thousand times over plains, lakes, rivers and forests, and are known as "ecosystems".

Pyramids of Life opens a window on nature, taking Africa, with its unique richness in pattern, structure and process, as its focus. Examining every level of existence, and taking into account the recent interference of man and the emerging science of adaptive systems, behaviourist and ecologist Harvey Croze has joined forces with the renowned photojournalist John Reader to offer a fascinating perspective on the natural world.

This definitive book is an indispensable guide for all those with an interest in ecology, as well as a beautiful portrait of wildlife in Africa and indeed in every other wild region of the world.

Cover photographs by John Reader

ISBN 1 86046 613 3

THE HARVILL PRESS
LONDON

www.harvill.com

Natural History/Afri
UK £19.-
US $32 _

ISBN 1-86046-613-3

9 781860 466137